FIVE

AnnaLisa Grant

For the best readers a girl could ask for.

Happy Reading!

Chapter 1

A gust of warm August air mixed with exhaust hits my face as I exit the cab. The wind blows my long, blonde hair in my face so I pull the band off my wrist and pull my mane into a pony tail. I followed my father's instructions and had the cabbie drop me off on Constitution Avenue, near where I'm supposed to meet him. Constitution Gardens isn't far from the Reflecting Pool that stretches beautifully in front of the Lincoln Memorial, but you wouldn't know it to sit on one of the benches or under a tree next to the pond. The Gardens are so secluded that you often feel like you're in a neighborhood park instead of in the middle of Washington, DC.

I come up the sidewalk and begin looking for my father in the direction of our favorite spot by the Garden pond. It's dusk and most people have cleared out for the night already. It's also Wednesday and there usually aren't that many people here this time of night anyway.

I spot my dad sitting against our favorite tree. He's been bringing me to this spot since before my mom died. I was only ten when she lost her battle with breast cancer. It was really tough, but Dad was always strong. Looking back I realize just how strong he had to be for the both of us, and I've shed more than a few tears at the thought of Dad crying himself to sleep at night after holding everything in all day.

Bobby Matthews loved Elise Medcalf from the moment they met. They had always been a match made in Heaven. Even though Dad was the typical "boy from the wrong side of the tracks," Mom always saw the good in him. She didn't see the thug who had a rap sheet as long as your arm or the guy who beat the shit out of someone if they looked at his buddies the wrong way. She saw the sweet boy who always respected women, especially his mother. She saw the guy who literally took his leather jacket off and laid it over a puddle so my mom's shoes wouldn't get wet. She saw the guy who, when she asked him to leave his trouble-making friends behind so they could have a future together, did it without question.

They had a good life together. Mom was a secretary for the same law firm from the time she graduated high school, and Dad took his lock-picking expertise and starting using his skills for good by becoming a Master Locksmith. We never had a lot of money, which sucked at times because DC is so damn expensive, but we had a great life together.

Dad's fellow-gang-member-turned-business-partner, Oz, became even more like family after Mom died. He ran their locksmith and security business while Dad took almost a month off from work, and kept it running as if Dad had never left. He maintained the clients they already had and landed a few new clients as well. Oz never married, which is a shame because even though he still looks like a bouncer, he's a teddy bear and an amazing cook. I told Dad I was going to refer to Oz as my other dad since he took just as good care of me as he did, but Dad told me I better not as he didn't want anyone to think he and Oz were *that* kind of partners.

Overall the last nine years since Mom's death have been as good as could be expected. Each day things got a little better to where we could talk about her again and not cry. It's been hard at times, and losing Mom's income has been a source of many head banging nights doing the bills. Dad has had to do some things he promised Mom he would never do again, but you gotta do what you gotta do when the mortgage is due and your hungry eyes are staring at an empty refrigerator. We don't talk too much about that, though. It makes Dad sad to think about how disapproving Mom would be about what he's been doing for a certain Senator for the last few years.

I smile as I approach Dad but it fades quickly as I see that he's not well. He's slumped over and looks like he's going to be sick.

"Dad! Are you ok?" I ask as I rush to him. "Oh my God! What happened to you?"

Dad lifts his hand from his belly and even in the shadows of dusk I can see how bloody it is from what looks like a gunshot wound.

"I need you to listen to me. There isn't a lot of time. If you don't hurry, they'll be back for you," he says through winces of pain.

"Keep your hand there! We have to keep pressure on the wound. I'm calling 911!" I start to pull out my cell phone but Dad stops me.

"You haven't even started nursing school and you already think you know everything." Dad gives a muffled laugh. I don't know why he's trying to use humor right now. This is serious. I've got to get him to a hospital.

"Who did this, Dad?" I look him square in his brown eyes hoping he'll be honest with me. He looks at me and I immediately know the answer. "It was him, wasn't it? What happened?"

"I got caught. The detective on the case knew right away that I wasn't behind this or any of the other break-ins. He wanted a name or he was going to bring you in for questioning, too," he tells me with a strained voice. I have no idea how long he's been sitting here like this so I don't know how much time has been wasted. "Naming Dellinger was just the confirmation they needed."

"Oh, no, Dad. How many times did you tell me he was not to be crossed? How many times did you tell me that politicians like Dellinger are invincible?" I put my head in my hands and rest them on his should for a moment while I try to gather my thoughts. "Ok, ok, ok...let's just get you to a hospital and then I'll call that detective."

"We're not doing that, Ronnie. Dellinger made sure the road that detective was going down is a dead end. Now listen to me. You need to go see Oz. You knock on his door without me and he'll know exactly why you're there. He'll take you back to the house. You know *exactly* what to take with you," he says softly. "Everything is already set up for you to leave town and start over again."

"No! Dad, I'm not leaving you!" I protest.

"Yes, you are. You can do this. I taught you everything I know for a reason. You can protect yourself and you can get yourself out of any bind. You have to go. I won't let him trap you the way he did me. You deserve to live the life you've always dreamed of." Dad takes my hand in his as he winces with pain. I hate that he won't let me help him. "This is it for me. You have a long life ahead of you. Go live it."

"I'll stay with you until…" I can't say it.

"No. Go. You have to go now. They'll be looking for you. They will have already been to the house. When they don't find you there, they'll assume you've come to find me." His words are pained and his voice is struggling. My heart is breaking.

"Dad…Daddy…." I lean in gently and hug him as best I can without making the pain worse. "I love you."

"I love you too, baby girl. You were the best thing that ever happened to your mom and me. I'm sorry that this is the way it is, but…" He coughs and I wince at the pained expression on his face.

"I don't want to. How am I supposed to live with myself knowing that I left you here all alone to die?" Tears are streaming down my face and falling onto his blood-soaked shirt.

"You'll live with it knowing that you honored my last wish for you. Now, go, and do what Oz tells you."

"I love you so much." I lean down and kiss my father on his cheek. With all the strength he has he lifts his hand to my head and hugs it close to him for a moment. With nothing left to say I look my father in his dying eyes and then force myself to follow his directions.

I get up quickly and make my way back to Constitution Avenue, hailing the first cab I see. I give him Oz's address in West End and ring my hands the entire ride there. I can't believe I just left my father to die under a tree. *Please, God, let someone find him!*

I pull out my cell phone and stare at it, hoping to get a call from some stranger telling me they found him and are taking him to the hospital. Every second of the drive to Oz's is spent gazing at my phone, willing it to ring. It doesn't, and when the cab stops in front of Oz's building, I feel an emptiness greater than when my mother died.

I get off the elevator on the tenth floor of Oz's beautiful West End building. Oz was always really good with money. He inherited a huge sum from some distant relative a few years ago and has been investing it wisely. He offered to help me and Dad out, but Dad wouldn't have it. I wish he had because then maybe it would have been easier to walk away from the money he was getting from Dellinger.

The knock on the door is still echoing when Oz swings it open with a wide smile. His 6'4" football player frame is quite a sight in the black, flour-covered apron he's got on. When I was little I used to think they must have modeled Mr. Clean after him. He looks to my right expecting to see my father with me. When he doesn't, the smile fades and he grabs my arm, dragging me into his home.

"What happened, Ronnie?" he asks in his serious, baritone voice. The door slams behind me and I'm walking aimlessly into his condo. I circle the couch and stand in front of the window that faces the direction of the Lincoln Monument, just yards away from where my father is still probably dying, or is now dead.

"He got caught. He named Dellinger. Dellinger had him…" I can't hold it in any longer and I begin to sob. Tears are streaming down my face. They roll under my chin and I can feel the neckline of my t-shirt beginning to soak.

"It's ok, Angel. It's gonna be ok," Oz says pulling me into his ridiculously large arms. I'm enveloped in them, my face in his chest now soaking his t-shirt. "I wish we had more time, but we don't. We have to get moving." Oz takes me by the shoulders. "Are you listening to me?"

I nod and wipe the tears from my face, trying to ready myself to really hear what he's saying. I have to focus on the fact that every step I'm about to take is all part of my father's dying wish for me.

"Now listen carefully and do exactly as I say. No questions. Understand?" I nod again. "Good. I'm going to take you back to your house. You'll have exactly five minutes to put everything you can into *this* bag." Oz goes to the hall closet and pulls a large duffle bag from the top shelf. "If it doesn't fit, it doesn't go. Got it."

"Yes," I answer softly. "What happens then?"

"One step at a time, Ronnie," Oz says as he rubs my shoulder.

We pull onto my street, having taken the longest route ever to get here. Oz parks a block and half away and takes us through the back alley of row houses. We pass through the wooden gate quickly and enter the house through the back door.

"Five minutes, Ronnie," Oz reminds.

Dad said I would know exactly what to take with me so, with the duffle bag in my hand, I bolt upstairs. I hit my bedroom first and grab the obvious first: bras, underwear, clothes, toiletries from my bathroom, and every pair of dance shoes I own. They're already perfectly broken in and way too expensive to replace. I pull a couple of books off the shelf, grab some pictures, and put my mom's locket around my neck. I move to Dad's room and pull a few of his t-shirts from closet, the picture of the three of us from his bedside, and the box from the top shelf of his closet. I check the gun inside and confirm that the safety is on after I take inventory of the rest of the important contents. This box, among everything that I'm taking, is the most important.

"Can you help me shove my laptop in here, Oz?" I ask hauling the now heavy duffle bag in one hand and my laptop case in the other.

"Leave it. They'll be able to track the IP address," he responds flatly. He's pulling documents from a hidden panel in the pantry that I had no idea was there.

"What's all that?" I ask as I struggle and force the zipper to the duffle bag closed.

"A few things you need…a few things I'm taking for safe keeping." Oz opens the bag I finally got zipped closed and shoves one of the large envelopes in before closing it back much faster than I was able to. "You ready?"

"Yeah, I guess. Can I ask what the next step is now?"

"Now I take you to my sister's in Virginia. He won't look for you there."

"Why? Why would he come looking for me in the first place?" I ask, confused. My father said the same thing and I was just as curious then.

"Because your father had a big mouth. Did your dad ever tell you about the night he met Dellinger?" I nod, remembering that Dad told me his company was called to install a new, high tech lock and security system at Dellinger's home after a break in. "Your dad didn't just get mouthy about how great he was at his job, but that he had taught *you* everything he knew. That you were a chip off the old block."

My father could get pretty bold with his bragging, whether it was about me and my dancing or him with his ability to create a locking system no one could break into…no one except him. My father learned a lot about breaking and entering when he was running the streets with his crew back in the day. The first thing he learned quickly was how not to get caught. Dad wasn't about running fast or even talking his way out of things. Dad was about mastering skills that would leave no evidence you were there in the first place. Except, of course, for the missing goods. He thought it was so unnecessary for guys to smash and grab, leaving a mess everywhere. He told me he was classier than that. So, Dad would do things like seal up a glass display case and work for hours and days at a time to break into it without leaving a single scratch. That's what made him so valuable to a collector like Dellinger. And now that Dellinger knows I carry the same skills as my father, he'll be after me to pick up where my father left off.

"Are you sure it's safe for me to go to your sister's? I'm already

9

concerned about you! I don't want your family in danger, too," I protest.

"No one is going to look for you there. She's not really my sister. She's the sister of a guy your dad and I used to hang with. When he got pinched back in the day, your dad and I promised to take care of her, so, we're family. Our five minutes is up. Let's go." Oz opens the back door and I take one last look around the kitchen and into the living room before passing him and stepping outside.

Before I know it we're on the highway and crossing into Maryland. I pull my knees to my chest and rest my head, tired. I'm tired from crying. Tired from the whirlwind of the last hours. And already tired of running. I close my eyes thinking it best for me to give in to my need for sleep, but all I do is relive the moment I found my father dying from a gunshot wound under a tree that, up until that moment, held nothing but fond memories. I shudder at the thought of how many people were probably around at the time, totally unaware that a man had most certainly attached a silencer to his gun, walked up to my father, and shot him at close range without even saying a word.

We used to fly kites in the park, and Mom would read to me as we leaned against that tree. One year for my birthday we picnicked under the shade it provided. That was the year Dad got me one of those motorized boats. I barely had it out of the package before I was headed straight for the pond declaring that I just *had* to drive it in the water.

So many fond memories all washed away in a matter of moments.

"I just left him there, Oz," I whisper. "I just left him there to die." I begin to cry again and Oz puts his hand on my shoulder. "How could I do that?"

"You did it because he told you to. Bobby would have been so mad at you if you stayed there and watched him die. Even madder if Dellinger's guys had come back and found you," Oz tells me in a soft, but straightforward tone. I know he's right, but it doesn't make this any easier.

"You pulled two envelopes from the kitchen wall but only gave me one. What's in them?" I ask deciding to move onto the logistics of the situation.

Dad had those files hidden for a reason. They must contain some pretty important information.

"Get some rest. We'll be at Paulina's in about an hour. We'll talk then." Oz puts both hands back on the wheel and all his focus back to the road. I agree only in my lack of objection and rest my cheek back on my knees, sure that I won't be able to fall asleep because of everything that keeps running through my head. I stand corrected, though, when the car stops and Oz nudges me awake.

"We're here already?" I ask as I rub the sleepy saline from the corner of my eyes.

"Yep." Oz is out of the car and pulling my bag from the hatch in a flash. "Ronnie, let's go. C'mon," he rushes.

I follow quickly from the car to the front door as it is being opened by a woman who looks more like she belongs on the Jersey shore than she does in north Virginia. Her dark brown, almost black hair is big and poufed up in the front. Her leopard print leggings are only slightly less distracting than the ultra-plunged neckline of the black top she's wearing, and the gold chains that are tucked awkwardly into her cleavage. Her chest is huge and I can't help but think that if I were a guy my eyes would be glued to that golden trail. However, her distracting exterior is quickly overshadowed by her warm and inviting personality as she embraces me and Oz and moves us into the large kitchen.

"I've got your favorite meat loaf and mashed potatoes ready for you, Ozzy. I hope that's good for you, dear," she says in the most warm and motherly voice. It's sweet and kind, and if this is where Oz has taken me to start a new life, then I think I might be ok.

"Yes, that's great, thank you," I tell her.

"You're the best, Paulina," Oz says. She just smiles and nods and goes about finishing making our meal. Oz pulls out the envelope he stuffed into my bag and puts it on the table.

"What about the other one?" I ask him, curious as to what is in both of these mysterious envelopes.

"The important things you need to know now are in here." Oz opens the envelope and pulls out a small stack of papers and a smaller, letter-size envelope. He takes a deep breath and closes his eyes for a moment before he speaks. "You know that when I offered to help you guys out financially Bobby immediately shot me down. What you don't know is that six months later Bobby came to me with a compromise of how I could help." Oz slides the papers he took from the large envelope so they're right in front of me. He nods, giving me permission to view them.

I flip through the pages, not fully understanding what I'm seeing. All of the papers and forms I'm staring at have someone else's name on them. I open the smaller envelope and pull out a Social Security Card with the same name as is on all the paperwork: Jenna Rockwell. I sort through the rest of the cards and find credit cards with the same name, finally finding a driver's license with my picture, bearing Jenna Rockwell's name.

"I don't understand, Oz," I say quietly.

"Bobby came to me and asked me to have a new identity created for you. He didn't know when, but he knew that his term with Dellinger was going to end badly. Once he was gone, he knew Dellinger would come after you. He had me put every penny I offered him into an investment account for you, well, for Jenna Rockwell. You've got plenty of money to start your new life wherever you want, Ronnie." Oz's delivery is straight and unwavering. It makes me wonder how many times he thought about, or even practiced, what he was going to say to me when the time came.

"What if I don't want to be this Jenna Rockwell? I *like* being Veronica Matthews," I tell him in protest. "Why can't I just stay here with Paulina?"

"Unless you want to become an indentured servant to Dellinger, too, Veronica Matthews has to cease existing," he answers.

"So, what? I'm supposed to just, what, start over? Where?" I fluster at

Oz, picking up the pieces of my new identity then tossing them back on the table.

"You can go wherever you want. You can do whatever you want. There are high school transcripts and an impressive SAT score for Jenna Rockwell. You can get into any school in any city and do anything. You may not have a choice in starting this new life, but you have a choice where you start it." I don't ask because I probably need to maintain plausible deniability, but it's most likely that one of Dad and Oz's old friends knows how to manipulate computer systems and forge legal documents, giving me my new identity.

I take a deep breath and let what Oz just said soak in. I don't have a choice about starting over because I've decided I never want to be connected to Senator Dellinger in any way. I saw what he did to my father. Dad had been full of life, even in the face of tragedy with Mom. Once Dellinger roped him in to doing his dirty work for him, Dad died a little with ever job, knowing how disappointed Mom would have been.

"So…what do I do now? How long do I have to decide where I want to go? What I want to do?" I ask Oz as I surrender to the reality of my circumstance. I'll handle the logistics of everything now and then resolve to crying myself to sleep every night for the rest of my life.

"Do you still want to be a nurse?" Oz asks softly, seeing my defeat. "Had you already decided where you wanted to go to school?"

"Yeah, actually. Dad and I had been saving. I was hoping to apply and start at Radians in January. But…there are some really great teaching hospitals in Chicago. I had wanted to go there, but didn't want to leave Dad," I tell him.

It was during a writing assignment on the greatest cities in the world during my senior year that I discovered the greatness of Chicago. A lot of people wrote about London, Paris, New York and LA. I started to write about New York, too, but stumbled across an article about the shopping on Michigan Avenue in Chicago. That article lead to another and before I knew it was learning all about the Windy City and totally falling in love with it. I decided that one day I wanted to visit so I scanned a copy and kept every article I read saved on my computer, along with the paper that I got an A+ on.

"Write down all the specifics and I'll take care of everything." Oz slides the envelope he hasn't shown the contents of to me and pulls a pen from a drawer in the kitchen. "I'll be back in a minute."

Oz leaves me sitting in the kitchen, staring at this large, blank envelope. *How did this happen?* I ask myself. I know how it happened. Senator Henry Dellinger happened. It's probably best that I'm leaving DC for good. It wasn't just Dad's lock-picking skills he taught me. I became a really good shot with the gun in the case in my bag, and I spent more than enough time in the gym training to know how to kick ass if I had to. If I ever see Dellinger again I'll be putting all my skills to use.

"Here you go, hon," Paulina says sweetly as she fixes a plate of meat loaf and mashed potatoes and sets it in front of me.

"Thank you," I tell her with a small smile. "It smells and looks delicious."

"It's Ozzy's favorite. I was glad I had everything on hand when he called." Paulina smiles warmly and a part of me wishes that I really could just stay here with her.

"When did he call?" I was with Oz the whole time and I never saw him call her.

"He was talking all hushed, so I think you must have been sleeping," she tells me.

"Paulina, this is amazing. I've tried to make your meat loaf a hundred times and it never comes out this good!" Oz kisses the top of her head as he comes into the kitchen. She's already got a plate with a double portion ready for him. "How ya doin', Angel?"

"I'm ok, I guess. At least I still have you, Oz." I smile weakly, a mix of sadness and joy filling me. I'll be eternally devastated at losing Dad, but am finding a level of joy at knowing I have my second dad in Oz.

"Actually...you don't." Now Oz looks sad.

"What do you mean? Why won't I have you?" Fear fills my eyes and begins to overflow.

"You can't have any contact with anyone in DC. It's too risky. Dellinger will most likely have me monitored and if I start getting calls from a Chicago number he'll put it together. I know it sucks, but it is what it is. I'm so sorry, Angel." Oz takes my hand in his two huge ones and looks into my eyes. "Even though I can't be with you, I'll always take care of you. You're the daughter I never had, Ronnie. I hate it that you're having to do this, but I know that you can do it. Your dad did a great job preparing you for anything."

It's not fair. I'm giving up everything of my life in DC. What are the few friends I had going to think? And my dance instructors? They'll think I walked away from the one thing that I loved more than anything. But...this is it. I either stay in DC and let Dellinger control me like he did my father, or I become Jenna Rockwell, which means I get to have the life my father wanted me to have.

I breathe a sigh and extend my hand to Oz, taking the first step in assuming this new life. "Jenna Rockwell. It's nice to meet you."

Chapter 2

Six years later.

I stand here, watching them as I have so many times before. Mothers, fathers, sisters, brothers, and sometimes grandparents. They all look on and wait for this person whom they love dearly to die, too many of them long before their time. They cry and get angry, letting rage fill them at times. I saw a sweet looking mother in her mid-50s clock the hospital chaplain in the jaw with a pretty good right hook one time. Her 31-year-old daughter died from Lupus that day.

Today though…today is one of those times when a family has chosen to have peace. I'm always amazed at these families. I understand the right-hook-momma a lot more. The patient's parents and siblings have all gathered around this once vibrant and handsome 38-year-old man to watch cancer take its final bites out of his life. Mom strokes his hair, while his father holds his hand. They both whisper how much they love him and how proud they are of all that he accomplished. He gives them the faintest of smiles that I know took every single ounce of energy he has in him to give. He'll slip into an unconscious state soon, and then it really will just be a matter of time. But…as I see the look on his family's faces, I know they're going to be some of the luckier ones who grieve and are able to keep living their lives.

I sigh as the hospital chaplain comes in and the patient's nurse comes out. "You doing ok?" I ask Mercy. She's been a nurse longer than I have and I see the same look on her face every time she's about to lose a patient.

"Yeah, I'm ok. Thanks, Jenna. I've been doing this for eight years and it just never gets easier. They're a sweet family, and he was a sweet guy," she says. Mercy is a doll of a girl at just 5'3". Second generation Italian-

American, she's the living example of "you can take the girl out of Brooklyn, but you can't take Brooklyn out of the girl." She's smart, feisty, and the kind of girl you want to have on your side. She's turning 30 this weekend but still looks like she's 20 with her soft features and brown eyes. She gets carded every time we go out, and would tonight, too, if we weren't going to our regular hangout, Duke's.

"Ok then. I'm gonna take off. You should too. I've already gone over everything with the new shift. I'd wait for you but I want to catch the morning dance class before I head home," I tell her.

"How can you go dance? It's 7:15 in the morning and you just worked a 12-hour shift?" Her eyes are wide and she's shaking her head. "I get home and I'm asleep before my head even hits the pillow!"

"I normally *do* go home and straight to bed, but it's a rare weekend off and I love the people in this Saturday morning class." I grab my purse from the cabinet and round the nurse's station to the open hallway. "I will see you tonight at 7:30. Don't be late to your own party. Jerry said he'd hold our favorite table for us but can't do it all night." I give Mercy a hug and say goodbye to the other staff either on their way in or out as I take the stairs from the fourth floor to the parking lot.

If someone overheard our conversation they might think we're kind of insensitive for brushing over the impending death of a patient so quickly. The truth is, we have to. It's not that we don't care. It's that if we got torn up every time a terrible diagnosis came in, or a patient died, we'd live in a constant state of heartache. For some, becoming a nurse was a pragmatic decision. We'll always have a job somewhere and the hours, while a little on the crazy side, can actually be pretty flexible. For others, the major reason they became a nurse was because they wanted to be able to comfort others and help in their healing process. I suppose I fall somewhere in between. I love being a nurse for all the emotional reasons, but I also know that if I have to pick up and move, I can find a job most anywhere.

I found this dance studio four years ago and have become almost obsessed with everything they teach there. I had been in Chicago about two years already and was in desperate need of a place I could release the stress of being in the midst of nursing school and still looking over my shoulder. Dancing had always been my passion and I put in on the back burner while I got settled and felt like I was in the clear, that I wasn't going to have to run. Sometimes I make it for the ballroom dance, and other times its Latin dance, but my passion had become contemporary before I left DC. Sometimes I get to use the studio to work on some freestyle contemporary pieces, but that happens so rarely that I think I'm beginning to forget the art of contemporary. I love the instructors and since I've been working on a sporadic schedule of attendance, I've become familiar with several of the regulars at most of the classes throughout the week.

The train stops four blocks from my apartment, but the dance studio is another three blocks past that. On days when I work, I have to haul ass to get to the morning class in time to change. I thought about skipping this morning, but if I don't go today it'll be late next week before I make it. I'm off the next two days, but then on two, off two, and then on three. I know after tonight's birthday festivities, I'll be sleeping off a good time all day Sunday and definitely won't make it then.

I love Chicago. I couldn't have picked a better place to start the life I always dreamed of. It's the middle of July and not sweltering. The way the wind whips around and through the city cools everything off just enough. Not to mention the breeze that we get from Lake Michigan. And the people! I love the people!

"Hey you! I thought you had given up on the craziness of coming here straight from an overnight shift?" Marco says with his beautifully sexy Latin accent. He and his wife Carina opened this studio 15 years ago when then moved here from Miami. They're just the sweetest, most attractive couple I've ever known.

"It'll be too late next week if I didn't come today. I've got the weekend off and I wanted to kick if off right!" I shout as I scurry to the back of the studio where there are a few dressing rooms so I can change in a hurry. I brought my jazz dance shoes since I didn't have time to check the calendar online and see if this morning was ballroom or Latin. "Besides," I say to Marco as I emerge. "You would miss me too much!"

"True, true, mi amor," he says with a kiss to my cheek. "Ok, everyone, today we're going to cover the basics of Salsa! Find a partner and give yourself plenty of room. Jenna, would you and Carina help some of our new friends?"

"Sure," I say.

"Thank you, love. There are only a couple of new people today. Can you work with Sam? He's been coming for a little while, but still a little clumsy. I'll work with the other guy. It's his first time." Carina casually points to "the other guy" standing nervously on the other side of the studio.

"Holy hell! Who is *that*?" I whisper to her in shock. Standing there, fidgeting like a boy at an eighth grade dance, is the best looking guy I've ever seen. He's tall, definitely over six feet, has brown hair, and has that sexy *I haven't shaved in a few days* look. He's wearing jeans and a fitted shirt with a faded Captain America shield on it and what I can already tell is a totally badass tattoo peeking out from his left sleeve. He's also wearing, of all things, Chucks. Sneakers of any kind are the worst shoes you can wear to dance in. The rubber soles catch and I've watched more than my share of first-timers plow face first onto the floor. Marco and Carina have been very happy to have me here when that's happened. I'm their unofficial staff nurse.

"I know, right? I think he said his name is Landon. Want me to get his story?" Carina asks with a wink. I love how passionate Latin people are about all things, but especially romance. This is probably the 20th guy in four years that Carina has tried to set me up with. I haven't actually been out with very many of them. We talk after class and most of them come on too strong. There have been a few who actually sparked my interest enough to give them a single date, but that's all I'm willing to give. I don't know why I can't bring myself to get emotionally involved with anyone. Maybe it's my still-present fear of Dellinger, or maybe it's just me. But I'm 25 years old for crying out loud. I want to settle down one day and have an awesome life like my parents did. That's never going to happen if I don't start giving a guy more than one or two dates.

"Um…ok," I say to Carina with a smile. "Why not?" Just because there wasn't a spark with many of the guys here at the studio doesn't mean there couldn't be with this one. There are the guys at work who have asked me out, a couple of doctors, too, but I have this thing about dating people you work with, especially at a hospital where the politics are ridiculous. Let's hope that once this hot guy opens his mouth, he doesn't flush his chances with me down the toilet.

I smile briefly at Landon from across the room and he gives more of a sexy smirk. Flustered, I turn quickly to find Sam while Carina draws Landon's attention.

Sam is an average guy, good looking. He's definitely your boy next door. When I ask him about why he's taking dance lessons, I have to admit that my heart swoons just a little.

"I've been dating my girlfriend for almost two years now and she comes from this really great Cuban family. I'm going to ask her to marry me in a few months at her parents' anniversary party. There's always dancing when her family gets together, and I'm always on the sidelines. She's never said anything to me about it, but I just want her to know that it's important to me that I at least try…for her." A huge smile spreads across Sam's face and he glows. He's clearly so in love with this girl.

"I think that's awesome, Sam! We're going to make sure you've got moves she didn't even know you had!" I tell him with a hug.

"More like moves *I* didn't know I had!" he laughs.

Marco starts the music and does the basic steps for the class to follow. He shouts the directions out in his passionate accent and I can tell the really new people don't totally understand him yet. He's a trial-by-fire kind of teacher. He believes in throwing the music on and letting the beat move us. Unfortunately, some people and the beat don't get along very well.

Carina wasn't kidding about Sam being clumsy. He's got two left feet, but I applaud his persistence. He's working so hard. If he sticks with it, I think we can whip him into shape in time for his big proposal.

I can't help but sneak a few looks at Landon. He's not doing too badly for his first time, if this is his first time. Carina has him spinning her around and he's following her really well. Some people have natural talent, and his natural talent is *really* sexy.

The class of about ten follows Marco's lead, with a few pauses so he and Carina can show us in slow motion what the moves are supposed to look like. When the hour is almost up Marco comes and whispers in my ear.

"Dance with me. Let's show them how this is *really* done," he says. He cocks his chin down and his head to the side and looks at me from the top of his eyes.

"Not the Latin smolder! You know I can't resist the Latin smolder!" I hang my head, knowing I have no argument.

"Oh, do it, Jenna! You and Marco make a great dance team!" Carina says with a bright smile.

"Ok, ok! I'll do it…but only because I love you dearly," I tell him with a faux defeated voice.

We take our place at the center of the room while the rest of the class gathers around the perimeter. I don't have my best dance shoes on so I'm praying that I make it through this dance without falling on my face. The music starts and I immediately feel good. The beat and the music just start to move through me and a feeling of being invincible takes over.

Marco takes my hand and spins me once before I dip down and let him spin me several times. I pop up and we move together, hips shaking, legs kicking. We even work in one of those moves where I lean back and Marco catches me by the back of my neck. When we're done the room erupts in applause and cheers, and Sam's jaw is on the floor. I look at Landon and he's got the sexiest smirk on his face.

I grab my stuff from the back dressing room and come out to the studio and do my best not to make it completely obvious that I'm looking for Landon. When I find Carina she tells me that he had to leave for a work commitment.

"He was definitely interested in you, though. I didn't have to say anything. He asked about you first," Carina say. She likes to put on her sexy Latina voice whenever she talks to me about men.

"It'll be later next week before I'm back, but not on Saturday. So…if he asks, and *only* if he asks, I guess you can give him my number," I tell her. "I've gotta run. I really do need to go home and sleep. It's Mercy's birthday and I've got a night of celebrating ahead of me. Thanks for the dance, Marco!" I say as I push the door to the studio open. "I'll see you next week!"

I walk back to my apartment both exhilarated and exhausted. I don't think I'll have any trouble falling asleep. My roommate Spring will still be asleep so it'll be perfectly quiet. She'll be gone with her boyfriend Matt by the time I wake, too. Between my third shift work schedule, and Spring's time with Matt, I have the apartment all to myself a lot.

I take a quick shower just to wash the grime of a long shift and an hour of dancing off me before I climb in bed and tune the rest of the world out completely. When I wake up at 3:00, I think that maybe I should dance first thing off my shift every time. I slept so solidly and feel amazingly rested.

I wash my hair during shower number two and actually take the time to straighten it. It's a long mane of soft curls, brown now. It lives in a bun or braid between the hours of 7:00 pm and 7:00 am for work three to four days a week. Thank God I had it cut a couple of weeks ago. The last time I straightened my hair it was all the way down to the small of my back. Now it's just past my shoulder blades. It still takes me almost an hour to do, but it's worth it. I love the sleek look, and Mercy asked if I would please straighten it for her birthday. How could I say no?

With jeans, wedge sandals, and my favorite pink top with the fluttering sleeves on I'm ready to leave. I would normally walk the four blocks to Duke's, but I'm running a tad later than I planned so decide to catch a cab.

I pull the heavy, solid wood door open and walk inside, heading straight to the tables in the back corner closest to the bar. As promised, Jerry held our favorite spot for us. And as expected, Mercy isn't here yet. Our best friends, Jack and Demi are already here, along with Mercy's sister, so I give Jerry a wave as I pass the bar and approach the table with open arms.

"Hey!" I shout as hugs go around. "Of course your sister is not here!" I say to Mercy's sister, Grace. I laugh every time I think about the first time Mercy introduced me to her sister. They said their mom named them thinking they might offer a little bit of each, but was left sorely disappointed.

"You expected her to be on time? You know she wants to make a grand entrance!" Grace says above the noise the growing crowd is causing.

Before I know it, Grace's declaration has become a reality. Mercy has stormed through the door, waving a pink feather boa. "I'm here and I'm ready to get my birthday on, bitches!"

Lots of laughter and more hugs all around. I offer to get the first round so I leave Mercy to her personal parade and head to the bar.

"Hey Jerry! Thanks for holding the table for us." I step up on the brass foot rest and reach across the bar to hug him. Jerry is a Chicago boy through and through. He loves this city and looks every bit like he belongs here. A buff guy, he's shaved his head rather than pretend he's not balding, and he truly has one of the greatest smiles I've ever seen. He reminds me a lot of Oz, which is one of the reasons why I think I love him so much.

23

"Anything for you!" he says in his gruff voice. "First round is on me."

"No! Jerry I can't let you do that!" I protest.

"You guys are family. It's Mercy's birthday…I want to buy the first round so be quiet and go sit down. I'll bring the usual pitcher over in a minute."

"This is why we love you so much! You're the best, Jerry!" I pop over the bar like I did before and give him a quick kiss on the cheek before heading back to our table.

Jerry runs Duke's Bar. His dad was the Duke and opened this place before Jerry was even born. When Duke died ten years ago, Jerry swore he'd never let anything happen to the place. He's done some things to keep it up and running that his dad would never have done, like adding some better items to the menu and opening early on the weekdays. He opens two hours earlier Monday through Thursday and added free Wi-Fi for all the executives who would find that 3:00 report a little more tolerable with a beer in their hand. He also brings in local bands on Saturday nights. That's why we had to have him save our table. Band night has become crazy popular and if he didn't save it, or we got here too late, we'd never get a table.

"Alright ladies and gentlemen! Jerry is bringing over the first round as a birthday gift to our birthday girl. Perhaps you can *thank him* later?" I tease. Jerry has asked Mercy out countless times, but for some weird reason she keeps turning him down.

"Back off, Jenna! It's my birthday. I get one day of you not hounding me about going out with Jerry," she says rolling her eyes.

"I don't get why you don't go out with him either," Jack tells her. "I mean, I know he's not as awesome as me, but…" Jack and Mercy went out a couple of times and had one heated night when they realized them dating was a bad idea. They both have a tendency to thrive on drama and there was too much competition to see which one of them could be the bigger drama queen…or king.

"Enough!" she shouts playfully.

"Ok, guys, here you go," Jerry says with a smile as he brings us a pitcher of Bud and frosted glasses. "And these are for you." Jerry hands Mercy a small bouquet of tulips and from what I can see in the dimmed lights, her cheeks actually blush.

"Oh, wow…that's really sweet of you, Jerry. Thank you." Mercy pauses for a moment before she leans up on her toes and gives Jerry a long kiss on the cheek.

"It was worth it just for that," he says before walking away.

"Don't say it!" she says to me.

We mill around the table drinking, talking, and eating for a while before the band comes up to play. Mercy thinks that Sharper Image just happens to be playing tonight, but the truth is that I got Jerry to book them special for Mercy's birthday. They're her favorite local band because they hardly do any covers and their original stuff is really good.

"Holy smokes! You didn't tell me Sharper Image was playing!" Demi shouts. "Their bass player is ridiculously cute!" They're Demi's favorite band, too, and she has a hard time not salivating over the bass player. He *is* pretty hot.

"Hello! Sitting right here," Jack whines. He and Demi have been an item for a few months now. I'm wondering how long it'll last. They seem pretty happy most of the time, so I guess I'm optimistic.

Hours go by and this literally is the best night I've had in a really long time. I've been working my regular hours and working a little bit of overtime covering for the short staff in the ER on occasion, so while my wallet is happy, my social life has taken a hit. We dance and sing along with the band and Jerry continues to provide us with free food. He argues with me, but I insist on keeping a tab open for the beer. I've lost count on how many pitchers we've had, and somehow I doubt Jerry is going to give me the accurate total when we finally settle up.

"Hey! I heard you went to your dance thing today after work!" Demi shouts to me above the noise. "Are you crazy?"

"I'm not crazy, I just love to dance!" I spin around in my festive mood and that's when I see him. He's standing by the bar, holding a beer in one hand, and looking in my direction.

Landon. Oh my God! He's here! What is he doing here?

"You know him? If not, I suggest you get to…he's hot," Demi says, catching me staring at Landon. She yells right into my ear since I think Jack is done hearing Demi's opinion of other guys.

"I met him, well, I didn't *meet* him, today at dance. We didn't talk, but I guess we know who each other are," I tell her into her ear without taking my eyes off Landon. "You know what? I'm gonna go talk to him!"

I turn and put my beer on the table, straighten myself out, and begin the walk to the other side of the bar where Landon is standing. I'm about five feet away when some assholes next to Landon start pushing each other and break into a fight. I move back and to the side to get out of the way of the onlookers and make room for Jerry who's jumping the bar to break them up. Clearly these guys are new here because *no one* gets in a fight in Jerry's bar. It takes Jerry and some of the regulars to wrestle the guys off each other and hustle them outside.

After all the commotion, I pull myself together again and take one step in Landon's direction, my eyes searching for him among the crowd milling back into the bar.

"Shit! He's gone."

Chapter 3

I walk back to the table completely deflated. I had pulled together those 20 seconds of courage everyone talks about and attempted making the first move with Landon. I thought for sure he had seen me, but I guess not. I can't imagine he would just walk away if he had, especially after Carina said he had been asking about me. Oh, well. I guess tonight wasn't the night for me.

"So, where's hottie guy?" Demi shouts at me above the music.

"I don't know. He left in the scuffle," I tell her with equal volume.

"His loss!" she smiles.

I grab the beer I put down before I went after Landon and finish it in a few gulps. It's almost one and even though I slept this afternoon, I'm pretty wiped.

"I'm gonna head out," I tell Mercy in the lull between Sharper Image's songs.

"Do you have to?" Mercy whines. "The bar doesn't close for another hour, and Jerry said we could hang out until he leaves."

"I think he really just wants *you* to hang out until he leaves," I smirk. I wish she would just give him a chance. He's been nothing but awesome to us for the last three years, and I've never seen him with or heard about him dating anyone else. He's had eyes for Mercy from day one.

"Goodbye!" Mercy is totally avoiding the Jerry issue again. I'll have to keep on her about it at work when she's more lucid. I think I'm finally beginning to wear her down.

"Alright! Alright! Happy birthday! I'll see you guys later. I'll settle up with Jerry but you're on your own for the next hour," I tell them with hugs and kisses. I pay Jerry for the pitchers and, as I suspected he would, he totally jips himself. I'm sure we had at least eight pitchers, but he only charges me for five.

I step out onto the sidewalk and begin the four block walk home. The city is still bustling with Saturday night activity. There are a few other bars on this block and some around the corner the other way, along with three or four great restaurants. I *excuse me* my way through a group of guys as I've done countless times on the walk home from Duke's and keep walking until I reach my building.

I can't get Landon out of my head. I keep seeing him dancing with Carina. It was definitely not his first time taking lessons. He was way too good. She said he asked about me and the thought of that makes me blush for some reason, which, I realize, has never happened. I have *never* thought about a guy like this. Maybe this is what happens when you're ready to stop messing around and look for an actual relationship, not just someone to date.

Ok. Enough of this. He's just a guy. A really, super-hot guy who can dance and who asked about me, but just a guy nonetheless. Pull it together!

I approach my building and, as usual, am struck with just how awesome it is. It's everything I dreamed living in Chicago would be like. I was so lucky to find this place right after I started nursing school. Had I not met Spring when I did, I'm sure I would have been living out of a hotel for months. Her roommate had just gotten married and moved to Ohio when we met in an anatomy and physiology class. It's a great two-bedroom, two bath apartment with an incredible view of the city. There's a grocery store, bakery, and coffee shop all next to each other on the ground level, so it really doesn't get much better than that.

It took a lot of courage on my part to even engage Spring in conversation those first days of class. I was still really unsure of myself and scared about the new life and lie I was beginning to live. She made it easy, though. She's the kind of girl who, when she wants to get to know you, you pretty much have to surrender to it and let her become your new best friend. I'm glad I did. Between Spring, Mercy, Grace, Demi, and Jack, I've been able to create a new little family for myself here in Chicago. It's the best I could have ever hoped for. I don't know what I'd do if anything ever happened to any of them.

I'm extra quiet when I enter the apartment. Spring isn't as much of a night owl as I am even though she has normal hours at an Ob/Gyn office. I pull my shoes off and feel the comfort of my bare feet on the carpet before falling onto my bed. I lay there for a minute knowing I can't fall asleep in my clothes, but enjoying the soothing coolness of my quilt against my skin and through my clothes.

When I get up, I do something I haven't done in long time. Opening the bottom drawer to my dresser, I remove the false bottom and take out the box I have hidden there. I leave the gun in the box but pull out the rest of the contents and set them on the bed.

"Hi Dad," I say with a sigh, brushing my thumb against his face on the picture in my hand. "I miss you a lot." I pick up another picture, this time of both my parents, and turn it over. *Me and Bob on our 5th anniversary. Veronica on the way!* "I miss you, too, Mom." I open the gold locket hanging from an extra-long chain and smile at the pictures of my dad and me. She wore this around her neck until the moment she died. *Stupid cancer.*

I put everything back in the box and hide it again in the bottom of my dresser drawer. I try not to visit too often because I can't have the walk down memory lane cloud the mind of my life now, but…a girl needs to see the face of her mommy and daddy every once in a while.

*****

I have two patients, both of which were here during my last several shifts. Patient one is a 300 pound woman in her 40's with multiple medical problems. She's on a ventilator and in a coma so I wasn't expecting her to have gone anywhere unless she died. She has a history of spiking temps to

107 and is on 70% oxygen. We're basically keeping her alive until her mother can get here in the morning.

Patient two is a man in his 50's with an infected toe. He came to us in the Critical Care Unit because his blood pressure in the ER went to 70 *one* time, which made the doctors worry about sepsis. Every vital sign that he had taken in Critical Care Unit was normal and stable. We're monitoring him, but I suspect he'll be gone soon.

"I have six meds due for my coma patient at 9:00 pm. I had problems getting one of those meds from the pharmacy and it looks like the other staff nurse did, too! Geez! What is going on down there," I rant to Mercy. "Tonight, I checked as soon as I got here and it's not there! I'm going to have to re-order it now! I wish those pharmacy techs would get their heads out of their asses!"

"Whoa! Did you run out of Nutella or something because you are seriously on edge tonight!" Mercy has a look of shock mixed with *you better calm the hell down* on her face.

"Sorry...I'm just distracted and I'm pretty sure the med situation, at least during my last shift, is my fault," I tell her apologetically.

"What's on your mind?" Mercy rolls a chair next to me at the nurse's station and slaps the charts in her hands down. "Spill it!"

"I don't know..." I begin. "It's so dumb, but...I've been thinking about that guy Landon."

"That's not dumb. From what Grace said, he was totally hot. And if you know him from the dance studio, it sounds like you've already got something in common," she says.

"It's not really about him, although, I wouldn't say no to him if he asked. I'm *distracted* by being *distracted* by him," I tell her with some trepidation. She's only a few steps below Carina when it comes to matchmaking.

"Finally! Maybe you'll stop going out on one or two dates before you find something terribly wrong with the guy," she says with a glowering eye.

30

"I don't know what you're talking about," I say wryly, pretending to go back to my paperwork.

"Oh really? Mark?"

"His feet were ridiculously small for a man that tall."

"Steven?"

"He had matching tattoos with his mom."

"Paul?"

"He always smelled like baby powder. What *man* smells like baby powder?"

"Andrew?"

"He wanted to wear his ex-girlfriend's yoga pants out to dinner on our second date because, and I quote, *my package looks really huge in them.*" I raise my eyebrows at her as if this should be obvious to everyone.

"Ok. I'll give you Andrew," Mercy concedes.

"Look, don't go reading anything into it. Landon is just a guy with the most *amazing* smile who dances really well. I've never met a guy who had those things wrapped up into one, super-hot package. He caught me off guard. That's all."

"Ok...for now. In the meantime...Dr. Fisher was asking about you again last week!" Mercy doesn't like to miss an opportunity to set me up, especially with a doctor. "You want me to talk to him?"

"No. You know my rule on going out with people I work with," I say.

"You don't technically work with him. He works an opposite shift from you." Now Mercy is the one raising her eyebrows like this is a no-brainer.

"Fine. It's a firm *maybe*. Let me think about it," I tell her as I surrender.

"Ok, but he'll be here at six to start his rounds, so you better tell me yay or nay before then otherwise it's a definite yay," she smiles. Mercy picks up her charts and heads down the hall to check on her patients before I have a chance to argue with her.

I head down to the pharmacy and tell the person helping me that I am there to pick up the meds I re-ordered for my patient. She gives me a quizzical look and asks if I checked the bin where that med is held. I start to lose it a little bit but contain myself for the greater good. I may still be a little on edge from my recent personal revelation, but this whole thing with them not having the meds for my patient is what's really irking me.

"Yes," I say in a controlled voice. "Of course I checked. There wasn't any there, which is why I re-ordered it, even though I ordered it the first time two hours ago."

The pharmacist steps in and takes care of getting me the medication I need for my patient and assures me that the daily order for it is now updated and that we shouldn't have any problems in the future.

I give patient one her meds and check her temperature. It's about 103, so I check the cooling blanket that she's laying on. The blanket is warm so there is no cold or cool water circulating. It might be because the nurse before me didn't clamp the blanket before putting it under the patient. The patient's weight will have pushed all the water out and seeing as how she weighs 300 pounds, it's not going to refill until I take it out.

I manage to grab Mercy and another nurse to help me roll the patient over so that I can take the blanket out. The other nurse can't lift more than 25 pounds due to a recent injury so she's the one that takes the blanket out. We watch the blanket to see that it fills now that it's free to. Nothing. No filling. So, I order a new blanket, and new cooling machine, just in case.

"Oh, dear Lord, it's only 10:30," I sigh, putting my face in my hands.

"It can only get better, right?"

"Dr. Fisher! I didn't know you were on call tonight," I say with both surprise and nervousness. I'm hoping with everything in me that Mercy hasn't gotten to him yet. I haven't had a moment to think about if I'm going to break my cardinal rule.

"Dr. Wallace had a family emergency, so he asked me to cover for him. Tomorrow is going to be rough since I still have rounds at six," he says with a smile and a breathy laugh. Dr. Adam Fisher is attractive for sure. He's tall with broad shoulders, wavy blonde hair, and blue eyes. He's kind of dreamy. Wrap that up with him being the head of the spinal surgical team and he's every mother's dream for her little girl.

"So…Mercy said I should ask you something," he tells me with a soft tone. I'm going to kill her. "I know our schedules are a little crazy, but, would you like to have dinner with me this week?" Dr. Fisher smiles and my heart does that thing where it feels like it skips a beat. If I'm going to break the rules, I suppose Dr. Hottie is a good place to start.

"Sure. Yeah, that sounds really nice," I tell him with a smile, surprising myself with how quickly I agreed.

His eyes light up and a smile beams across his face. "Awesome! After tonight I've got normal people hours this week, so you just let me know when you're available and we'll call it a date."

"How's Thursday night at seven?" I suggest.

"Thursday at seven is perfect," he says still smiling like a fool. Maybe I should have said yes ages ago. "It's a date."

"I'm looking forward to it, Dr. Fisher," I smile as I write down my address and phone number and give it to him. "Here you go."

"Please, Jenna, call me Adam."

"Of course…Adam."

Adam takes the paper I handed him and tucks it in his front shirt pocket. He holds his gaze on me for a long moment before he heads down the hall to see Dr. Wallace's patients and I get lost in the stack of charts in front of me.

"Excuse me?" I hear a small voice say. I turn and there's a young girl standing to the side of the nurse's station.

"Can I help you? It's a little late for you to be out, don't you think?" I ask.

"I'm here with my gramma to see my aunt," she tells me as she points to patient one's room. She and her grandmother must have slipped in while I was talking with Dr. Fisher.

"Oh," I say softly. "What's your name?"

"Heather."

"Is she gonna die?" the little girl asks. I can see the pain and confusion in this little girl's eyes. She's not any more than eight or nine and this may be the first time she's experienced the death of a loved one.

"What did your gramma tell you?" I ask. I want to tell her the truth that her aunt is most likely going to die, and soon, but the last thing I need to do is scar this child for life if gramma has been holding out hope.

"She said Aunt Lola is gonna die."

"Well, Heather, your gramma is right. Aunt Lola is going to die," I tell her softly. "Shouldn't your mommy or daddy be here with you and Aunt Lola?"

"I don't know where my mommy and daddy are. I used to live with Aunt Lola 'til she got sick. I had to go live with my gramma far away." Heather's delivery of the facts of her life is flat and makes me sad. "Is Aunt Lola gonna go be with the angels?"

Whoa! This kid is full of questions that I'm not sure I should be answering.

"Do you think that's where she's going to go?" I ask Heather.

"Yes. I think so."

"Then that's where she's going. And if you believe that she's up with the angels, then that means she'll be looking down on you and watching over you, so she'll always be with you." I smile at Heather and she smiles at me, seemingly comforted by my confirmation that Aunt Lola will be going to a good and happy place. "You think maybe you're ready to go in and be with your gramma and Aunt Lola?"

"I think so," she says thoughtfully.

"Tell you what…I'm going to be sitting right out here. If you need to come out, you can come sit with me. Sound good?" I offer.

"Yes. Thank you." Heather turns and walks slowly into patient one's room, taking her grandmother's hand as soon as she enters.

I remember being that small, standing with my grandmother next to my mother's bedside, my father on the other side, clutching Mom's hand as she died. It was the worst day of my life. My mother's death was the worst experience of my life. Coming in second is leaving my father to die in under a tree while I ran for my life. At least I got to say goodbye to both of them, and hear them tell my they loved me.

Poor Heather. No mother or father, and the only parent she's known is about to die. I just pray her grandmother lives a very long life.

The rest of my shift goes off without incident. Aunt Lola, patient one, makes no changes and Heather and her grandmother end up leaving a little after midnight. Heather fell asleep so I helped her grandmother put her in a wheelchair to get her down to the car without having to wake her, and also because there's no way she could have carried Heather.

This morning is one of those mornings where I fall asleep on the train countless times. It doesn't happen very often, but sometimes an emotional time like I had with Heather can drain me. I keep waking myself up out of fear that I'll miss my stop. I did that once and ended up walking 12 blocks back to my apartment.

I make it to my stop and trudge to the sidewalk. It's almost eight so I know the bakery will still have some fresh croissants. I secure my bag over my shoulder and pull the door to the bakery open. A gust of delicious air attacks my face as I inhale deeply. There is nothing like the fresh, buttery, organic smell of fresh baked goods.

"Hi Jenna! Haven't seen you in a while. You doin' ok?" Amy says from behind the counter. She's always got a sweet smile, no matter what time I show up.

"Hey Amy! I've been by in the afternoon, and sometimes before work, so

I haven't gotten to see you. I'm good. How are you?" I peruse the case to see if there's anything else I want in addition to my croissant.

"I'm great! What can I get you?" she asks, prepping a bag.

"I think I'm going to go with a couple of plain croissants and a couple of chocolate ones," I tell her. My mouth is salivating just thinking about them. Add the coffee I'm going to get next door and I'll be set for a perfect little breakfast before bed!

"That'll be $8.65," she tells me. I pull a ten from my wallet and we exchange the croissants for the ten and my change. "Thanks, Jenna! Enjoy! Hope we get to see you soon!" she calls as I push the door open.

"Thanks, Amy!" I call back. I'm crossing in front of the grocery store and approaching the coffee shop when I stop in my tracks. Landon is sitting at one of the café tables outside the coffee shop. It's impossible for me to enter the coffee shop, or the building to get to my apartment, without passing right in front of him, so I suck it up and smile.

"Hi," I say nervously.

"Hi," he says with equal nervousness as he stands.

"Um…what are you doing here?" I ask him. It seems strange that he would be here…at my coffee shop…where my apartment is…right now.

"Would you freak out if I told you I was waiting for you?" he says with a coy smile.

"*Are* you waiting for me?" I ask a little hesitantly. I'm a little freaked out, but more excited than anything. After he disappeared that night at Duke's I wasn't sure if I'd ever see him again.

"I'm only waiting for you if you think it's sweet and charming. I just happen to be here if you think it's creepy," he says with a timid smile.

"The fact that you just said that makes it kind of sweet and charming," I tell him with a smile I'm trying not to let split my face.

"Great! We haven't been formally introduced," he says. "I'm Landon Scott."

"Jenna Rockwell. It's nice to meet you, Landon," I tell him as we shake hands. *Oh, God, his hands are strong. Shut up, Jenna!*

"It's more than nice to meet you, Jenna. Can...I...buy you a cup of coffee?" he asks motioning to the door to the coffee shop.

"Sure," I answer with a little bit of an embarrassed smile. I'm still in my scrubs and my hair is in a crazy bun on the back of my head. And coming off a 12-hour shift, I know I look really tired.

He opens the door to the coffee shop and we walk into an aromatic sea of the greatest scent on earth. We stand in line, both quiet as we wait for the few customers in front of us to move along. I do my best not to stare at him, but it's difficult. He's got this thing about wearing fitted shirts and I'm pretty sure it's because he knows he looks totally hot in them. His tattoo is peeking out again and I fight the urge to lift his sleeve so I can see what it is. It looks Celtic, but I could be wrong.

"You want something other than coffee? A latte or something? I'm buying, and I don't mind saying I'm a *pretty* generous date," he smirks.

"Just a regular coffee is great, thank you," I giggle. *I giggled! Oh, my God, what is this guy doing to me?*

We automatically walk back out to the table where I found him and sit down. He's comfortable, casual. Totally at ease as he leans back in the metal chair.

"Would you like a croissant? I have plain and chocolate," I offer.

"I like a girl who brings something to the table," he chuckles. "I'll take one of those chocolate ones if you can spare it."

"Here you go!" I take a chocolate croissant and place it on two napkins in front of him. "They're fresh. Just got them next door."

"Holy crap! This is the best thing I have ever put in my mouth," he says with muffled joy.

"I know, right?" I take a bite of a plain croissant and it practically melts in my mouth.

"So, Jenna, tell me about yourself," he inquires as he takes a sip of his coffee.

"C'mon, Landon. You don't strike me as a small talk kind of guy. I mean,
you *did* find a way to know exactly where I was going to be this morning. And you *were* at Duke's on Saturday night. So why don't we start with you telling me how we came to be having coffee and croissants this morning." I say to him. It's too early to go into the vague backstory of my life and I want to know more about this guy who has seemed to magically pop into it.

"Well played, Jenna, well played. Well…I saw you at Carina's and, as cheesy as it sounds, I was just drawn to you. You came scurrying in like a frazzled schoolgirl, but then you *owned* that dance floor." I blush as I recall the dance Marco and I put on for the class that day. "I did some digging – and by digging I mean I just asked Carina where you hung out, where you lived, and where you worked. Don't tell that woman anything you don't want anyone to know." We both laugh because that is absolutely true.

"So you knew I was going to be at Duke's? And you saw me there?" He nods and gives me a tightlipped smile. "Why did you leave?"

"I don't know. I started feeling like a creeper. You were there with your friends and I thought maybe you were just coming over to tell me I was intruding," he tells me.

"That didn't stop you from waiting for me this morning," I challenge.

"This morning is different. This morning I get you all to myself." Landon smiles and a nervous lump appears in my throat. I take a sip of coffee in an effort to push it down.

"You really *aren't* about the small talk, are you?" I say, biting my lip so I don't grin like a total fool.

"Not at all. Have dinner with me," he says. It's not a question.

"My schedule is kind of crazy…" I begin.

"When? When are you free?" Landon leans forward in his chair and

38

locks his eyes on mine. They're this beautiful shade of brown, so rich and velvety.

"I, um…" I clear my throat, caught off guard by his directness. "I'm free tomorrow night," I tell him.

"Perfect. I already know where you live, sort of. Tell me which apartment is yours and I can pick you at your door properly." He leans back in his chair again, the intensity of the moment is gone now that I've surrendered to his *I have to meet this girl* techniques.

"How about I just meet you down here 7:30?" I propose.

"No."

"No?"

"No. I don't meet girls for dates and I don't go Dutch. I'm the guy. I pick you up at your door, take you out and pay for it, and then I drop you off at your door. So…I've already proven that I can find out where your apartment building is. How hard do you think it'll be to find out which apartment is yours?" There's that smirk again. I've known this guy for 30 minutes and I already love his smirk.

"Well played, Landon, well played," I say, mirroring his smirk. "It's apartment 420."

"Wonderful. Now, I imagine you have some sleeping to do, so I'm going to tear myself away from the best coffee and croissant date I've ever had and let you go." We both stand and I move to the other side of the table, toward the entrance to the building.

"Thank you, Landon…for the coffee. I'll see you tomorrow night." I reach out my hand to shake his and he looks at me like I'm being silly. Eventually he takes my hand in both of his and grins.

"Thank *you*, Jenna." He holds my hand with his for a few long seconds, gazing into my eyes, before he lets it fall.

I walk to the entrance to the building and open the door. "Oh, wait, um…I feel like I should give you my number, just in case."

"I already have it," he says with that smirk.

Of course he does.

Chapter 4

"I can't believe I'm doing this." I lay another outfit on my bed in a pathetic attempt to find something to wear on my date with Landon. I decide against a skirt since my idea of a good time does not include having my skirt fly up and flashing him. "I barely know this guy and I'm totally freaking out about what I'm going wear!"

"What about this?" Spring hands me a top from my closet that still has the tags on it. "This would be great with your white jeans."

"You are a life saver! I totally forgot I had this!" I pull on the blue striped top over the white cami I already have on and then paint myself into my white jeans. "Have they always been this tight?"

"Oh please! You look great. He's going to flip," Spring says reassuringly. I determined early on that Spring's hippy parents knew what they were doing when they named her. She really is the most chipper person I know. She's a little shorter than me with an athletic build from her competitive swimming days and just the cutest girl ever.

There's a knock at the door and I freeze. "Shit! He's here!"

"Calm down, crazy! It's just a guy. I'll go let him in," Spring says. I hear muffled greetings and Spring is back in my room within two minutes. "Ok. You're screwed. That is not *just* a guy."

"Not helping!" I grimace.

"Just don't catalog this one's faults too quickly. I wouldn't mind seeing him stick around a little longer than the others." Spring nudges me, raising her eyebrows like a caricature.

"Yeah, I'm sure your boyfriend will love that," I say as I nudge her back. "Ok. Deep breaths. I'm good. I can do this." I repeat this four or five more times before opening the door and walking out into the living room.

Landon is standing in my living room with a bouquet of flowers in his hands. I thought his whole fitted shirt thing was hot, but the black vest and white dress shirt with the sleeves rolled up tops that by a million percent. He hasn't shaved and is still wearing the same sexy, scruffy beard he wore the morning I first saw him at the studio.

"Wow. You look incredible," he says. "These are for you." He hands me the flowers and I'm immediately impressed. The bouquet is filled with tulips and irises, my favorite flowers.

"Thank you. That was so sweet of you," I tell him, feeling the petals of the flowers. I've never had a guy bring me flowers. Even Brian Parker who took me to my senior prom didn't get me a corsage or anything.

"I'll take those and put them in some water for you," Spring says.

"Oh…I'm sorry. Landon, this is my roommate, Spring. Spring, this is Landon," I say a bit flustered.

"Yeah, we met at the door when I opened it for him, Jenna." Spring gives me a sideways look and the two shake hands anyway before Spring says her goodbyes and goes into the kitchen.

"I guess we should be going?" Time for me to regroup from my frazzled state.

"Yes. I made a reservation. I hope you like insanely good Mexican food," Landon tells me as I open the door.

"It's my favorite, so that's perfect." I smile and let Landon open doors for me as we make our way outside.

"I thought we'd take a cab there, and then maybe you'd let me take you for a walk after." He smiles at me and I'm distracted for a moment. He crooks his head as if to ask me again and I'm brought back to the moment.

"Can we walk now?" I smile hopefully at him.

"Yeah," he smiles, pleasantly surprised at my suggestion.

We're quiet for about a block before I have to break the silence. It's hard to concentrate on anything with Landon's scent lingering in the air and him walking so close to me. I'm trying not to be alarmingly distracted by him, but it's difficult.

"Carina said it was your first time at the studio, but it clearly wasn't your first time doing the Salsa. How long have you been dancing?" I ask.

"You picked up on that, did you?" There's that smirk. *Must...look...away.* "My mom was a dance teacher. She used to take me to her studio with her when I was little. I watched in between coloring. Then when I got older, she made me learn all the dances she taught. Everything from Salsa, to Swing, and even some ballroom dancing." A soft expression covers his face as he recalls those days with his mom and my heart swells a little.

"So how long has it been since you danced or took a lesson?"

"I haven't really danced in about seven or eight years. I moved to Chicago about a month ago and thought I'd give it a shot. I was actually pretty surprised at what I remembered," he tells me as we continue to walk.

"Well, you were pretty great for a guy who hasn't danced in that long," I say.

"I knew you were watching me," he teases.

"I was only watching you because you looked like you were so nervous you were going to pee your pants. I didn't know if you were going to fall on your face and, *as a nurse*, I would have been obligated to help bandage you up!" I say in my defense. It's only partially the truth, though.

"I was only nervous when you looked over at me," he says quietly. "I told you I was immediately drawn to you, Jenna."

I smile shyly at him and watch the curb as we cross the street. I try to think of something clever to say, but Landon puts his hand on the small of my back as we cross the street. Now I'm too consumed with the warmth of his touch.

"How long have you been dancing?" he asks.

"I used to dance when I was little, then I took a break after my mom died," I tell him.

"Oh, I'm sorry. Can I ask how old you were when she passed?" He's walking and looking at me with concern at the same time. It's nice.

"I was ten. She had breast cancer and it was pretty aggressive. It took a while after I she died for me to be ready to get back into dancing. When I did, I danced all the way through high school and after."

"What about your dad?" he continues.

"He died a while ago. Can we not talk about my depressing past, please?" I beg. This is about the time I stop giving information about my past. It's generic enough. I mean, lots of people lose their parents. Lots of little girls take dance.

"Sorry. I just…I just want to know you, Jenna," he tells me with a bit of an apologetic tone.

"It's ok. I want to be known." *Did I just say that? And mean it?*

We continue to walk and talk about various things. He tells me he grew up in Miami, which explains his mom's love of Latin dance, but that he went to college in Michigan. He has an older sister who still lives in Miami with her husband and kids, whom he adores. His grandparents played a pretty heavy roll in his life. With his mom being Latina, it's very much a part of their culture. They both passed away several years ago. His grandfather had a heart attack while scuba diving, which I think it pretty remarkable for a 70-year old man. Landon's face shows his sadness when he tells me that his grandmother died just a few years later. His grandparents were so close he believes she died from a broken heart.

"Can that happen?" he asks, stopping me to ask again. "Can someone die from a broken heart?" He's being so transparent with me, so real. I've seen people watch their loved one die right in front of them and they've not been this real about their emotions.

"Actually, yes. Well, it's not a medical diagnosis, so a lot of doctors and nurses don't believe in it. But…I do. When the love someone had that was keeping them going is no longer there, it's hard for some people to want to exist in a world that doesn't include that other person. They just give up their will to live. They become weaker, and sometimes get sick. Without the will to live, the sickness takes over and they die. If you trace it back, past all the medical stuff, they really did die of a broken heart."

Landon stares at me, his brown eyes diving into my ocean blue ones. He takes a step closer to me and moves a piece of my hair out of my face before he runs his hand down my arm. My heart is racing. Now I *know* I've never felt this.

"I think we passed the restaurant," he says softly, holding his gaze for only a moment longer.

"I think we did, too," catching my breath and looking around. "Oh, my gosh, we walked all the way to Navy Pier!"

"It's a good 12 blocks from the restaurant, and your place was nine blocks! Your feet must be killing you in those shoes," he says, noticing the heels I'm wearing.

"Oh, please! I walk 21 blocks in these shoes all the time!" I tease.

"I have an idea. What do you say we skip the restaurant, grab a burger and park it on a bench on the pier?" His eyes are hopeful and I can't think of a better way to improvise our date.

"I say that sounds great." I smile and hope I'm not being too agreeable. It's been so long since I've been on a date where I think I care if there's a second date. I don't remember the rules of playing hard to get.

"Awesome!" Landon grabs my hand and leads me down the pier. He's threaded his fingers through mine, which in my mind has always seemed like a much more intimate grasp. We stop at a burger place with outdoor seating, but Landon places our order to go. I don't hear him order because it's pretty loud, but figure he just ordered a couple of regular burgers and fries.

We walk the length of the pier to the last bench facing the water. It's a gorgeous night. The pier is lit up by all the restaurants and attractions. There's a special light hovering over the pier from the Ferris wheel, while the dinner cruise ship on the lake is adding a romantic glow to the water.

"Well, this is some first date, Landon Scott," I tell him while I unwrap my burger.

"You said *first*," he says flirtatiously.

"I...uh..." I let out a defeated breath, not knowing how to recover from that.

"It's ok, Jenna. I've already been thinking of where to take you on our second date." He's smiling this ridiculously sexy smile and I realize I want to kiss him. I mean, really kiss him. But...I contain myself and take a sip of my soda.

"This is Dr. Pepper," I say in shock.

"Yeah...is that not ok?" Landon looks worried.

"It's my favorite," I tell him with a grin. I take the bun off the top of my burger to pick off the onions, but there aren't any. In fact, it's made just the way I like it. No onions, extra pickles, one super fresh tomato slice, ketchup, mayo, and extra mustard. "How did you..."

"This is the part where I ask if you would find it sweet and charming, or creepy," Landon says tentatively.

"Just be honest with me, Landon. You've hit the nail on the head with my favorite things, down to how I like my burger. What's the deal?" How could he possibly know how I like my burger, or that Dr. Pepper and Mexican food are my favorites?

"I...dug a little deeper than the resume Carina gave me. I hope you don't think I'm some kind of creepy stalker. I just really wanted to make sure that if you let me take you out, that it would be perfect for you." He looks nervous now, maybe a little afraid that he's blown it.

"Who did you talk to?" I ask. I haven't decided if this will be a list of people to thank or punch.

"The cook at Duke's knows how you like your burger. And, uh…I talked to the guy at your grocery store. He's how I knew you were a Dr. Pepper girl," he tells me.

"What about the Mexican food?"

"According to your grocer, you make *a lot* of guacamole." Landon looks at me with hopeful eyes, wanting to hear me tell him again that his efforts to meet me and get to know me are sweet and charming. They are…mostly.

"Ok. Let's just…now that you've met me, you ask me anything you want to know. No more snooping around. Do what normal guys do and unknowingly make a reservation at a restaurant I hate…and don't have a plan B. Can you do that?" I tell him, satisfied with his answer.

I'm not concerned about Dellinger. If Landon was working for him, a list of my favorite things would be the last thing he'd need to confirm who I really am. That, and Dellinger wouldn't use such benign tactics. No, Landon is just a guy smitten with a girl. It's kind of nice to have a guy be this interested in me. I wonder if any of the guys I gave a date to would have become this interested had I given them the opportunity. I really like Landon and, oddly enough, I do think it's sweet that he tried so hard to meet me and make sure this night was perfect.

"I can do that. No more snooping. Scout's honor." He lifts his hand and gives the Boy Scout sign. We both chuckle nervously, and I make a conscious decision to move forward.

"So…you know what I do…why don't you tell me what you do, Landon?" I ask. I pick through my fries finding any that are overdone and super crunchy. Those are my favorite.

"I work for a securities company," he says.

"Like, installing security systems?" I inquire between crunches.

"No, more like protection. For example, a company might be bought or sold and dismantled into several smaller companies. There's always information that can't be leaked to the new facets of the agency, so I work with the CEOs to protect them and the information their company values," he explains.

"Sounds boring," I tease with a straight face.

"Oh really? What would be more interesting to you to talk about?" he asks, laughing with me as I break my poker face. The last guy I teased about having a boring job took it very personally and developed a sudden headache, thus ending our date before either of us had finished our dinner. It's nice to see that Landon doesn't take himself too seriously.

"I want to hear about your dancing!" I tell him.

"Great! I knew that was going to come back and bite me in the ass!"

"It's too late now, Fred Astaire! I want to hear about your ballroom dancing days," I declare with a huge smile.

"I am not going to *tell* you anything. I'm going to *show* you." Landon stands and holds out his hand to me. "Dance with me."

I don't hesitate for a second and immediately take my shoes off and stand up, taking Landon's hand. He leads me to a more open area of the pier near where we've been sitting. People are looking at us, but I don't care. There's something about being with Landon that makes me want to embrace all the things I've been holding at arm's length.

"Waltz?" he says, wrapping his hand around to my back above my waist and holding our extended hands together. His touch is amazing.

"Tango." I counter with a smirk of my own.

"You're killing me here, you know that." He tosses his head back and laughs. "What the hell! You ready?"

"I was about to ask you the same thing?" I raise my eyebrows and realize that I am officially flirting. I position my hand on his shoulder and we bow our arms, putting ourselves into proper dancing posture.

Landon starts counting and we start to move. He stops counting after a few sets as we both realize that we're moving together perfectly, both hearing the music in our heads. A few more passes like this, and with our eyes locked on each other's, Landon lets go of my hand and puts his arm around my waist. I move my arm to his waist and we spin, Landon still holding onto my eyes with his.

I've danced this dance a hundred times with Marco and other experienced dancers at the studio and it never felt this way. I've heard professional dancers say that dancing with a partner should be almost as emotional as having sex. You have to connect with your dance partner so that the emotions and message of the dance come across to your audience. If this isn't a connection, I don't know what is.

This connection seems apparent to the onlookers around us on the pier because as we stop and I don't remove my eyes from Landon's, whistles and clapping erupt. I'm trying to catch my breath when Landon's mouth is suddenly on mine. I part my lips to receive his kiss, but hold back, unsure of myself. I feel our bodies move in line with each other, his arms wrapping around me.

"I don't usually do that on a first date," he says, now catching his breath.

"Tango?" I smile.

"I *definitely* don't Tango on a first date. Then again, I've never had such a worthy partner." Landon's face is still so close to mine. I can feel his breath against my mouth and all I want to do is kiss him again.

"Well, you *did* refer to our meeting yesterday morning as the best coffee and croissant date you'd ever had. So, technically, this would be our second date," I reply softly.

"Well played, Jenna, well played." Landon kisses me again and this time I don't hold back. I part my lips again, letting us explore each other in a kiss that's a show in and of itself for the onlookers. He grabs the back of my head and a fistful of my hair with it and a noise escapes from the back of my throat. I have never, ever, been kissed like this.

More clapping and whistling brings us back to reality and we both chuckle with just a bit of embarrassment.

"I really hadn't planned on that, Jenna. I just want you to know that…considering our earlier conversation. It was a bonus, though," he says. I think he's sincere. I look into his eyes and think he's just one of those passionate guys, and when he wants something, he dives right in.

"I believe you. It's been a while since…well…it was nice," I tell him.

We pack up our leftovers and walk back down the pier to the circle where there are a dozen cabs waiting. Landon suggests we take a cab back to my place since he's thinking neither of us is up for walking 21 blocks back. I agree and scoot into the cab first.

"This night was way more than I expected, Jenna. I hope you had just as great a time as I did." Landon takes my hand and threads his fingers through mine and a shiver runs across my body.

This is insane. How could I possibly have this kind of reaction to someone I just met? This has never happened before. I'm giddy and excited and totally acting like a 16-year old girl on the inside.

"I did. I had a really great time, Landon. Thank you," I tell him honestly. I like being open to more than just a date or two. I like the hopeful feeling that comes with being willing to look at the potential in a relationship. Regardless of what happens with Landon, it feels good to be here in this emotional place.

"I want to see you again, as soon as possible," he says sitting up as if this is an epiphany.

I smile at his enthusiasm. "I'd like to see you again, too."

"Tomorrow," he declares. "Are you working tomorrow night?" He looks at me with anticipation of my answer and I feel myself fill with as much anticipation for when I'll get to see him again, too.

"I'm not working tomorrow," I tell him, still smiling. "Oh, but wait. I can't."

"Why not?" Disappointment coats these two little words.

"Um…I have a date." I watch for his reaction, not sure what he'll say or do. He doesn't say anything, but sits back against the seat. "It's one of the doctors at the hospital. I agreed to the date the other night, before I saw you at the coffee shop. He's kind of been asking me out for a while, so I'll feel bad if I back out." *Why did you tell him that?*

"I understand, Jenna." He takes a deep breath and lets out a rush of air. "This is just our first, uh, second date. I don't have any expectations."

I cock my head to the side, questioning his statement. I don't believe him. I think he felt the connection between us as much as I did. That kiss he planted on me said as much.

"Ok," he says, giving in to my questioning look. "I have an expectation, well…more of a hope. I didn't want to say anything after our whole conversation about what I did to meet you. I don't want to scare you off, Jenna."

"I don't think you're going to scare me off," I say quietly. I want to tell him about the connection I felt so he knows the lengths he went to get to know me weren't in vain. That right now I really wish I wasn't going out with Adam Fisher tomorrow night. That, in fact, I wish tonight would never end so I didn't have to eventually say goodnight to Landon. But it's too soon and saying any of those things will only paint me as some desperate chick that doesn't have a clue what she's doing.

"I like you, Jenna…a lot." Landon caresses the back of my hand with his fingers. That same shiver I got earlier returns and makes me smile.

"That's $15.70," the cabbie says as he stops in front of my building. Landon gives him a twenty and tells him to keep the change.

We make our way upstairs to my apartment and stop outside the door, standing silently. I examine his face and notice a small scar above his right eye and make a mental note to ask him about it sometime because something in me wants to know everything about him. I suddenly become very aware of just how unfair that would be since he'll never get close enough to know everything about me. No one ever will. But at least I'm finally willing to let someone into the world of Jenna Rockwell.

"Do you want to come in...maybe continue this conversation?" I ask with a hint of coyness.

"I would love to come in," he says, running his fingers down my arm again.

I turn and unlock the door, trying to be as quiet as possible. It's after midnight and Spring is going to be in bed already. We enter the living room and I reach to turn on the table lamp so it won't be too bright.

"Can I get you something to drink? A glass of wine maybe?" I set my purse on the kitchen table and turn around face Landon.

"I'm good," he says with the sexiest smile.

"Ok..." I move to the couch and sit sideways, tucking my leg under the other one. I take my heels off and set them next to the end table. Within seconds, Landon is facing me, mirroring my posture. He rests his arm across the back of the couch and plays with a lock of my hair while we sit close.

"Earlier you said that it had been a while. What did you mean?" Landon takes my hand and moves it to his leg while holding it. I lose concentration for a moment with a brief vision of all the places my hand could travel within seconds.

"Oh, that...it's nothing. It's a little embarrassing," I begin. Landon lowers his chin and looks at me over his nose. "Fine. It's been a really long time since I've been kissed like that."

"I'm sure your idea of *a really long time* really isn't that long at all."

"Oh, Landon, you don't want to know..." I start, but Landon gives me that look again, convincing me to divulge my pathetic dating history. "Truth be known...I've never been kissed like that. Not that I've really given anyone the chance in the last several years," I admit.

"*That* is a tragedy," he says, perfectly serious.

"I sound totally pathetic, don't I?" I close my eyes and shake my head, disbelieving that I'm actually having this conversation.

"Not at all. It's a shame someone hasn't felt strongly enough about you to kiss you the way you deserve to be kissed. And, I'd be lying if I said my ego didn't just get a huge boost." He smiles and runs his thumb along my jawline."

"Your ego could have taken a boost earlier if you hadn't disappeared on me at the dance studio that day, *or* at Duke's," I tease.

"Alright, alright! I get it! I was slow…but not anymore." Landon takes the hand that's been playing with my hair and reaches behind my head, pulling me into him. He kisses me and I feel a surge of nervous excitement rush through me. Landon is still holding one of my hands, so I reach up and touch his face and then run my fingers through his hair with the other. He moans and I think I'm going to jump out of my skin. It is by far the sexiest sound I have ever heard.

Landon lets go of my hand and runs his fingers up my leg to my waist. Another rush of electricity runs through me and I shift my body, pushing Landon against the back of the couch and straddling him. He takes my face in his hands and kisses me even more deeply than he already was. His hands brush the sides of my breasts as he skims my body, causing me to moan. He starts to unbutton my shirt when something clicks and he stops abruptly.

"Jenna," he says my name breathlessly and I want to crush my lips to his. "I, um, we…I should go." Embarrassed, I move my body off of him, not sure what else I should do, or what I should say.

"I'm sorry, Landon. I didn't mean…" I stutter.

"No. It's nothing you did, Jenna. I just…I have a work thing tomorrow and…" he stammers.

"Of course." We stand and I walk him to the door.

"I had an incredible time with you tonight," he says, brushing my cheek.

"I did, too." *Obviously.*

"I *do* want to see you again. I'll call you. Have fun with the doctor." Landon opens the door, kisses me on the cheek, and is gone.

I close the door behind him, mortified I acted the way I did. I practically attacked him on the couch on our *first date*! Add the fact that I told him I had a date tomorrow and I batted a thousand tonight! *Way to go, Jenna.*

I am never hearing from Landon Scott again.

Chapter 5

I pour my coffee mindlessly, rehashing the last 30 minutes of my date with Landon last night. I didn't sleep well and I now I'm trying to convince myself that I didn't totally blow it with him.

"Hey! How did your date go?" Spring asks in her usual chipper morning voice. Even on my best morning, I am nowhere near this cheerful.

"It went," I say, sarcasm oozing from me.

"Oh, my God, what happened?" Spring grabs a cup from the cabinet and quickly fills it with coffee and a ridiculous amount of creamer and sweetener. She plops down on a bar stool at the counter and holds her cup with two hands at her mouth, waiting for me to spill the beans. "Please don't tell me he picks his nose or smells like feet when you get up close!"

"No! He doesn't pick his nose and he smells as amazing as Ryan Reynolds looks. It was an incredible date...until I unleashed six years of sexual frustration on him." I lean on the counter, putting my face in my hands.

"What did you do?" Springs eyes are wide.

"Ok...so, we were going to walk to the restaurant, but we just kept talking and walking and before we knew it we were in front of Navy Pier. Then we got burgers and sat on a bench and talked. *Then*...he danced with me on Navy Pier. I mean, *really* danced...like, *the Tango* danced. It was the most incredible dance I'd ever danced. He moves like, oh, my God...then he kissed me, and I mean *really* kissed me." I decide not to tell Spring about the lengths Landon went to meet me. I've already chosen sweet and charming over creepy and I don't want to have to convince her otherwise if she chooses creepy.

"So far it sounds as amazing as I hoped it would be for you," she says.

"It gets better...then it gets worse. We came back here and talked for a little bit before he kissed me again. It got hot and heavy and before I knew it I was…" I bury my face in my hands again so I don't have to see Spring's reaction when I say the words. "I was straddling him on the couch."

"Who would blame you, Jenna? Landon is seriously the hottest guy I have ever laid eyes on," she says without missing a beat.

"I wouldn't tell Matt you said that!" I chuckle. Matt and Spring have been dating for over a year. Things are going really great between them and I'm afraid *I'll* be the one looking for a new roommate soon.

"Seriously! Don't be so hard on yourself, Jenna. You said it yourself…you haven't had any real action since before you moved here. You can't be surprised when a guy as great, and as hot, as Landon comes on to you that you explode. If you'd stop pushing guys away, you might not be so frustrated. When did he leave? Oh my gosh! Is he still here?"

"No! I may have bottled up frustrations, but I wouldn't have slept with him on the first date! Geez, Spring! No…that's the mortifying part. *He* stopped us and then he left. Said he had to work today, but that he'd call me. He also told me to have fun with the doctor tonight." Spring paints a puzzled look on her face. "That was the other *super great* part of the night. When he asked to see me tonight, I told him about my date with Dr. Fisher."

"What is wrong with you?" she asks with a deadpan face.

"I'm a moron. Next question."

"You're not a moron. You just don't know what you're doing. But…if this guy really is as great as you think he is, he'll call. And if he's not, then maybe he was just your catalyst guy. The guy to get you off your ass and back into the dating world without finding the stupidest things wrong with every guy you go out with. The guy that makes you realize you're done with casual dating and that you're ready to be a big girl. I gotta run. I'm meeting Matt after work, so I won't be here to meet the good doctor, but I'm sure you're going to have a great time." Spring kisses my cheek, grabs her lunch from the fridge and her purse from the hook by the door and is gone.

With a deep breath and a swig of coffee, I right myself and get ready to go dance. I'm hoping I can get some endorphins flowing and start feeling more positive about how things ended with Landon last night.

The 9:00 am studio class today is ballroom and I can't help but hope that Landon will be there…that he's figured out a way to see me today since I can't see him tonight. I enter the studio fully aware that a stupid look of anticipation is spread across my face. I scan the room and check out each of the eleven students' faces before I'm left with nothing but disappointment.

"He's not here," Carina tells me. She's tightening the long, fringed scarf around her waist as she approaches.

"Yeah, I can see that," I say. She follows me to the side of the room where everyone dumps their belongings. "We went out last night," I tell her.

"Aye! I knew it! He came back later on Saturday and asked a hundred questions about you! How did it go?" Carina asks with immediate excitement.

"It started out as the most amazing date I've ever had, but…I blew it in the end." I sit and put my ballroom shoes on.

"How could you have blown it?" she says with disbelief.

"Let's just say I came on a little too strong and sent him running. I may have also told him about the date I have tonight with one of the doctors I work with."

"A doctor! My goodness, Jenna! You're on a roll,'" she says with that sexy tone.

"Yeah, I'm hot stuff," I reply blankly. "Has Landon been back to class?"

"No. I haven't seen him since Saturday. I'm sure he's going to call you. He's a fool if he doesn't!" Carina's hopeless romanticism is endearing. I just nod and work to convince myself that she's right. I never told Landon that my class attendance is sporadic, and that I won't be back at the Saturday morning class for three weeks.

I make it through class, doing my best to let the euphoric feeling I usually get from dancing take over. I think about my Tango with Landon last night and remember just how ridiculously in sync we were. All that seems to do is wash me with embarrassment for my behavior last night.

I walk home and slowly approach my building, hoping to find Landon waiting for me again outside the coffee shop. No such luck. The sidewalk tables and chairs are empty. I let out a big sigh and walk into my building and up to my apartment with the intent of finding something terribly fattening to drown my sorrows in. Spring and I are both relatively healthy eaters, so there isn't much in the way of totally fattening in the kitchen, but my search does reveal that I have everything I need to make a hollandaise sauce. So…eggs benedict it is!

I stuff my face and drown my sorrows with the freshly made orange juice Spring made the other day. I hope she doesn't get mad that I drank almost all of it. It literally took six bags of oranges and two hours to make this one pitcher.

Feeling a surge of energy, which I can only attribute to the massive quantities of Vitamin C I just consumed, I take to cleaning the entire apartment. I turn on the mix playlist Mercy, Spring and I made one night after too many bottles of red wine and start fluffing the pillows on the couch from where Landon and I flattened them. Not able to look at this couch any longer I grab the supplies from under the kitchen sink and scrub and scour the bathrooms. I dust and polish the furniture, and finally vacuum every room before I collect our laundry.

We're fortunate to have a closet for a full-size washer and dryer in the apartment so I spend the next two hours doing all of our laundry, folding it and putting it away. I pause only a few times when random songs play as proof to our drunken state when we make the playlist. Like when KISS's *Rock and Roll All Nite* ends and Barry Manilow's *Can't Smile without You* begins.

There's a knock at the door precisely at seven just as I'm deciding which shoes to wear with my dark jeans and orange top. I know Dr. Adam Fisher is standing on the other side of that door and I wish I felt the same kind of crazy butterflies as I did when it was Landon. It's not that I'm not excited. He's a well-respected, attractive doctor for crying out loud. I just don't feel that same spark as I did with Landon.

"Hi, Adam," I say opening the door with a determination to enjoy myself tonight. Adam is standing there smiling wide and wearing a suit, with a baby blue tie and everything. I feel terribly underdressed and Adam's quick-changing facial expression tells me he feels the same way about my choice of clothing.

"Hi, Jenna. I'm sorry…I really should have told you where we were going. We have time for you to change," he says, the smile returning to his face.

"Oh, uh, ok. I'll be just a minute. Make yourself at home," I tell him. I close the door and motion to the living room before going back to my room to change. I would never have done this before my new resolve to grow up and start looking at the potential a date has. I would have rightfully used his rudeness to end the date right then and there.

Now I really have to be determined to have a good time tonight. Adam clearly isn't a go-with-the-flow kind of guy. He's got a plan and we're going to stick to it. *Don't compare him to Landon. Don't compare him to Landon.* I make this my mantra for the night and choose a black pencil skirt, a blue top that nearly matches his tie, and a pair of black patent heels. I check myself in the mirror and, feeling good about being up to par with Adam, I find him standing in the living room.

"Oh, that's much better. You look lovely, Jenna," he tells me.

So glad I meet your approval, I think. "Thank you. Let's go."

We step outside onto the sidewalk and I almost suggest walking to the restaurant, but decide against it since Dr. I've Got It All Planned Out is in charge. Adam grabs a cab and we're quickly being whisked away. It doesn't take long before we're pulling up to an Italian restaurant about two blocks from Navy Pier. I sigh to myself remembering how Landon and I walked all the way from my apartment just last night.

Adam and I are seated at a quiet table for two in this restaurant I didn't know existed. After we order and our server brings the bottle of wine Adam ordered, we settle in for what I hope will turn into a lovely evening.

"So, Jenna, tell me about yourself," Adam asks. *Standard first date question number one!*

"There's not much to tell, really," I say. I take a sip of my red wine. It's delicious and obviously more expensive than the cheap stuff Mercy and I usually drink. "How about you go first? Did you always want to be a doctor?" I avoid asking about his family for now. I have a rehearsed answer I give about mine, but think maybe I'll wait it out before I open the door to that conversation. Since I'm trying to be more open to things, I may be able to tweak my answer and provide a little more of a personal spin on it.

"Yeah. I was the guy studying my ass off in high school so I could get into a great college and go pre-med. I used to want to have a family practice and then thought about pediatrics, but decided that I didn't have the patience for it. Some people go to the doctor for every sneeze and then some don't come until it's turned into something worse. And don't get me started on pediatrics!" he huffs.

"You don't like kids?" Him not liking kids is going to diminish any potential I'm working to find here. So far this date is going the exact opposite of how I had once hoped it would. I'd blame it on me being preoccupied with thoughts of Landon, but that is definitely not the case. Dr. Adam Fisher has taken us on the a-hole train and I'd like to get off.

"Oh, no, I like kids," he says with a smile. "It's the parents that would drive me crazy. I have a good friend in pediatrics and you wouldn't believe the ignorance and arrogance of some parents. They don't want to vaccinate because they think they know better. Then their kid gets sick and they wonder why. Then some parents think their home remedies are better than FDA approved medicine that's gone through a decade of clinical trials. I think I'm better off with patients who have serious issues."

"I suppose that's one way of looking at it," I tell him. "Don't you think that parents are just doing the best they can? They don't have all the information we do, and sometimes the information we give them is confusing."

Adam just stares at me for a long minute. I don't know if I've stumped him or if he thinks I'm as crazy as the parents he just referred to. "I'm sorry," he finally says.

"Why are you sorry?"

"I don't think I'm getting off on the right foot here. Work is an intense topic for me, so let's start over and avoid talking about work like the plague. What do you say?" He looks at me with a sweet smile and morphs into the nice guy who stood on the other side of the nurse's station and asked me to dinner.

"That sounds good," I tell him. The waitress brings our dinners and we ease back into conversation.

"So, Jenna…what changed your mind?" I look at him quizzically and he answers my unspoken question. "Any time I asked Mercy about you, she was very clear in telling me that you were not interested. Then, all of the sudden, Mercy finds me in the hall outside a patient's room and tells me that I need to strike while the iron is hot."

"Thank you for reminding me that I owe Mercy a swift kick in the ass." I give a breathy laugh and Adam smiles. "I was just really focused on my job for a long time. Well, nursing school and then my job. I know me and I knew that if I got involved with anyone while I was in nursing school that I'd get distracted, and I didn't want to be distracted." This is one of the rehearsed answers I've been giving about dating for six years. Most people thought I was being extreme, but it was an explanation they could believe.

"So what happened after nursing school?"

"I guess I was just really focused on my job until…until you made me break my rule," I smile.

"And what rule is that?" he mirrors my smile and I think that maybe I could find potential here since I'm sure I scared Landon off.

"Not to date anyone I work with…especially doctors."

"Oooh! I'm hurt! What's wrong with doctors?" he asks with mocked disappointment.

"You know how your people are. Obsessed with your jobs, crazy hours, God complex," I tease.

"Wow, this keeps getting better! So what was it about me that made you break your rule?" Adam takes a sip of his wine and sets it down before he focuses all of his attention on me, sending a little surge of nervous excitement through me.

"I don't know. I guess you seemed like you might be the kind of guy worth breaking the rules for," I say with a smile. His eyes are locked on mine and I see all of the arrogant doctor attitude slip away. Sitting in front of me is just a guy who likes me who happens to be a doctor.

The conversation the rest of the night goes much better. Adam doesn't ask me about my family or my past, and I steer any discussion that looks like it might even remotely lead to work to something different. We talk about my love of dance and Adam's fascination with NASA. When we arrive at the door to my apartment a few hours later, I'm tempted to invite Adam in, but decide against it. The rest of the date went really well, and I could see myself getting caught up with him. I don't really want to spend another night lying in bed thinking of all the things I should not have done.

"I wish we could have stayed out a little longer, but I have rounds in the morning and I always underestimate how quickly 6:00 am arrives." Adam takes my hands in his as I lean against the door. "I had a really nice time tonight, Jenna. I'm sorry we got off on the wrong foot. I didn't mean to come across as a total ass…not on the first date at least," he chuckles.

"I had a nice time too, and you weren't a *total* ass," I smirk.

"I'd really like to see you again. And you should probably say yes because
if you don't, things are going to be very awkward at work." Adam smiles and I can't help but smile back, biting my lip so it doesn't get out of control.

"Well, we can't have that, can we?" I tell him.

"Great. I'll call you." Adam's smile fades into a contemplative expression. His lips part and his takes in a rush of air before leaning down to kiss me. I kiss him back, waiting to feel a swell of cosmic connectivity but the whole thing falls flat. The kiss is fine, but there's no spark, nothing that makes me *want* him. My heart sinks. Knowing I ran Landon off, I wanted to feel something, anything with Adam.

The kiss ends quickly and he smiles, satisfied. I smile back, not quite as satisfied. Adam waits for me to walk into my apartment and doesn't leave until he hears me lock the door. I go to the living room window and watch him hail a cab. I plop, defeated, onto the couch.

After a few minutes I walk back into my room and take note of the outfit I had on when Adam arrived. A funny feeling rolls around in me and I'm suddenly unsettled. I like Adam, but is it going to be like that all the time? He didn't even ask me if I minded changing because of where we were going. He basically just told me to change. What about talking about work? He was kind of an ass when we started talking about work at dinner. Are we supposed to avoid that subject forever?

I walk back out into the living, grab my keys, and walk outside. I don't stop walking until I reach Duke's. I pull on the heavy door and feel a rush of complete comfort come over me as I cross the threshold into the bar. It's Thursday night, so the place isn't too crowded at all, although most of the tables are full. I begin to find a place at the bar when I notice Mercy sitting at the other end near the corner where our favorite table is. I make my way along the bar and find her cozied up with a guy. As I get closer I see that it's Jerry. It's clear what's going on between them and she is so busted.

"Well, well, well…what do we have here?" I tease.

"Jenna! What are you doing here? I thought you had your date with Dr. Fisher tonight!" she says as she abruptly pulls herself out from Jerry's arm.

"I did, but it didn't go so great so I thought I'd come get a drink. That is beside the point. How long has this been going on?" I ask, pointing at both of them. Mercy stares at me with a blank face and I raise my eyebrows to prompt her answer.

"Just tell her, Mercy," Jerry says.

Mercy sighs. "About six months," she says.

"Six months? Why wouldn't you tell me? I mean, especially since I've been on your case to give the poor guy a shot!" I'm shocked. I don't understand why they would keep this from me.

"I'm gonna go check on something." Jerry excuses himself and I take his seat next to Mercy.

"I didn't want to tell you because I didn't know where things were going. Jerry and I agreed that it might make things awkward if we told everyone and then it didn't work out. We didn't want you or Jack and Demi to feel like we couldn't come here anymore. I'm sorry I didn't tell you," she explains.

"I guess that makes sense," I reply. "The only way we wouldn't come back here is if Jerry absolutely ripped your heart out. But…now that I think about it…if he did that, we'd have to kill him, so then it wouldn't matter if we came back here or not because Jerry would be dead." I smile sweetly at Mercy and she smiles back.

"Thanks for understanding, Jenna," she says as she hugs me.

"Soooo…how have things been going with him?" Jerry swings by and puts a beer in front of each of us. I wink at him to tell him that we're all good. He smiles at me, relieved.

"Really good. I meet him here a lot, and then we go out when Rocco can cover and close the place. He's really good to me and, well…I think I'm totally falling for him." Mercy rests her elbow on the bar and lays her head in her propped up hand.

"That's awesome, Mercy! I'm so happy for you! I've always thought Jerry was a great guy. You deserve this happiness."

"What about you? What happened with Dr. Fisher?" she asks with a shocked tone.

"He's kind of a control freak. Well, maybe not a complete control freak. He showed up dressed in a suit, which he looked really good in, but…he made me change my clothes," I tell her, a little surprised at what I'm actually saying.

"He did what?" Mercy's Jersey Girl persona is coming out and I think that Dr. Adam Fisher should be glad he's not here right now.

"I had on my dark jeans and this really cute orange top. I opened the door, he said hello, and then he told me I had time to change. The night got better. He took me to this Italian place near Navy Pier. The food was great, the wine was even better. But then he was a total ass when he talked about work and patients. The worst part was that when he kissed me, there was no spark at all. It's not like I'm not attracted to him. I am. He's just…"

"He's no Landon," Mercy says, finishing my thought.

"No, he's not. The night did turn out fine, but I think he's just a bit too planned and rigid for me. I don't want to compare them. It's not even an apples to oranges comparison. It's apples to the most decadent, not good for you, but too good to put down dessert," I say, remembering exactly how Landon tasted.

"So what's wrong with a little not-good-for-you? Cut yourself some slack. You don't have to find Prince Charming right away. Have some fun! Go out with both of them if you want." This was Mercy's rule of thumb for dating for as long as I've known her, until I discovered her secret relationship with Jerry.

"All I've been doing is having fun! I want…I want something more than that, Mercy. I don't like the idea of dating more than one guy at a time. I had friends in high school who did that and it never worked out," I say.

"Oh, my God! Did you actually just reference your life before Chicago?" Mercy almost shouts. She's right to be astonished. I never, I mean *never*, talk about my life before Chicago, except to give the answers I've rehearsed about my parents being dead and me having no other family.

"It's not a big deal, Mercy. We all went to high school. It's not like any of us really want to relive those terrible years by chatting about them," I say to play down my slip.

"Ok, ok. So now that you've passed my test and refused to continue on the non-committal highway, why the change of heart?" she asks swallowing a sip of beer.

I sigh. "You guys are right. I need to stop cataloging faults and give somebody a chance," I tell her. It's a strange thought to me to allow myself to get close to someone. *It's been six years. If Dellinger wanted to find you he would have by now.* "I like them both. They're really different. But I don't like the idea of dating more than one guy at a time…"

"Jenna…listen…you know I love you but you have to get off your ass on this. You've got to start letting people get close enough to you to really know you. With guys, you've acted like you don't want more than just a date or two, but I know you and I know you want more than that. Just give someone a chance to come up next to you and spend a little time there." Mercy is honest to a fault. Sometimes she adds the word brutal to how honest she's going to be, but not this time. I know she's right. Maybe one day I'll be able to tell someone about my past, but it doesn't mean I can't get close at all. I'm just nervous about feeling like I want more. I've spent so long being guarded that I'm not sure I know how to do this.

"Ok. You're right. So...how about this: the first one to call me will be the guy I give more than a half-ass try with. What do you think?" I tell Mercy with some level of confidence rising in me.

"Does he have to call? What if you saw him?" she asks.

"Yeah. That would work too, I guess," I tell her.

"Well, by the way that guy is looking at you, I think your answer may have just walked through the door." Mercy smirks and pushes my chin to the left toward the door of the bar.

Standing there, staring at me with a huge, surprised smile is Landon.

Chapter 6

"I'm not stalking you, I promise," Landon says as we meet each other halfway between the door and where I was sitting.

"What *are* you doing here?" I ask him with some suspicion.

"Truth?" I nod with a sarcastic look on my face. As if I would want him to lie. "I knew you had your date with the doctor tonight, so I was just coming by here to see if I could meet anybody you knew. You seemed pretty friendly with the bartender the other night so I thought I'd start with him. I thought it would be kind of a good-faith effort on my part to get to know your friends," he explains. "Sweet or creepy?"

"I'm still deciding," I tell him with a wary look.

"Really. The bartender looks like the kind of guy who would totally kick my ass if I did you wrong, and I figured he hears enough people talking shit that he'd be able to read me well enough to know that I'd never intentionally hurt you, Jenna."

"How did you know the doctor didn't bring me here?" I challenge.

"I didn't, but that would have been awkward," he smirks. "Especially after I embarrassed him for the totally unclassy move of bringing you to a bar on your first date."

"Hey! You took me for burgers on Navy Pier," I counter with a smirk of my own.

"That was plan B. Plan A was insanely good Mexican food, remember? Besides, if dancing on the Pier didn't outweigh the burgers…that kiss certainly did." Landon's smoldering eyes are staring at mine and I know I'm totally gone. I don't know how this happened, but this is the first guy I've ever wanted more than something superficial with. There's something about him that, while I totally want to rip his shirt off, makes me interested in so much more than that.

"Sweet."

"Awesome." Landon kisses me on the cheek and takes my hand to walk back to where I was sitting with Mercy. She's made her way to the other side of the bar with Jerry where she's pretending not to be watching us. "Where *is* the good doctor?" he asks.

"Early morning rounds means an early night," I tell him.

"So how did it go?" he asks, scoping out the competition.

"You're really asking me how my date went with another guy?"

"Listen, Jenna...I know this is going to sound fast and really presumptuous, but...I'm not the kind of guy who dates more than one woman at a time. I don't know everything you're thinking or feeling, but if what happened at your apartment is any indication, I'd say you're feeling for me the same thing I'm feeling for you. If you're interested in seeing where this goes, which by the way I am hoping to God you are, then, you need to know that I would prefer that you not see the doctor, too."

Landon's words are echoing in my head. They are exactly what I just said to Mercy.

I remember what my mother always told me about when she met Dad. They had both been attending a party of a girl they both knew from school. Dad and Oz were playing some drinking game when Mom and her best friend Sarah walked in. Dad was so distracted by her that he missed his mouth all together when he took his next drink. No one had ever looked at her, or made her feel that way before. When she looked in his eyes she didn't see the underage hooligan drinking with his buddy. The point, Mom always said, was that when she looked at him, she saw the potential of who he could be.

Landon sharing the same sentiment as me feels like that moment Mom talked about. I feel like I can see the potential of what could be. And, for the first time, I feel like I'm ready to be open to that.

"I'm not interested in seeing anyone else right now either, Landon. And I'm not the kind of girl to date more than one guy at a time. In fact, if I'm honest, I've spent a long time not giving any guy more than one or two dates at most. And just so you know, what I did last night, how I basically attacked you...I don't do that."

"Does that mean you're not going to do it again?" Landon fakes a disappointed frown. "That was the highlight of my evening."

"I thought I scared you off. You ran out of there so fast." I feel shy recapping the most mortifying moment of my life. Landon brushes his hand down my arm and takes my hand.

"I'm sorry about that. I really did have a work thing and I knew if I didn't get out of there...I would have been making you breakfast," he explains. "As much as you are going to love my ham and cheese omelet, I didn't want to rush into that."

"Well...that was very sweet of you, I suppose," I reply. "So now what? I've never gotten this far before."

"How about I walk you home? It's late and I really don't like the idea of you walking home alone," he says sweetly.

"That would be nice. I'd really like to introduce you to Mercy and Jerry before we go, if that's ok," I tell him. He did say that was why he came to Duke's tonight in the first place.

"I would love that!" A smile spreads widely across his face and he actually takes my hand and drags me to the other side of the bar where Mercy is whispering something in Jerry's ear. I never had a guy be so enthusiastic about meeting my friends. I guess that's my fault since I never suggested he meet them before.

Mercy pulls away from Jerry's cozy arm and stands when she sees us approaching. Jerry looks behind him and stands with her, extending his hand to Landon.

"Well, this is a first. Jerry," he says with a straight face as he shakes

Landon's hand.

"Be nice, Jerry!" Mercy smacks Jerry's arm as she scolds him. "Sorry about him. His charm is a mixture of protectiveness of Jenna and just pure ass-hat. You'll get used to it. I'm Mercy," she laughs.

"Don't worry about it. I'm Landon. It's really great to meet both of you." Landon chuckles, shaking both of their hands.

"But…you better be good to her…or I'll kill you." Mercy is serious. Over the last several years, Mercy has become the older sister I never had. She's honest with me to a fault, and more protective than I ever imagined a friend could be.

"Oh, my God, Mercy!" I roll my eyes.

"Someone has to be the mother in your life. Like it, or not, that person is me!" Mercy smiles, reminding me that everything she does, she does because she loves me.

"It's ok, Jenna. Really," Landon says. He puts his arm around me and a warm rush of emotions floods through me. "I'm glad you have such great friends. It must be nice."

"If you're ok in Jenna's book, you're ok with me," Jerry says. "It'll be nice to have another guy around. Jack's a little too metrosexual for me. You don't do all that girly stuff like get pedicures and facials do you?"

"Uh, no," Landon tells him, his face showing his confusion.

"Then we're good! Come by the bar any time. I've got you covered. I gotta get back to the kitchen. Sam's having some trouble with the new bus boy." Jerry leans down and kisses Mercy quickly. "I'll be back in a bit, babe. Night you two."

"Goodnight, Jerry," I call.

"Night. Good to meet you," Landon says.

"Landon is going to walk me home. I'll call you tomorrow," I tell Mercy, but she seems uneasy.

"Can I have a second with our girl here, Landon?" she asks. She's put on a super sugary voice so I know something is up.

"Sure. I'll run to the bathroom and be right back."

"What?" I don't even hesitate or act like I don't see that the wheels are turning in her head.

"Nothing. But... You've never done this, Jenna. You've never been so quick to give a guy a real chance. I just want to make sure you're not rushing into anything," she warns.

"Are you kidding me? You're the one who just said ten minutes ago that I needed to open myself up and let someone get close enough to me. Why the immediate change of heart?"

"I meant everything I said. I just...I don't know. Sometimes I do feel like your mom. You don't have a mom to be worried sick about you, and everyone needs one of those. I just want you to be sure you're not rushing into anything." Mercy's tone is soft. It's rarely ever soft, and usually only happens when she's comforting a patient's family, so I know she's being totally sincere with me.

"We have no idea what's going to happen with us. All we're doing is acknowledging the obvious attraction we have for each other and are willing to see what happens. This is not as big a deal as you're making it out to be. Really. I appreciate you. You're my family, Mercy, and what you think matters to me. But there's nothing for you to worry about. He's just a guy...and he's keenly aware of Jerry's ability to kick his ass." I give a breathy laugh as I take Mercy in my arms. "Thank you," I whisper.

"Everything ok here?" Landon asks as he returns.

"Everything is great. Take care of my girl," Mercy tells him.

"You got it," he replies.

Landon puts his hand on the small of my back and leads me to the door. Leaving Duke's, we walk at a slow pace down the sidewalk toward my apartment.

"Carina said you haven't been back to class. Did you give up?" I ask him.

"I didn't give up. I realized that while it was fun seeing if I still had any moves left in me, the real reason I'd be going would be to see you." He takes my hand and laces our fingers together, smiling at me softly.

"Yeah, I guess you don't need to go then. I'll be sure to tell Carina I'll be giving you private dance lessons then," I smile back.

His hand is strong around mine. The way our fingers are intertwined makes me feel secure and wanted, but mostly it makes me wish I hadn't been so afraid for so long. I had a right to be concerned, though. When I first moved to Chicago, I was still getting used to being Jenna Rockwell, and looking over my shoulder all the time. I worked hard not to stand out and to make friends so I would look like a normal girl who came here to go to nursing school. I even started going out on dates, mainly so I wouldn't look weird and give anyone cause to question why I was so noncommittal.

The reality is I could have stopped playing offense years ago. If Dellinger wanted to find me, he would have long before now. I just got so used to not being vulnerable that finding reasons not to let guys in became my thing. When I met Spring and Mercy, it became easy to let them into my life because it wasn't about sharing the details of my past. Friendships are different than intimate relationships. If I'm honest, at times I was scared that I would meet someone who would sell me out for whatever Dellinger was paying, but mainly I knew that if I were to get emotionally involved with someone it would mean putting them in danger by telling them the truth.

Landon and I make small talk as we stroll down the sidewalk. We discuss our favorite things about Chicago and what he misses about Miami. We both love Navy Pier and that this great city sits right on Lake Michigan. I swore it would be super cheesy when Mercy made me go, but I ended up loving the architectural boat tour of the city. The rivers that run right through the city are one the most romantic things about Chicago. It's why it's often called Little Venice.

Landon tells me about Miami and how rich the Latin culture is there. He says it gets a bad rap because immigration is always in the news, but the people in those communities are some of the warmest, most welcoming you'd ever meet. We talk about food and music and determine that we're officially on a mission to find *real* Cuban food in Chicago.

My growing up back-story has been that we moved around a lot with my dad's job. I did a little research on some metropolitan cities so I could have something to say about the iconic places people always talk about loving so I would never have to tell anyone I grew up in DC. I had us living in Napa Valley, California and loving the beauty of the wine country. I told people the Riverwalk and Tejas Rodeo were my favorite places to go when we lived in San Antonio. I even gave us a short stint in Canada in Niagara Falls. There was always a good, shared laugh about there being a Tim Horton's on every corner there from anyone who had ever been there. So I give Landon my generic thoughts on these places knowing that it's not like we're going to have this same conversation a hundred times. This is a *getting to know you* conversation that will live and exist in this moment and that will live on as a fond memory of this time.

I enter the code to my building and Landon pulls the door open, gesturing for me to enter first. When we get off the elevator on my floor I realize I don't have my keys. I'm still wearing the pencil skirt outfit I wore to dinner with Adam and there are no pockets anywhere. When I left to go to Duke's I remember just grabbing my keys. I didn't even bring my cell phone for some weird reason.

I stand at the door, contemplating my options.

"Everything ok?" Landon asks curiously. "It's a nice door, but I'm thinking going in is probably our objective here."

"Um…I left my keys at Duke's. I don't want to wake Spring, and I don't have my cell to call Mercy and ask her to bring them," I tell him.

"Oh, well, just use my cell." Landon takes his cell from his pocket and hands it to me.

"Like I actually *know* Mercy's number," I chuckle. "Once it's in my phone I make no effort *know* the number. I just press her pretty face and the magic, slippery germ brick calls her!" We both laugh.

"We could just walk back and get them then. Or we can take a cab, which would be faster," he offers.

We *could* walk back, or take a cab. Jerry won't be locking up for another hour. There is another option. I've only had to do this twice since I've lived here, but both times I was alone. *It's not a big deal*, I tell myself. *Just a party trick, right?*

"It's getting late and I have sort of a key under the mat," I tell him a little hesitantly. I'm not sure how he's going to respond to this.

"Oh, well, then that's good. What do you mean *sort of a key*?"

I crouch down as best I can in this tight skirt and take the pick and tension wrench I have hidden under the mat. I hold them up and raise my eyebrows as if to say "see!" I bend them open and begin to work the lock with both of them. It takes less than 30 seconds before we hear the clicking of the door being unlocked. Last one in bolts the door, so I know the top isn't locked.

"Shit." Landon's face is unreadable as he runs both hands through his hair.

"What?"

It takes him a second before he responds. "You are one badass girl. You're making me look bad!" He gives a breathy laugh and helps me stand after I put my tools back under the mat.

We walk into the apartment and I immediately grab my cell and text Mercy to ask if she can bring my keys by before she goes home. She responds right away and I leave my cell on the counter while I take my shoes off.

"What'd she say?" Landon asks, making himself comfortable on the couch. *Oh, God! Landon on my couch again could be very dangerous.* He doesn't seem to mind, though. He's sitting just as he was last night, beckoning me with his smoldering eyes to come sit with him.

"She said she'd be by in an hour," I tell him as I position myself to sit on my knees facing him on the couch. "So…how long have you been doing securities work?" I ask him.

"We're not making out?" he teases with mocked shock.

"That depends. If you only want to have two dates with me, then yes. If you'd like to see me again, then no," I tell him with a smile. I'm having to contain myself in major ways here. I would love to make out with him again, but if I'm going to grow up and look for the potential here, I can't let sex cloud my vision.

"Hmmm…" he purses his lips and looks up as he considers the choices I've given him.

"Really?"

"This is tough! You're hot and a *really* great kisser," he says in his defense.

"That's awesome," I say, teasing rolling my eyes at him.

"I'm kidding! I really want to get to know you, Jenna. But, is it ok that when I told you I was drawn to you what I meant was that I thought you were the sexiest woman I'd ever seen?"

I know I'm blushing and I almost don't care. "Well, I'd be lying if I didn't admit that I thought you were sort of good looking, too," I say.

"Sort of good looking? I'll try to kick it up a notch for you!" We both laugh and it feels really good. I've been out with so many boring guys that it's just really nice to laugh with someone.

"Why did you shave?" I ask, cupping his jaw with my hand. He closes his eyes for a second, seeming to enjoy my touch. I move my hand away quickly because I know if I leave it there much longer I'll throw my insistence that we keep things non-sexual out the window.

"I go through phases. Sometimes it's because I like the way a rough beard looks, sometimes it's because I'm lazy. I had an important meeting with a new client this morning – my work thing – so I felt like I needed to shave," he explains. "You don't like it?"

"I don't know. I think I might like it either way," I tell him. "The beard is a little rough on my skin, but I didn't mind so much." I touch my cheek and blush even more as I remember just how incredible it felt to kiss him. "Ok…enough about your good looks. You're avoiding my question about your job," I say, turning the subject back around.

"Well…I did a couple of tours in Iraq and ended up moving into an Intelligence position," he begins.

"You were in the military?" I ask, a little, but not totally surprised. Landon's physique is the definition of a lean and muscular soldier.

"Yeah. I was a Navy Seal," he tells me.

"Wow. That's pretty hard core. I mean, a soldier is a soldier, but a Navy Seal is as badass as they come. How long were you in?" I'm so totally impressed and absolutely turned on.

"Eight years. I had to get out. I lost a lot of friends after a raid on a compound where we thought some POW's were being held." Landon's expression turns sad and I can see just how much he really loved his fellow soldiers.

"Did you get the POW's out?" I ask him.

"No. It was a disastrous situation. We were 20 yards out, silent as we had ever been and they just started firing on us. A few of my buddies made it in to try and find the POW's. After 25 minutes of firing back and forth, the bad guys started blowing up the building piece by piece. I'm not sure the POW's were ever there to begin with. That's the problem over there. Sometimes you get intel that's purely meant to trap and kill American soldiers. When my time was up, I decided I had to go." Landon's eyes are pink as he works to hold back how emotional the memory of that time is for him. I have so much respect for what he and his fellow soldiers did and are continuing to do over there. It must be tough to live a life of simply following orders without question. But, I suppose if that's not what they wanted to do, they wouldn't sign their lives away to the United States Government.

"That's amazing, Landon. I'm sorry you lost such good friends, but I'm glad you made it out alive." I take his hand in mine and rest our hands on my lap. I want to comfort him. I don't want him to be sad at what he lost. I want him to happy at what he has. I know how hard it can be to focus on that sometimes.

When I first moved to Chicago I thought a lot about the life I had to leave behind. I thought about leaving my father to die under that tree. It took a lot of time before I could focus on the fact that I literally dodged a bullet by doing what my father told me to do. It was hard, but I was eventually able to start recognizing the life I had been given. Spring and Mercy are like sisters to me. My friends are my family now and I'm *home* here in Chicago.

"Sometimes I feel guilty for having lived," he says softly. "A lot of soldiers feel that way."

"I kind of know how you feel," I say tentatively. Landon looks at me inquisitively as if to imply that there's no way I could understand. "I told you my father died. What I didn't tell you was that he was murdered. If the timing had been different, it could have been me, too. I've…never told anyone that. Not even Mercy or Spring." Landon looks at me, taking in what I've just told him. I can't really read his expression. Is he shocked? Surprised? Does he think what I've told him is absolutely nothing like what he experienced in Iraq? I hope I haven't offended him.

"Jenna…" he starts, but stops to collect his thoughts. "I'm so sorry that happened to you. That is far worse than anything I ever experienced in Iraq."

"Oh, I don't know. Being shot at and having your friends die as buildings explode around you is pretty terrible." I give a breathy laugh as I try to downplay what I told him, beginning to regret having told him. I don't want his sympathy. I just wanted him to know that I could relate somehow.

"Those guys were my friends and it sucks that I lost them. But he was your *dad*. That trumps anything else." He squeezes my hand and runs his thumb across my fingers.

"At least when my mom died I had time to prepare for it," I tell him. It feels really nice talking about this with him.

"Your mom is dead?" His face is puzzled, as if he doesn't believe me or finds this hard to believe.

"Yeah. She had breast cancer and it was about six months from the time we got the news that treatment hadn't worked to the time she died. I was only ten," I explain.

"Oh...that's right. I remember you telling me that now." The questioning leaves Landon's eyes and a soft concern replaces it.

There's a knock at the door that can only be Mercy coming to bring me my keys. Landon helps me off the couch. This pencil skirt is not a good hanging-out-on-the-couch outfit. I open the door and Mercy is standing there with a raised eyebrow that immediately lowers in disappointment.

"What's that look for?" I ask her.

"I was kind of hoping you'd be buttoning your top so I could scold you," she says dissatisfied and trying to peer into the apartment to see Landon. "Hi Landon!" she says a little too loudly.

"Hi Mercy!" Landon calls back to her in a loud whisper, remember that Spring is sleeping.

"Sorry to ruin your plans to lecture me. We're actually doing what we said we were going to do: get to know each other." I take my keys that are now hanging from her extended finger. "Where's Jerry?"

"He's downstairs holding the cab for us," she tells me.

"Then you really didn't have time to lecture me anyway!" I tease as I give her a hug. "Get down there to your man. I'll see you tomorrow night at work."

"Bye Landon!" she calls to him.

"Bye Mercy!" he answers.

Mercy hugs me and is on her way.

"Sorry about that," I say. "Mercy is like a sister, and a mother, to me. She can be a little protective."

"No…I'm glad you have such great friends."

"You said something earlier about how it must be nice. What did you mean?" I ask him.

"Well…while I was in Iraq for eight years my friends from high school all moved on with their lives. They were all there at my big coming home party, but after that they went on with the lives they had been living. I started doing contract work and have been travelling with my job since. So…I'm kind of the loneliest 30-year-old out there. It's sad, I know."

"How long does that mean you're in Chicago?" Worry fills my eyes as I realize that all my determination to grow up and give Landon a chance could be all for naught if he's just going to pick up and move on to another contract. I'm way too new at this to think for a second that I could make a long-distance relationship work.

"I'm here indefinitely, Jenna. Once this contract ends, I'm hoping to have something else in place so I don't have to leave. I already love Chicago and…I don't want to leave you." Landon smiles, putting my mind at ease.

This is good. I can do this. And, for the first time in six years, I feel like I'm finally doing what my father's last wish was for me: living.

Chapter 7

It's been a relatively uneventful few weeks at work, which is good. There haven't been any more hold ups with the pharmacy and my post-surgery patients have all been dream patients.

The most stressful moment I've had was last week when Adam covered for another doctor again and was checking on those patients during my shift. It was the first time I had seen him since I told him I was seeing Landon. I avoided his calls for several days after our date because I hadn't known what to tell him. Mercy told me he had asked her about me one night when I wasn't working so I had to finally return his call before it became just plain rude of me not to.

I told him the truth about seeing him and Landon on back to back dates and felt like there was more of a spark with Landon. He was disappointed but said he understood. He also made sure to tell me if anything changed with Landon that I should call him. I told him I'd keep that in mind even though I don't foresee that happening.

Things with Landon are better than I knew they could be. He's really understanding about my crazy, mixed up sleeping schedule, and even arranges his life around it when he can. He's still living out of a hotel. His contract includes a stipend for housing and food, which means he's been able to stay in some of the world's most elite hotels and resorts. He said it would make him feel weird to take me back to his place since *his place* is a hotel, so we're typically at my apartment.

We've had some beautifully romantic dates, including actually going to the insanely good Mexican restaurant he intended for us to go to on our first date. I also made him take the architectural boat tour of the city. He loved it, of course. I try to cook dinner for him as often as I can. He said he's been living on hotel and restaurant food for so long he forgot what it was like to have a home cooked meal. One morning he met me after work and I made him eggs benedict. He loved them so much I think I'll make them for him this weekend. I'm not working, but I think I'm ready for our Saturday night date to extend into Sunday morning.

The best part has been how well he's fit in with my little family. Jack and Jerry like having another guy around. He's just metro enough for Jack and tough enough for Jerry. It's funny how Landon falls in the middle of the Jack-to-Jerry Spectrum.

He caught on to our version of Would You Rather quickly. Instead of it being a free-for-all on topics, we choose a topic and every scenario has to fit. The last time we played all the scenarios had to be about music. We threw things out like "Would you rather have to sing everything you say, or listen to everyone else sing what they said?" and "Would you rather be a one hit wonder, or an average singer for as long as you wanted?" Landon stumped us all when he posed "Would you rather be in a 90's boy band, or in Nickleback?" We were rolling with laughter and no one could decide which was the lesser of two evils. That was the night I knew things with Landon were better than I could have ever hoped. It makes me feel really optimistic about where things could go.

I'm reviewing the chart of a man the ER just brought up when a woman rounds the corner and enters the unit. She looks a little lost and a lot out of it. Her clothes are less than clean and don't leave a lot to the imagination. Her red bra is quite visible through her tight pink tank top, and I'm afraid of what I might see if she bends over in that short denim skirt. She's barefoot, carrying electric blue patent heels in one hand.

"Where is she?" the woman with stringy hair and sunken eyes says aggressively to me.

"I'm sorry. Who are you looking for?" I ask, trying to ascertain who she's referring to.

"My sister. Lola Washburn. I heard she was on this floor. Where is she?"

she says, clarifying who is she talking about.

I'm sure I know whom she's referring to but look up the chart anyway just to make it official. Yes, it's her: *Aunt Lola* from about a month ago. I spoke with her niece, Heather, for a few minutes on what would be the night before she died.

"I'm so sorry to tell you this, but your sister passed away about a month ago," I tell her solemnly.

"Where did they take her?" The woman has become more aggressive and I ready my hand near the phone to call security.

"Your sister would have been taken to the morgue, and…" I begin but am quickly cut off.

"I don't care about the fat fucking bitch! Where did they take my daughter?" she yells.

This must be Heather's mother. No wonder she was in Lola's custody. This woman is so strung out there's no way anyone was going to let her raise a child.

"I'm sorry, but I don't know where Heather is," I tell her.

"You know Heather?" she asks, her aggression increasing by my familiarity with her daughter.

"No. I don't *know* her. I just spoke with her briefly once when her grandmother brought her here," I tell her, immediately unsure if I've told her too much.

"So my old hag of a mother has her. Figures. Give me the address," she demands.

"I can't do that, ma'am," I tell her.

"Give me that address!" She's raising her voice now and I know I'm going to have to calm her down and call security.

"I'd like to help, but HIPAA laws don't allow me to release any information in a patient's chart. I'm sure if you're trying to find your daughter that the local authorities will be happy to help you. Why don't I call them for you?" I pick up the phone to call security. I glance down to dial the number and the phone gets knocked out of my hand. I look up, startled and see that the woman in front of me is now holding a switchblade about a foot from my face. The blade is rusted and jagged and has tetanus written all over it. God only knows where it's been.

"I swear to God I will cut that pretty face of yours if you don't give me what I want. She's *my* kid and I'm going to get her back!" She's waving the knife around aimlessly, clearly having no idea how to use it. That makes her more dangerous than a sober person with knife skills.

"Ok. Ok. Can you just pull that thing away from me? I can't exactly think straight with a knife in my face." I've lifted my hands up near my shoulders in surrender. "What is it that you want exactly?"

"I want my mother's address. She's got to be on there as some kind of, of, of... relative or, what do they call it?" she asks, confused.

"Next of kin?" I say, filling in her inebriated spaces.

"Right. Next of kin. Now give me the fucking address or I swear to God..."

"I know. You'll cut me. I believe you. Now, I have to get that information from another computer." I lie so I can get to the other side of the desk and do something about this woman.

Right about the time I'm rounding the desk and meeting the crazed woman, Mercy comes up the hall and enters the nurse's station from the opposite side.

"What the hell?" Mercy says in shock of what she's walked into.

"Back off, bitch!" the woman yells.

"I've got this, Mercy. Just stay there. I'm going to the other computer to pull the information this woman is asking for." Mercy just nods, recognizing what my tone and facial expression are telling her.

I approach the woman, planning out my strategy. She's so high or drunk, or both, that it won't be difficult to subdue her. I'm trying to figure out the best way to do that without causing the nearby patients to panic. I glance over at Mercy who is inching toward the phone, readying herself to call security as soon as she can. Even in her strung-out state the woman catches my signal to Mercy and she becomes even more agitated.

"Bitch!" she yells as she lunges for me with the knife.

I wasn't sure I would remember it or not, but the training my dad made me take when I was 16 comes back to me as if I just learned it. Dad said that as long as Dellinger had a hold on him, I had to be prepared for anything. I took months of classes that combined mixed martial arts, krav maga, wrestling, and basic self-defense. I hated it at first, thinking it was going to bulk me up too much for dancing, but after a while I started to like it. I actually found a few moves to incorporate into my contemporary dance pieces.

As the knife is hurling toward me in her hand, I throw my arm up across my body and block her arm. My left hand is in front of my face, with my forearm in front of my torso. I feel the sharp pain of the knife cutting into my right thigh before I'm able to grab her hand holding the knife. I tighten my grip and thrust my knee into her stomach. Hunched over from the pain my bloodied leg caused her body, she releases the knife with ease and falls to the floor.

I kick the knife away from us and fall to the floor in front of her limp body, my leg now throbbing from the wound. It's a deep cut and I apply as much pressure as I can to control the bleeding. Mercy is next to me in a flash as security is hauling the woman away.

"C'mon Jet Lee, let's get you sewn up." Mercy's use of sarcasm has always been one of the things I love about her. I try but can't put any weight on my right leg, so Mercy practically has to carry me to the closest unused patient room while two security guards subdue the crazed woman. The other two nurses on the floor are doing their best to calm the patients who heard the commotion. It's after eleven and all but a few were already asleep. "Ok, let's take a look at this." Mercy tears my pant leg where the knife cut it and we both examine the wound.

"Wow. That looks just as bad as it feels. Ahhhh," I wince as Mercy's now-gloved hands touch around the gap in my leg. "That crazy bitch cut into the muscle. It's going to be weeks before I can dance again."

"It doesn't look like it's that deep. Dancing is the least of your worries. She could have *seriously* injured you, Jenna. Where did you learn to defend yourself like that?" Mercy is questioning me and gathering supplies to clean my wound at the same time.

"I took some self-defense classes before I moved to Chicago. I was coming to a new city and didn't know my way around. I figured I should be able to take care of myself if and when I got lost," I tell her. It's not a complete lie, but the details of when and why I learned to defend myself aren't important.

"Well, you totally kicked her ass. I was impressed," Mercy smiles proudly.

"It wasn't that hard. I mean, seriously, she was so out of it. She came looking for her kid. Her sister had been a patient and had custody of her daughter. The patient died and no one told her. It's no wonder she didn't have custody of her kid. It's sad, really." I wince again as Mercy finishes cleaning the gash in my leg.

"Really. Ok...you're going to need a tetanus shot and a blood screen. God only knows where that knife has been. I'll get a doctor from the ER to come up and take care of you. Then I'm calling Demi and having her take you home," Mercy tells me with certainty.

"Fine," I say, immediately giving in. I know I'm not going to be able to walk on this leg for at least 24 hours. That means I'm going to have to be off tomorrow night, too, but I should be ok to cover that shift in the ER on Friday night. I'll be hobbling around, but at least they won't be short-staffed. I almost tell her to call Landon, but he's working a lot over these three days

that I'm working. I don't know if he has early mornings or had late nights. I don't want to worry him either. I'll call him sometime
tomorrow and leave him a message.

"Good girl. I'll get the doc and call Demi. She'll be happy for an excuse to be out of work tomorrow!" We both grin knowing just how right Mercy is. Demi hates her marketing job and is trying desperately to find something new in PR.

Mercy's gone about ten minutes before she comes back with Dr. Culpepper from the ER. He's an older doctor, in his 60s, and is the best of the best. He's also one of the sweetest people you could ever meet. He comes into the room applauding, which tells me Mercy physically went and got him and recounted the whole story to him. He commends my bravery and suggests I give the hospital security team some training.

He gives me a tetanus shot and an antibiotic shot, not wanting to wait days for an oral antibiotic to kick in. After stitching me up, he instructs me to stay off my injured leg for at least 24 hours, and promises that if I come to work in the ER on Friday night he'll make sure that I'm not running all over the place.

I'm finalizing the paperwork for the reports with security as well as the on-shift injury forms when Demi arrives.

"Dear Lord! You look like shit!" Demi says entering the hall.

"Thanks for the encouragement!" I laugh.

"I heard you were a total badass and kicked that junkie's ass," she beams. "Way to go!"

"Thanks. I'd prefer to not have had the encounter, but…yeah, I totally kicked her ass!"

Demi gets my pain meds from Mercy and wheels me down to the main entrance of the hospital where she hails a cab. I tell her the whole story from beginning to end all the way home. When we pull up to my building the cabbie tells us there's no charge for someone as brave as me. I give him a tip at least and Demi helps me from the cab and I get settled on my crutches.

We get off the elevator and round the corner to find Landon sitting with his back against my door. He's got his head hung over and he's wringing his hands. When he sees me he bolts up to help me, practically knocking Demi out of the way.

"Jenna! Oh, my God! Why didn't you call me?" he says putting an arm around my waist. He gives Demi the crutch he's just replaced.

"I didn't want to worry you. I know you've been working a lot," I tell him. "How did you know?"

"Mercy called me two hours ago and said you were getting stitched up and that Demi was bringing you home." He takes my keys from my hand and opens the door quietly knowing that Spring is asleep. "I've been here for over an hour, worried sick. I was about to call you!"

"I was going to call you tomorrow. I knew you were super busy," I begin.

"Thanks for bringing her home, Demi. I really appreciate it," Landon says with a smile. "I've got her from here."

"Alrighty then…I'll leave you with your Prince Charming and call you tomorrow." Demi smiles and gives me a hug. "I'm glad you're ok, Jenna."

Landon closes the door behind Demi and turns to me.

"I can't believe you didn't call me," he says with a hint of chastisement.

"I told you I didn't want to worry you. I know how busy you were supposed to be over these next few days," I tell him in my defense again.

"I don't care what I have going on, Jenna. If something happens to you I want to know. I *need* to know." He's boring his eyes into mine, driving home his message.

"Ok. I'm sorry," I tell him. He wraps his arms around me and holds me like he's hanging on for dear life.

"Good. Now, let's get you into bed." Landon releases his grip on me and takes my crutches, leaning them against the couch before he gingerly scoops me up in his arms and carries me to my room. With the pant leg missing where my bandages are, he can see the area of my leg to avoid so he doesn't hurt me.

He lays me gently on my bed and all I can think is how awful I must look. I'm wearing my scrubs, which is already not the most attractive look, but I've got blood on them and one of my pant legs has been torn completely off so I have one regular pant leg and one short-shorts pant leg.

"What's wrong?" he asks.

"I look ridiculous," I tell him, motioning to my torn and bloody clothes.

"You look beautiful, and brave. I'm so proud of you," he says.

"I'm glad you're here, Landon," I tell him, taking his hand as he positions himself next to me on the bed.

"This wasn't exactly how I envisioned the first time I took you to bed, but..." We both give a small, nervous laugh. "But I'm glad I'm here, too. Do you want to talk about it?" he asks.

"I'm not sure what Mercy told you, but there was this totally cracked out woman demanding the address for her mother so she could find her daughter. Her sister had custody of her kid, but the sister, who was a patient on my floor, died about a month ago and now the girl is with the grandmother," I explain.

"So what did you do?" Landon asks.

"I played along until I could get in a position to get the knife out of her hand," I tell him, playing down my krav maga skills.

"Well, like I said, I'm very proud of you, Jenna." Landon kisses the top of my head and pulls me just a tad bit closer to him. He's lying slightly above and next to me on the bed. My head is nestled between his shoulder and his chest and, despite the insanity of the night's events, I have an overwhelming feeling of peace.

"Don't you need to go? I know how busy you were going to be over these three days while I was working," I say. "I don't want you all groggy for work tomorrow. Oh, my gosh! It's 2:30 am!" I hadn't checked the clock at all since before the incident and am shocked at just how late it's gotten.

"I've already rearranged my morning appointments so I can be here to take care of you. Spring will be working and you'll need me here." His tone is so beautifully commanding. "Now, what can I get you? When do you need to take your pain medication? Mercy said it's every four to six hours but I don't know when you took it last." Landon stands and shoves his shoes off, making himself even more comfortable. He looks at me, anticipating my reply.

"Well, Mr. Bossy Pants...I took the pain meds right before we left the hospital, so only about an hour ago. I'm doing fine, but they're going to make me sleepy soon. Why don't you go back to your place, get some sleep, and then if you want to come back in the morning you can," I tell him. This seems like a reasonable plan to me.

"No."

"No?"

"No. You can barely walk, Jenna. What happens when you have to get up to use the bathroom in the middle of the night? You're going to need more pain medication in a few hours and I can't trust that you'll hear an alarm to wake you up for it. And what happens if I'm not here when you're ready to eat in the morning? You can't stand in the kitchen and cook! I'm staying." It's not a question, but a statement of intent. He's smiling at me because I have no defense. Everything Landon said is valid. Even if it wasn't, I'd still take it because I really don't want him to leave.

"Ok then. I guess you're staying. This isn't exactly how I planned on posing on the bed, but..." I smirk and Landon raises an eyebrow at me, smiling right through me. "I'd like to change. Do...you...think you can help me...with that?" It's going to be a feat to get my pants off without making me wince.

"Well, this night is just full of surprises! Again, not how I envisioned taking your clothes off." Landon takes my ugly, yet wonderfully comfortable clogs off my feet and tosses them in the corner before looking at my legs. "Hmmm…do you think you can use your left leg to lift yourself up a little? I'll hold you up on the right." He moves around to the side of the bed and we work together to lift me off the bed enough that I can start to pull my pants down.

"This is so embarrassing," I mumble.

"You're just not used to be the patient," he says, his free hand helping me with my pants while I hang onto him. "Do you want me to leave while you finish changing?" We've successfully moved the waistband of my pants past my injury so Landon pulls my pants the rest of the way off and throws them in the trash in my bathroom.

"Um…you could just turn around I suppose," I tell him. Landon just nods at my suggestion and turns to face the door while I pull off my shirt and take my bra off. "Oh, um, I forgot to ask you to get me a shirt. They're in the second drawer in my dresser there."

Landon pulls open the drawer and unknowingly takes out one of my dad's t-shirts. When he turns around I'm sitting up holding my scrubs in front my bare chest. We lock eyes and I feel my chest rise and fall with heavy breathing. At that moment I will myself to be 100% better by Saturday night. Nothing is going to keep me from following through on my plans to take my relationship with Landon to the next level.

"Thank you," I say softly as Landon hands me the shirt and turns around. He doesn't say anything. I think he's trying to calm his own hormones down, too. "Ok, you can turn back around now," I tell him after getting settled.

"Nice shirt." Landon smiles at my vintage Dr. Pepper shirt.

"It was my dad's," I tell him, feeling the worn material in my hands.

"That's nice." Landon moves to the bed and moves the sheets and blanket so he can pull them over me. Once I'm settled he pulls his shirt off and I think I release an audible gasp. "I'm sorry. Do you want me to leave this on?"

"No," I say quickly. "I mean, I'm sure you'll be more comfortable without it on." My heart is beating fast as I get my first view of Landon's body. We've been together for a month now, but have been very cautious after our first date when I attacked him on my couch. He's toned and cut and looks like he belongs on the cover of Men's Health. It's also my first full view of his tattoo. It's a symbol that I've never seen before, and it is just as sexy as I knew it would be. He starts to unbuckle his belt and I panic just slightly. "What are you doing?"

"I can't sleep in my jeans, Jenna," he says matter-of-factly. "I'm going to sleep in here on the floor. Are there extra blankets in the hall closet?" I suppose I should be relieved that he's going to sleep on the floor, but I'm actually a little disappointed.

"You can sleep up here, with me, if you want," I say. He tilts his head and gives me a suspicious look. "It's fine. With my injury it's not like anything is going to happen. It'll all be very PG…13." I smirk and flap over the covers to my left.

"If you're sure," he says quietly.

"I'm sure."

Landon finishes unbuckling his belt and his jeans are on the floor in a matter of seconds.

Boxer briefs.

Oh, dear God, help me.

He slides into bed and pulls the covers over him before he turns on his side to face me. He's got his arm crooked under his head and his tattooed left arm is now blanketing my stomach. I could lie like this forever.

FIVE

"Tell me about this tattoo of yours. It's the only one you have so I'm guess it means something." I trace my fingers around the symbol that looks slightly Celtic, but isn't. It's clearly an original design. It's a circle with an intricate design woven within it. It's beautiful.

"How do you know this is my only tattoo?" he smirks.

"Any guy that has a tattoo that can be completely covered by his underwear is clearly not capable of making good choices."

"Ouch!" we laugh. "No, you're right. This is the only one I have. My buddies and I got them after our first tour in Iraq. Andrew, Dave, Kyle and I met in boot camp and were brothers right from the beginning. All our last names start with S, so Kyle started calling us S Squad. One day he came up with this design. There are four S's, one hidden in each quadrant of the circle. Andrew suggested we get tattoos, so we did. I wanted to get the Superman symbol and call it the family crest, but that idea got shot down."

"Kyle is quite the artist," I say, hunting for each S on Landon's arm.

"He was. He, along with Dave and Andrew were killed in the explosion I told you about."

"Oh, Landon. I'm so sorry." I pull his arm closer to me and hug it.

"It's ok. It was a long time ago. I was the most hesitant about getting the tattoos in the first place, but, I'm glad we did it. Those guys will always be with me."

"You know, when I was in nursing school, I saw my fair share of tattoos," I begin. Landon is looking sad and that makes my heart hurt. I know he treasures those guys and to have lost them the way he did is tragic. I just can't stand him feeling that agony.

"I bet you did!" he says, turning his sad, introspective expression into something happier.

"You want to hear some stories?" I say with a yawn, my eyelids becoming heavy.

"Why don't you tell me tomorrow? I think your pain meds are really kicking in," Landon says, brushing his thumb over my cheek.

"No, I'm good. I can…" Another yawn escapes me and my eyes now feel like they're glued closed. I try to open them…try to speak again, but it's futile. I feel my body move and Landon's voice say something about making me more comfortable. He brushes my hair from my face and I feel his arm blanket me again. And, just as I'm about to be fully unconscious, I can almost swear I hear Landon whisper, "I think I love you, Jenna."

Chapter 8

I wake up to the smell of coffee. Landon must still be here because Spring can't make coffee to save her life. I move and stretch my stiff body. A hard night's med-induced sleep has left me feeling weighted and heavy. The clock reads 11:30 am when I'm finally able to turn my head and open my eyes. Oh, well maybe Landon isn't still here. He had a lot going on today and tomorrow with work. I'm sure he didn't mean that he was going to stay all day and that he's got coffee and breakfast waiting for me.

I manage to gather enough strength to shimmy myself to a sitting position without too much strain on my leg. I can move it. It's sore, but nothing like last night. I think if I stay off it as much as possible today and tomorrow, then I should be ok to cover in the ER tomorrow night. Dr. Culpepper will be there and I know he won't let me do more than I should.

I scan my room for a note from Landon, but don't see one. Then I check my cell to see if he texted me. Nothing there either. Maybe he left it near the coffee pot. I look for my crutches but don't find them. They must still be in the living room where we left them last night.

Last night.

I sigh and can't hold back the smile as I remember how insistent Landon was about staying to take care of me. My smile gets bigger and I bite my bottom lip to keep it from spreading from ear to ear. A shirtless Landon flashes across my memory and I close my eyes to keep him there just a moment longer. I wrap my arms around my waist, feeling the warmth Landon's arm created there.

"You're up and all smiles! That's a good sign!" Landon's voice rings in my room as he enters with a tray of food. He's shirtless, wearing his jeans without a belt so they're hanging a little low on his hips. It is by far the sexiest thing I have ever seen in person. Ever.

"You're still here!" I say with shock.

"Of course I'm still here. What kind of a guy would I be if I left my girl in her time of need?" He smiles and sets the tray down on my dresser.

He called me his girl. Wow. I had no idea two words coming out of Landon's mouth could cause such a stir of emotions in me. And am I remembering right in thinking I heard him tell me he loves me last night? I am *not* asking him that, that's for sure! If he did say it, he knew I was headed into a deep sleep, so he probably didn't mean for me to hear him. Not yet at least. And I'm not even sure if I can define how I feel about him as the same...can I?

Am I falling in love with Landon?

"Oh, well...I thought you had a ton of work stuff today. But, I'm glad you stayed." I smile as Landon leans down and kisses my forehead sweetly. "Can I have my crutches, please?"

"They're out in the living room. I'll help you," Landon says as he moves to take my hand and help me up.

"Um...I have to use the bathroom."

"I can help you with that, Jenna," he says matter-of-factly.

"No."

"No?"

"No. I'm really happy with how things are going between us. I'm not ready for whatever image you have of me to be totally shattered by helping me get on and off the toilet. Now can you *please* get my crutches?" I ask with sugary sweetness. I won't say it out loud, but that is not the image I had in my head of the first time Landon takes my panties off.

"As you wish." Landon gives me his smoldering smirk and I'm glad I'm on the bed. It melts me every time he does it. It has the same effect on everyone, though. On one of our "adventure dates" as Landon calls them, we crashed a convention at McCormick Place. We must have sat in on at least three panels on how to have a more profitable direct sales business before someone caught on that we were not part of the group. It was when we tried to sneak in to the lunch they were serving when the shit hit the fan. Lucky for me, *my guy* has the best smolder on the planet and used it to his full advantage in getting us out of hot water that day.

"How's your leg feeling?" he asks, returning to my room with the crutches. "It looked the same in the night when I woke you for your meds at 5:00 am."

"You woke me up?"

"Yeah. You were still pretty out of it, but I wanted to make sure to keep the pain meds in you. In fact, you're overdue for the 11:00 am dose." Landon moves to the side of the bed where he slept to retrieve my pain medication.

"I'm feeling good, actually. I can take some Ibuprofen and that'll be just as good now that I'm on the other side of the trauma. I don't want to be all drugged up and sleepy while you're here with me," I tell him.

Landon sighs heavily as he considers my refusal to take the pain medication.

"I'm a nurse, remember? I kinda know what I'm talking about," I smirk.

He looks at me warily, but finally concedes. "Alright. But if you even so much as *wince*, I'm going to pick you up and put you back in this bed. I'm also making you take the medication. Got it?"

"Got it. Thank you, Landon. It's nice being taken care of," I tell him with a soft smile. I'm a little overcome with emotion that I think I could cry if I let myself.

"I like taking care of you, Jenna." We look at each other for a long moment, both realizing that even though we've only been seeing each other for a month that what we have here is deeper than we thought it could become. For the first time since before I left DC, before I left Veronica Matthews behind, I feel really excited about the future.

Landon lets me pee in private and then insists on helping me out to couch to rest. I'm still wearing only my dad's t-shirt, so at least it's long enough to cover me, but it lifts up when I raise my arms for stability at Landon's side. I get situated on the couch and examine my stitches as I change the bandage.

"How's it looking?" he asks, bringing the tray of food he had taken to the bedroom out to the living room. He's put his shirt back on which is really disappointing.

"It looks good. Definitely not infected, thanks to that shot of antibiotics, and seems to be healing well. The cut wasn't as deep as I thought it had been. I'll rest it today and try walking on it later this evening," I tell him.

"Will Spring be here later? I was able to move my day appointments, but I've got appointments tonight and tomorrow night that I can't move." Worry paints Landon's face.

"She'll be home around six. If you have to leave before then I can call Demi or Jack. Mercy is working tonight." It's so sweet how concerned he is. As a nurse I know that this type of injury heals well if attended to quickly. As my guy, he's probably still reeling a bit from the whole incident. I know I'd be totally freaked out if anything ever happened to Landon.

"Ok, good. Now, you need to eat." Landon hands me a plate of food. It smells divine and I decide that I should keep him around for his cooking skills alone.

"Is this your famous ham and cheese omelet? Where did you get these berries?" I take a bite of the omelet and lay my head back on the cushion. "Oh, my God! This is amazing!"

"I told you you were going to love it. I ran downstairs this morning before you woke up and picked up a few things. Is it ok that I kind of stocked your fridge with stuff?"

"Sure. Well…what kind of stuff?" He's eyeing me nervously and I think I know what he's going to say.

"Um...I kind of put some food I like in there. And my favorite beer." Landon raises his eyebrows, asking me if it's ok that he's done this.

"So does this mean you're going to be spending more time here?" I ask hopefully.

"I'd like to. I mean, I'm not asking to move in, but, I'd certainly rather be here in any down time I have than at a hotel. And I wouldn't want to be here without you, so Spring doesn't need to worry that she's going to walk in one day and find me hanging out on the couch in my underwear."

"But *I* get to find you hanging out on my couch in your underwear, right?" I tease. I know I can't do much with Landon right now because of my leg, but I have this almost uncontrollable urge to kiss him. He's standing above me so I pull on the bottom of his shirt, forcing him to kneel on the floor next to me. My right leg is to the back of the couch so as Landon leans over me I don't feel anything but warm and tingly. "You know you haven't even kissed me since you've been here?"

"Well I guess I need to remedy that," he says, his lips brushing against mine.

I run my fingers through his hair, pulling him closer to me. Our mouths crush against each other and the passion is immediate. Our lips open and close, moving together as we explore each other. I hold his face in my hands and feel the roughness of his stubbled chin. Landon's hand moves up my leg and inside my thigh. He traces his fingers at the edge of my panties before lifting my shirt and running his hand across my stomach to my back. His hand is warm and just rough enough to make my skin feel every pass.

I grab the front of Landon's shirt and pull him even closer, but I decide that he's still not close enough so I pull his shirt off of him over his head. In that moment between the shirt coming off and resuming our increasingly intense make-out session, he stops and holds my face with his hand, running his thumb across my cheek.

"Jenna…I…" he begins. I don't know if he's trying to tell me he loves me or that he at least feels like he's falling for me. All I know is that I feel the exact same way about him.

"Yeah…me, too," I tell him with a breathy smile. He smiles and takes my face in his hands as he kisses me deeper than he ever has before. It's the kiss that seems to solidify the relationship. The one that says you both feel the same way about each other and have the same hopes for where you're going. For me, it says, yeah, I am definitely falling in love with Landon Scott.

At some point I realize Landon is probably really uncomfortable kneeling on the floor and leaning awkwardly over me so he doesn't hurt my leg. He's kissing my neck when I place my palms on his bare chest. The moan that escapes his mouth tells me he likes it when I touch him there, so I let him continue kissing me and allow myself a few more moments of feeling his strong body over mine. I almost don't say anything at all and see how far we can take this, but I can't stand the idea of Landon uncomfortably hunching over for much longer. I can't have his back hurting on Saturday night when my leg is better and we redo all the first-time moments we had from last night as well as continue on where we'll be leaving off tonight.

"I'm fine, really," Landon says, pushing his face back into my neck. He kisses and bites along my jawline, sending goose bumps rising like mountains across my body.

"I know you're fine, but…" I lose my voice when he covers my mouth with his, kissing and exploring me with such intensity. "I have plans for us on Saturday night and I can't have you injured, too!" I say quickly when Landon begins to trail kisses down my throat to my chest.

"Plans?" Landon pops his head up and spreads a huge grin across his face.

"Yes. Plans. I'm doing my part to have my leg all better, so you have to do your part and not stay hunched over here so that your back is, well, so that you have full use of every inch of your body." *Oh, my God! Did I just say that…out loud?*

"Best. Girlfriend. Ever." Landon's smile is even bigger now, and I can feel my face spread with a huge grin, too.

"Wow. I knew I had to be in the top five at least, but best? And I graduated from your *girl* to your *girlfriend*. This has been a tremendous 17 hours!" Landon stands and stretches his back before helping me shift into more of a sitting position.

"Is that ok? I mean, I wasn't sure if the whole boyfriend/girlfriend title was appropriate once you left your teens," he asks.

"It's totally ok, Landon. We've been seeing each other pretty consistently for a month now. I'm not going anywhere, and I'm pretty sure you aren't either. It seems like a natural move to better define us," I tell him.

"Awesome," he smiles.

"I need to get up and move around. Can you help me up?" I move my body so my legs are off the couch. The muscle in my right leg only hurts a little, but I can definitely feel the burn. Landon bends down and puts his arm around my waist while I use him as a human crutch. "I should get dressed, too."

We move to the bedroom, with me not putting any pressure on my leg. I'm a stickler for following doctor's orders, so it'll be after midnight before I attempt hobbling around without a crutch of any kind. I'll have to determine then if I can work my cover shift in the ER tomorrow night. I hate to leave them hanging, so I'm sure I'll go in and be everyone's paperwork lackey so I can sit the whole time.

Landon gets me settled on the bed before approaching my dresser. "What do you want to wear? You should probably put on some shorts, right?"

"You know what? I want to take a shower first. Can you…" I begin, but Landon cuts me off.

"No."

"No?"

"No. I'm here to help you with anything you need…but that." Landon sighs, collecting his thoughts for a moment and sitting next to me on the bed. "Jenna, the first time I see your naked body, I want it to be part of an incredible experience between us. Last night we had to alter some first-time experiences. Please don't take this as me not wanting to help. I just don't want to alter *that* first time. It's too important to me. Also, if I help you take a shower, I'm not going to be able to control myself, and you're in no condition for what *I* have planned for us."

I almost can't breathe. Damn that crazy bitch for slicing my leg up! Although, were it not for her, I wouldn't have spent the last 17 hours straight with the man I am clearly falling in love with.

"Well, I suppose I can't blame you. I mean, look at me. My hair is a ratted mess and I'm rockin' one sexy, surgical grade bandage on my leg!" We both laugh and the intensity of the moment is gone. I'm afraid to say anything that matches his passion right now because I'm certain that I'll forego the healing of my leg and rip his clothes off.

"I love your ratted hair. And no one rocks a surgical grade bandage like you," he laughs. "I have to leave soon so I can get back to the hotel and get ready for my meeting tonight. And I hate that I wasn't able to move my appointments around tomorrow. I won't get to see you until Saturday night."

"It's fine. I'll rest tomorrow, and by then I'll be able to hobble around without the crutches. Besides, I'll be better to work tomorrow night so I'll need to sleep in the middle of the day anyway."

"Are you sure you're able to work tomorrow night?" he asks warily.

"I'll be fine. I'll sit at the nurse's station and do everyone's paperwork. They'll love me!"

"Ok. I guess that makes me feel a little better. When will Spring be home? Can she help you with your shower or should I call Mercy or Demi?"

"Spring will be home in a bit. It's Thursday and she usually isn't out on a week night. I'll text her though just to make sure. If she's going to be out with Matt I can call Demi," I tell him. "Thank you, Landon. I really appreciate you being here. It's meant a lot to me." I lean in and kiss him gently on the lips. It's not a moment to be passionate, but to really express my gratitude.

"I'll always be here for you, Jenna," he says.

"I know."

*****

I texted Spring and found out that she did in fact have plans with Matt tonight. So I called Demi and she was quick to come help me in my time of bathing need. Landon stuck around until she got there so I wouldn't be alone. He gave me one hell of a kiss goodbye and we agreed that we would both live in a heightened state of anticipation until Saturday night.

Demi has been a great help since she got here, but she definitely seems out of it. She's usually not this preoccupied. She's usually wonderfully cynical and sarcastic, which is why I love her so much, but tonight she's abnormally quiet.

"So are you going to tell me what's going on or do I have to guess?" I ask as she helps get me situated at the kitchen table. We ordered pizza and I'm dying to dive into the ham and pineapple deliciousness that sits before me.

"I'm fine. Eat your weird pizza." She doesn't look at me, but goes into the kitchen to get drinks for us.

"C'mon, Demi. You were fine last night when you came to get me at the hospital. What happened between then and now? Did something happen at work? Oh, my God! Did you get fired?" Demi desperately wants to leave her job, but getting fired is not part of the plan. That doesn't exactly bode well with future employers.

"I didn't get fired. But thanks for that," she says. She fills our glasses with Dr. Pepper and sits back down.

"I'm just going to keep asking until you tell me. So, you should probably give in now and spare yourself the nagging." I take a bite of my pizza and think I've gone to heaven. I rarely eat pizza so when I do it feels like a real treat.

"Fine. But you can't say anything to anyone. Especially Jack. Ok?" I nod in agreement. "I'm pregnant."

"Wow. Not what I was expecting you to say. Are we excited or scared about this?" I ask. I can get on board with whichever it is, I just want to make sure I'm supporting her the way she needs me to.

"I haven't decided yet. Jack and I have known each other for a long time, but we haven't been dating six months yet. I'm 25 with a good job. I hate my job, but it's not like I'm 16 and still in high school and trying to figure this out. But still…" Demi puts her face in her hands. "I don't know what to do, Jenna."

"Have you told Jack yet?" I ask.

"No. I just confirmed it this morning at the doctor. I've been late before, but never this late. I thought maybe I was just really stressed out with work. Working for Cruella will do that to you."

"You have to tell him, Demi. He should have at least some input in what you do," I say. I'm all for women's rights, but I think the father of the baby should have some say in what happens. "What do you feel like your options are?"

"There are only three options any woman has in this position. You either keep the baby, give the baby up, or terminate the pregnancy. I can't have an abortion. I just…the whole idea of that gives me the creeps. I think I want to keep it, but I don't know…I don't know if Jack is ready to give up the things you have to give up when you become a parent. So then I wonder if I want to do this with him or not. I don't want to be one of those women who gets all aggressive about not needing a man to take care of her and her baby, but seriously…I might as well do this by myself if Jack can't let go of his bi-weekly manicures. Who wants to do this alone? No one! I don't. I don't want to do this alone. I don't want to do this alone, Jenna." Demi starts to sob and I reach across the table and take her hands in mine.

"Hey…you're not alone. I'm here, and Jack will be, too. You have to talk to him and give him the opportunity to help you figure this out." I rub her hand, trying to comfort her. I can't imagine how scared she must be right now. "Weren't you two being safe?" I ask her now that she's stopped crying. She's picking at her pizza and starting to eat a little something, too.

"I'm on the pill, but you know how it says it's only 99% effective. Guess I'm the 1%! And you know Jack is going to be all manly about his sperm being so strong that they defy the pill." We laugh at the truth of Demi's statement. I'm glad to see even the smallest smile from her right now.

"You know, I always think things happen for a reason. Sometimes it's unpleasant, but ultimately it happens for a greater reason in the grand scheme of life. If even the pill couldn't keep you from getting pregnant, I can't help but believe that there's a purpose," I tell her.

"You're probably right. Maybe my baby will grow up to find the cure for cancer…and then become President," she says with a breathy laugh.

"And at the very least, it's Jack's baby, so you know he or she will have great hair and impeccable style." Demi laughs again and we begin a lighthearted conversation about all the qualities Jack possesses that she hopes their baby gets. I have to steer her away from picking herself apart with all the things she hopes her baby doesn't get from her. Demi is a beautifully giving person who any child would be lucky to model themselves after.

I know she's scared, but it seems talking about it has helped calm her down and put her in a place where she can think more clearly about what she wants. She's not having an abortion, so now she and Jack have to decide if they're going to move forward in this pregnancy together, or not. I know Jack well enough to believe he won't bail on Demi. But this is a huge deal and he wouldn't be the first guy to freak out and run as fast as he could. Regardless of what Jack decides, Demi won't face this alone. Mercy and I will be there for her. And, if Jack does run, I think he'll have to outrun Landon and Jerry first.

Chapter 9

Demi spent the night with me last night, partly to help take care of me since Landon couldn't be there, and partly because she didn't want to be alone. She took a sick day and hung out with me while I began working my leg and putting pressure on it around the apartment. By lunch I was hobbling around just fine without her and feeling totally confident in my ability to come into work tonight. She'll tell Jack about the baby tonight when she sees him. I'm sure I'll get a text at the very least.

It's only 10:00 pm and it's already been one of those nights in the ER. No real emergencies, as in no ambulances, but plenty of fodder for break room conversation. I feel really sorry for the older gentleman who came in earlier after having mistaken a tube of very minty toothpaste for his hemorrhoid cream. And then there was the tatted up girl with purple hair who ended up with acute appendicitis. Her "keep off the lawn" tattoo above her died green pubic hair had us rolling. I think Dr. Culpepper is going to leave a note on her chart apologizing for having to mow the lawn.

Dr. Culpepper has kept his word and I have been pretty immobile for the most part tonight. He said he wants me to save my strength for if they really need me up and about, so I've been doing basic paperwork and tag-teaming on some calls in the triage office.

"How's it going, gimp?" Tim, one of the other ER nurses says to me. "I can't believe you came in tonight! I would have totally milked it!" Tim's a tall, lanky guy from Missouri who talks like a surfer. He's a walking contradiction, and one of my favorite people in the ER.

"I know, I know. Mercy told me the same thing. I just didn't like the idea of leaving you guys short staffed. You never know when the shit is going to hit the fan around here! Besides, the ER has the best stories ever!" I tell him. "Did you see *keep off the lawn* appendicitis girl?"

"Oh, my God! Yes!" he laughs.

"That's one of the best stories yet!" I say.

"Did I ever tell you about when I was working at a rehab center? I was giving an 87-year-old male patient a sponge bath. I stood him up so I could wash his family jewels. He looked down and said 'Have you ever seen anything so big?' I didn't know exactly what to tell him, and tried to think of an appropriate response. But before I could say a word, he shook his head and said, 'My brother-in-law told me once that these have got to be biggest damn feet he has ever seen.'" Tim barely gets the last part out before bursting into laughter. I follow quickly, grateful I didn't take a swig of my soda before he gave me the punch line.

"Oh, my God! That is hysterical!" I shout.

"I'm not sure what's going on here, but I'm fairly sure I'm going to want to hear this story later," Dr. Culpepper says as he approaches Tim and me. "Tim can you check on room four? Jenna, there's a head trauma in room seven. If you're up to it, can you check on him please? Make sure he's not falling asleep?"

"Of course. It's about time for me to get up and stretch," I tell him. Tim makes his way to room four and I hobble my way to room seven. It's getting easier to walk, and I do my best not to limp. Limping too much could lead to hip problems and that's worse than the healing process for this gash in my leg.

I pull the chart from the file hanger on the outside of the room and almost scream as I throw the curtain open.

"Landon! What are you doing here? Oh, my God! What happened?" I practically yell as I shuffle quickly into his room. He's lying there with an ice pack on his head wearing a disheveled suit. His tie is extremely loose around his neck and the top two buttons on his dress shirt are undone. He looks rough and I'm so scared that I feel like my heart is going to beat out of my chest.

"Jenna! What are you doing here," he says shocked. He tries to sit up but it clearly makes him dizzy so he lies back down.

"I'm working…covering in the ER tonight," I tell him as I check his vitals. His heart rate is elevated, but I think that's just because I startled him.

"Oh…I didn't know," he says.

"When did you get here? I must have been in the triage office when you were admitted."

"Um…maybe an hour. They hooked me up to this IV and got fluids going even though I told them I was fine. I'm still fine. I got clipped by a cab tonight. I'm fine, really. In fact, I'm going to check out right now." Landon is anxious and fidgety. I've never seen him like this.

"Fluids are standard procedure. But, you're obviously not ok, Landon. Now, I can't attend to you due to conflict of interest, but I'll get Tim in here in a minute to check your fluids and that bump on your head, ok?" I take his hand that isn't connected to an IV and run my thumb across his knuckles. "I'm sorry I freaked out. I shouldn't have reacted that way. I was just really scared."

"It's ok. I…I guess I was just taken by surprise to find you here, too." Landon squeezes my hand and smiles. "I'm going to be fine. I'm in the best ER in Chicago, right?"

"Right." I give him a quick kiss and head out to the nurse's station to wait for Tim so I can send him in to take care of Landon. When Dr. Culpepper comes back I'll tell him why.

About ten minutes goes by before Tim and Dr. Culpepper come back from checking on patients. I tell them about Landon and Dr. Culpepper sends Tim to do a full check on him before heading off in another direction. I'm in the middle of documenting why I had to pass Landon off to Tim when a woman enters the ER. She's got long, wavy blonde hair and is wearing a striking blue dress. She's scanning the loop of ER rooms when she approaches the nurse's station.

"Can I help you find someone?" I ask.

"Yes, I'm looking for a guy. Tall, really handsome? We were on a date when he got clipped by a cab as we started to cross the street," she says.

My heart stops and I immediately begin to think of any of the other patients that have been in tonight. *Were there any other head injuries? Maybe more than one came in while I was in the triage office.*

"Do...you...have his name?" I ask hesitantly. I know it didn't come out very professional, but I'm working really hard right now to will her into saying any other name.

"Yes, of course. How silly of me. His name is Landon Scott."

No, no, no, no. This is not happening. Maybe she thinks it was a date, but really they're just business associates. I can't blame her for being interested in Landon. I'll just take her to his room and get this all cleared up.

"Sure. I'll take you to his room." I stand up slowly, still hoping with everything in me that the status of their evening is a misunderstanding on her part. "A date, huh? So how did you two meet?"

"A dance class of all places! I take a Latin dance class on Wednesdays and one day I showed up and he was there. He was really good! We've only been out a few times, but, you know...you get that feeling like it could be more. It's like he knows how to read me. He's figured out all my favorite things. Like, tonight, he took me out to the most amazing Mexican restaurant," she tells me with bright eyes.

"Yeah..." I say trying to keep from throwing up my heart.

I walk into Landon's room and his eyes light up the moment he sees me. The light quickly fades, though, as blondie enters behind me.

"You have a visitor," I tell him before turning and walking out of the room. Dr. Culpepper is back at the nurse's station when I return. I hear Landon shouting my name but I ignore him completely.

"Everything ok, Jenna?" Dr. Culpepper asks.

"I know I said I was fine to work tonight, but I'm just in too much pain to stay," I tell him. I wish I was talking about my leg, but it's my heart that feels like it's burning and being clamped in a vice. "Will you be fine if I go?"

Dr. Culpepper looks back toward Landon's room and looks at the tears filling my eyes. "Will *you* be fine if you go?" he asks. He's got this fatherly way of looking and talking sometimes. It's part of what makes him an excellent doctor.

"Better than if I stay," I tell him, choking back tears.

"Go. Take care of yourself. I don't know what's going on, but I hope it works out, Jenna." Dr. Culpepper squeezes my shoulder before I walk behind the nurse's station and grab my purse.

I leave the ER, walking and crying for two blocks before I realize how much my leg hurts. I hail a cab and slide in, squeaking out my address just loud enough for him to hear me. I can't believe this is happening. I thought we felt the same way about each other, especially considering he took care of me just 36 hour ago. I think of all the things I told him, all the things I shared with him. I even considered telling him *everything* about my past!

I wipe the tears from my face as I open the door to the apartment just before midnight. It's dark and I know Spring is already in bed so I do my best to be as quiet as possible. I drop my purse on the couch and go straight to my room. My phone has been buzzing for the last 45 minutes with calls and texts from Landon. I haven't read any of them since the first one that told me he was sorry and just needed to explain.

Changing out of my scrubs, I find a shirt and a pair of sleep shorts to put on because all I want to do is crawl in bed and not get out until I have to be at work again on Monday night. I've just pulled my hair back up into a pony tail and am about to brush my teeth when there's a knock at the door. It could only be Landon so I'm not going to answer it. He knocks again, a little louder this time. I still don't answer. My phone buzzes again and this time I look at his text that tells me he's going to stay out there all night banging on my door if I don't answer him.

I ignore his text, not believing he'd actually do that. It's the middle of the night and he knows Spring, along with all my neighbors, is sleeping.

I was wrong.

The next thing I hear is a loud bang on the front door. I rush to it as fast as I can before he wakes anyone.

"You're an asshole. Go away, Landon," I say through the door.

"I'm not going anywhere, Jenna. You have to hear me out," he pleads. "Please. Please just let me explain." The tone in his voice is sad and it sounds like maybe he's been crying, too. Good.

"No. You hurt me. You lied to me, Landon. How could I ever believe anything you have to tell me?" I say through my tears. I don't want to cry, but I just can't seem to stop.

"Please, Jenna. I'm going to stay out here all night if I have to. After you hear what I have to tell you, you'll understand." The door knocks once and I think he's put his head to it out of fatigue.

I take a deep breath and calm myself. I've been through worse, endured worse. I can handle breaking up with a guy who just broke my heart in the most heinous of ways. I open the door slowly and just look at him. He looks tired, but he did get hit by a car tonight and spent some time in the hospital. His dress shirt is untucked and his sleeves are carelessly rolled up, one longer than the other. His tie is missing altogether.

"Can I please come in?" he asks carefully.

"Fine." I open the door all the way and Landon walks in. There's blood on his shirt and he notices me eyeing it with concern.

"I ripped my IV out when they wouldn't take it out for me. I got here as fast as I could."

"Where's your girlfriend?" Sarcasm drips from me with absolute intention.

"She's standing in front of me," he says. He looks at me with sad, but hopeful eyes.

"Like hell she is. You lied to me, Landon. You played me, and that poor girl. You used all the same moves on both of us. Are there more Mexican-food-loving dancers out there that you've got swooning over you?".

"It's not like that, Jenna. Sarah is…she's just part of my job," he says, trying to explain but failing miserably as far as I'm concerned.

"Part of your job? Bullshit! She said you two met in a dance class, and that you took her out for Mexican food, just like us."

"She just happens to like Mexican food. It's not that unique." He has the audacity to look at me with even the smallest amount of condescension so I reach for the door.

"I'm not doing this, Landon. You need to go," I say not looking at him.

"You won't let me explain," he argues.

"You're not *trying* to explain! All you're doing is making excuses!"

Landon starts to pace around the living room, sighing and breathing heavily. I'm actually kind of concerned about his head trauma and the damage he's done to his arm by ripping his IV out. It looks all dramatic in the movies but can cause some serious damage to the vein. And I never fully read his chart, so I don't know if he had a concussion or not. He shouldn't be getting worked up like this. As a nurse, I want to tell him to sit down before he faints or throws up. As the girl whose heart he just ripped out, I hope he pukes his brains out before fainting and cracking his skull open.

"Ok. I'm going to tell you what I should have told you weeks ago. I just…I didn't want to tell you because I knew as soon as I did that I would have to let you go. That you'd have things you would need to focus on and I would just be a distraction." He takes a deep breath, looks down to collect his thoughts, and then looks at me again. I can see the fear in his eyes and, even though I hate him right now, I can see that he really is afraid of losing me. "It has to do with my job."

"I don't care about your job, Landon. I care about why you were seeing someone else when you were so clear about not being the kind of guy who dated more than one girl at a time. That's how we began this relationship for crying out loud!" I'm doing my best to stay calm because I don't want to wake Spring up but I'm afraid if we continue this conversation in the living room it'll be inevitable. "Follow me." We walk to my bedroom, which is in the back of the apartment, and close the door.

"I wasn't lying. I don't date more than one woman at a time. Sarah…she was just part of…I was seeing her because…I didn't…"

"What? Spit it out!" I demand.

"I didn't want you to be *her*." His words and facial expression are both cryptic. I can't read him and I don't understand what he's trying to tell me.

"Are you spewing out some commitment-phobic excuse at me? You're afraid? You don't want me to be *the one*?" I stare at him with confusion. I know I didn't mistake his care and passion for just an attraction. I was certain he was falling in love with. I was sure I was falling in love with him. My anger is turning to sadness and I feel like I might throw up. How could I have been so wrong?

"No, that's not it at all. I *want* you to be the one. I *know* you're the one, Jenna. When I said I didn't want you to be *her*…I meant that I didn't want you to be Veronica Matthews."

Oh, my God.

"What…what are you talking about?" I put on my best confused face and take a step back. "I don't know what you're talking about. Who…who is that?"

"I know it's you. The dancing…nursing…Chicago. Veronica Matthews from Washington, DC. Your father was a master locksmith before…"

"He sent you to find me," I say, giving in to the fact that I'm going to have to run again. I don't know where I'll go, but I'll have to see if Oz can create a new identity for me again. How can I do that without putting him in danger, too?

"Yes, and he doesn't want you to be mad."

"He doesn't want me to be mad?" Shock rings through my voice. How could Senator Dellinger not want me to be mad? He destroyed my life! "He knows that the circumstances under which you had to leave were upsetting, but he misses you and…" Landon is using a calming tone, like he's trying to get me to understand Dellinger's side, but none of what he's saying is making sense.

"Wait. He misses me?"

"Yes. Your father misses you, Jenna."

"What?"

"Your father. He sent me to find you," Landon says.

"My father is dead," I remind him.

"Your father is alive. He feels terribly about making you believe he was dead, but he wanted me to tell you that it's safe to come home now."

My father is alive? Why wouldn't he come get me himself, or have Oz come get me? He's known where I've been all along. Oh no! Maybe something's happened to Oz and he didn't know how to find me. I haven't seen anything about Dellinger being dead, so how is it safe to come home? Maybe Dad finally has something on the Senator that will keep him more than an arm's length away. It doesn't matter. Dad is alive! Wait. Dad is alive.

"You've known all this time that my father was alive and you kept it from me?" I shout, now not caring who hears me. Landon has had the most life-changing piece of information in the palm of his hand for over a month and he never told me.

"I'm so sorry. I know, I should have told you sooner. I wanted to tell you. I tried to tell you so many times. But, I was already crazy about you when I realized that you were her and I knew as soon as I told you, you'd be making up for all that lost time with him and I'd only be a distraction. I just didn't want to lose you, Jenna," Landon explains.

"Why do guys always think that keeping the truth from us is somehow a good thing? You wouldn't have lost me, Landon, if you had been honest when you first found me. How *did* you find me?" I ask. Oz was so sure of his ability to create a new life for me and hide me. I chose Chicago, so it's not like anything Oz has indicates that I'm here.

"Your father gave me your laptop. I looked through your old high school papers and internet searches. Your med-tech class papers were excellent and you wrote a very convincing paper on why Chicago is the greatest city in the world. When your father told me about your passion for dance, I figured I'd start there once I got here. I must have been to every dance studio in the city, all 192 of them. Your father gave me some old pictures of you. You used to be blonde. I like you as a brunette." Landon looks at me, waiting for me to respond, but I'm not sure how. I'm torn between being angry with him for lying and keeping the truth of my father being alive, and throwing my arms around him in gratitude for bringing my father back to me.

"I don't know what to say, Landon."

"Just tell me you know that I wasn't cheating on you. I never got close to any of them like I did you," he says softly.

"Any of them? How many were there?" I ask, afraid of the answer.

"There were five over the course of about six months. You and Sarah were the last two. I knew it was you before I even found Sarah. I think I just didn't want it to be you so badly that I kept searching and following leads," he explains.

Five? He dated five women in his quest to find Veronica Matthews?

"How did you know it was me? I mean, when?"

"The night you picked the lock. Your father told me he had been a bit of a thug back in the day, and that he taught you everything he knew. Not many women have that party trick up their sleeves." Landon smirks as I recall that night. He had looked at me with amazement as I jimmied the lock and I just

116

brushed it off. "So, please, Jenna, tell me you understand I wasn't cheating on you, because…I'm in love with you. And I know you're in love with me, too."

"Landon…" I can't think clearly.

"Tell me." Landon takes a step closer and takes my face in his hands. "Tell me you love me."

"You lied to me, and you kept the truth about my father from me." My voice is small. I'm finding it hard to fight him, even with the truth.

"I never lied about being drawn to you. And I wasn't lying when I spent the night taking care of you." He runs his thumb across my cheek and my body won't let me be angry with him. "Kissing you was never a lie. Touching you was never a lie."

"I don't know what to think…what to feel right now," I mumble.

"Well then let me remind you." Landon leans in and covers my mouth with his. I don't respond at first but then, as if by instinct, my lips part and move with his. My hands reach his waist and I find myself grabbing his shirt to pull him closer. His slow, passionate kisses are overwhelming and I'm not sure that I can contain myself.

I do love him. I'm absolutely in love with him.

Landon pulls me closer and a shiver runs down my spine as I try to get as close to him as possible. My body responds immediately to his touch and Landon takes quick note of it, moving us to the bed.

He lays me gently on the bed, positioning himself above me carefully so as not to hurt my leg. I claw at the buttons on his shirt, working my way down until the white cotton is hanging open and giving me the most perfect access to his body. He slips his hands under my shirt and starts to lift it off me. I realize immediately that I'm not wearing a bra and would be completely exposed to him. This seems to wake me from my Landon high, making me aware of the truly terrible timing this would be for our first time together. Landon's lips brush my neck as he begins to trail kisses from the back of my ear down my throat. My hand holds his as he grips my shirt halfway up my stomach, keeping him from completing his task of beginning to remove my clothes. After a moment Landon stops and stares into my eyes.

"What is it?" he asks, noticing the obvious change in my intensity. "Am I hurting you? Did I hurt your leg?"

"No…you're not, I'm fine," I tell him.

"Then what? What's wrong, Jenna?" he asks with concern.

"I just…I have a lot to process here, Landon. It's not that I don't want to do this. It's just…"

"No, you're right. I'm sorry." Landon moves his body off of mine and lies facing me, propping himself up on his elbow. "I've just told you your father is alive and all I'm concerned with is making sure you know how I feel about you."

"It's ok. I'm a pretty willing participant here," I say with a breathy laugh.

"I just need you to believe me. I never lied about how I feel about you, Jenna. I love you." His brown eyes are warm like hot chocolate and all I want to do is dive into them and stay there forever.

"I do believe you. And…I love you, too," I say. There's a flutter in my stomach as the words leave my mouth, followed by a smile on my lips. I reach over and run my fingers through his hair, fixing the bit of a mess I made it only moments ago.

"That is the greatest thing you have ever said to me." Landon smiles and relief covers his face. He takes a deep breath before he speaks again. "Well…now that my crazy profession of love isn't hanging out there like a bad high five, let's regroup."

"Yeah…I feel like I need to stop and regroup now that I'm not completely furious with you. I thought I'd have a ton of questions for you, and I suppose I will, but I realize everything I really want and need to know is going to have to come from my father. I guess all I need to know from you right now is…when can I see him? I mean, are we going back to DC? Is he coming here?" My eyes light up as I think about seeing my father again. Warm memories of my life with him run through my mind and I can't help but feel a little giddy.

"You're so cute." Landon leans down and kisses me sweetly. I can't wait for my father to meet Landon in a non-employee way. He really is going to just love him. "He said as soon as I told him I found you that he'd be on the next plane out."

"You didn't contact him before you came over here?" I ask. I would have thought that since Landon's cover was blown he would have immediately called my father.

"No. I had to make sure we were good first. I just couldn't stand the thought…" Landon begins but I cut him off. We've been down this path and I just don't see the sense in travelling it again.

"It's ok, Landon. You know, it's late and we both need to get some sleep. Well, I'm going to *try* to sleep. My father will be here tomorrow. I'm going to see him again after *six* years." Tears begin to sting my eyes. "I wish you had been honest with me from the start, but…you brought him back to me, Landon. My dad was the only family I had left when I lost him. I felt so alone for a really long time. It took years for me to let Mercy and Spring and everyone in even in the smallest ways. They became my family but I've always had this little empty place inside because my dad was gone. You changed all that and it makes me love you even more."

"It makes me really happy to hear you say that. I guess we've got a big day tomorrow. I'm meeting my girlfriend's father and I'm just a little nervous about that. Oh, my gosh! I've never been so happy to have not had sex. I don't think I could look your father in the eye tomorrow knowing I had seen his daughter naked the night before," he chuckles.

"Eww! Aaaand on that note…" I interject.

"Oooh! Maybe I should play the white knight and tell him we're waiting until we're married!" Landon says raising his eyebrows at me.

Married? That's a pretty bold, off-the-cuff comment for a guy to make. One day I think I could entertain the thought of marrying Landon, just not today. But now that the idea has been planted, I'm sure it'll pop up when I'm least expecting it.

"Oh, please! My dad was a hooligan on the streets of DC and Maryland long enough to know how the world works. He actually gave me condoms when I started dating at 16. As if that wasn't bad enough, he also gave them to my dates," I tell him. My dad was always the most honest man I knew. He did his best to be both father and mother to me. Sometimes it was awkward, but at least you never had to guess where he stood on things, even contraceptives.

"Ok, now *that* is eww!" We both laugh and recognize that this is really the end of the conversation. It's late and there's not much left to talk about. The emotional roller coaster of the night has left me puffy-eyed and tired. I'm sure I'll have more questions for Landon in the morning, but for now all I can think about it going to sleep. Getting off the bed, we pull the sheets and blanket back and Landon undresses as he did before and we both crawl in.

Landon was right that once I knew my father was alive I'd be focused on that. What Landon underestimated was how much a part of my life he already is. There's no way I can reunite with my father without Landon by my side. I've been building my life and really living, just like my father wanted, especially over the last month with Landon. I'll never be Veronica Matthews again, but I have my father back and I know that I'll have an amazing future as Jenna Rockwell. That amazing life starts right now as I lay here in the arms of the man I love completely.

FIVE

Chapter 10

It's 8:30 am when I wake up and find myself still wrapped in Landon's arms. A smile spreads across my face as I realize just how perfect my life is right now. I'm lying in the strong arms of the man I love, and today I'm going to replace the last, terrible memory I have of my father. Today I'll throw my arms around my dad and tell him how much I love him and have missed him. I'll tell him all about nursing school and Spring and Mercy and everyone. I'll tell him how I've kept up with my dancing, and how I've been doing my best to live a full life like he told me to.

I move so I can look at Landon fully and realize that I'll also yell at my father for going to such extremes to find me when he could have just asked Oz. I'm reminded of the frightening thought I had last night and consider that something may have happened to Oz and that's why Dad hired Landon. He wouldn't have had the money to do that before, but maybe Oz provided the finances in some fashion. I don't want to think about that.

I have so many questions for my father. Why did he wait six years to find me? What deal does he have with Dellinger that is allowing him to do all this? What happened that night when I left him under that tree in Constitution Gardens?

I think about all the things I want to tell him about my life here and hope that he's going to be proud of all that I've accomplished. I find I'm also a little sad, too, because I know I can never go back to being his daughter…I can never be his Ronnie again. Veronica Matthews died the same day I thought he did, but I think Jenna Rockwell is pretty great and I hope Dad loves her just as much.

I get out of bed and quietly go to the kitchen. I can hear Spring making coffee and I want to apologize for the disturbance last night. I find her still in her PJ's fiddling with the coffee maker. Afraid she's going to make us suffer

121

her lack of coffee-making skills, I intervene before she gets too far.

"Hey! Everything ok?" she asks, a mix of concern and confusion painting her face. "I thought you were working, but then I heard you and Landon fighting last night. It got quiet so I came out to make sure you were ok. Then I heard other noises coming from you room, so I figured you were, um, getting over whatever it is he did."

"I'm so sorry about that. It was a huge misunderstanding," I tell her.

"So…is he still here?" Spring raises her eyebrows in that goofy way that only she can and get away with it.

"Yes," I tell her hesitantly.

"Oh, my God! You two *did* it!" she laughs.

"Shh! And, no, we didn't," I say. "The circumstances weren't really right for optimal enjoyment. I have *a lot* on my mind. He was totally great about it though. I'll eventually make up for it," I wink.

There's a knock at the door and Spring and I look at each other, puzzled. No one we know would be here this early on a Saturday morning. Even when Spring does something with Matt, she always meets him at his place so he gets to sleep in a bit longer.

I open the door and a frazzled Mercy is standing before me. She's wearing scrubs and her hair is pulled back, so she'd obviously come here straight from work.

"Oh. My. God! I cannot believe you didn't call me! I had to hear from Tim in ER that your ass-hat of a boyfriend cheated on you? Jerry has already sworn to kick his ass!" Mercy is channeling her inner New Yorker and I need to calm her down before she wakes Landon, and all of Chicago.

"Landon cheated on you?" Spring responds to Mercy's rant with wide eyes.

"Ok, first, shh! Second, Landon did not cheat on me. He had a work thing last night with a woman who thought their business relationship was more than that," I tell them. It's partly true. Of course, Landon *lead* her to believe he was interested in her in his effort to find Veronica Matthews, but I can't explain all of that to them just yet. "I overreacted and Landon followed me home and explained everything. We're good so call Jerry off before he shows up here with a baseball bat!"

"Really, Jenna, I didn't realize you were that stupid! If it looks like cheating, it's cheating! He comes here and gives you his sob story and just like that you two are all good?" Mercy cocks her head to the side in disbelief.

"Yeah, we're all good," Landon says entering the living room. He's wearing his dress pants with his white dress shirt completely unbuttoned. Spring gives a quiet, but still audible gasp when she sees him. I can't blame her. My boyfriend is undeniably hot. "I explained everything and Jenna knows I told her the truth. I can understand your protectiveness of her but don't ever refer to my girlfriend as being stupid again. Ever." Landon puts his arm around me and the tension in the room becomes palpable. I have to give Mercy credit for the restraint she's showing.

"I swear to God, if I find out you *were* cheating on her, or if you *ever* do *anything* to hurt her…I wasn't joking. I will kill you." Mercy gives Landon a dagger-filled stare before addressing me. "You're going to have to explain this to me, but clearly now is not the right time. I'm exhausted and hungry. I'm going to go home to eat and sleep off the fury. I'll call you later when I've calmed down."

Mercy doesn't bother with a goodbye. She just turns on her heels and closes the door behind her. I've seen Mercy mad before, but I've never seen her like this. It's because we're family. She's been my mother and sister rolled into one cute little Italian package for the last few years. Once I have all the answers from my father I'll know better what's happening and be able to tell Mercy everything. She won't apologize for her rage because she never apologizes for protecting the ones she loves, but she'll be so happy for me to have my father back.

"If Jenna believes you, that's good enough for me," Spring tells Landon.

"Thanks, Spring. I appreciate it. I'm really sorry if our arguing woke you last night." His sincere apology and smile are enough to make me weak in the knees right there.

"No worries. I'm an excellent judge of character and I have a feeling you're the real deal. But…if by some crazy fluke I'm wrong, you know I'll have to side with Mercy, right?" she smirks.

"I'd be disappointed if you didn't," he smirks back.

Spring excuses herself to her room to get dressed, leaving Landon and me alone. I finish making coffee and pull some breakfast items from the fridge.

"How's your leg? You don't seem to be limping at all." Landon stands behind me and rubs my shoulders.

"It still feels a little tender, but it's fine. I'll still have to wait until I feel zero pain before I can dance again. I need to know that the little muscle she cut has healed completely before I work it like that," I tell Landon as he sits on one of the two stools at the counter bar.

"I'm glad you're feeling better. I've hated watching you in pain. I was…I was really scared that night, Jenna." Landon rests his face in his hands for a moment before running his fingers through his hair.

"Hey…I'm ok. We're ok. We've dealt with everything else and now we're moving forward physically and emotionally. Ok?" Landon takes a deep breath and nods. "Good. Now, I hope I didn't wake you. Are you hungry?"

"I felt it when you got up. I wasn't nearly as warm." A sexy smile appears and his eyebrow rises with suggestion. "I waited a few minutes for you to come back, but then I heard you and Spring talking so I figured I'd go ahead and call your father. He's going to call me back when he's got his flight secured."

"Wow. I can't believe this is happening." My stomach flips and I'm not sure if I'll be able to eat breakfast or any other meal today.

"I can't believe you haven't asked me a million questions. What's up with that?" Landon gets up and assumes my breakfast-making tasks seeing that I'm now quite distracted.

"I have *more* than a million questions. It's just that I plan on holding my father hostage and asking him every single one of them. The last time I saw my father I was watching him die. I plan on replacing that memory." Landon kisses my forehead, causing a rush of warmth to run through me.

"That sounds great," he says.

I come back to the moment and Landon and I work together to make breakfast. I soften some cream cheese in the microwave to mix with the eggs I'm going to scramble while Landon gets started on the turkey bacon. The first time I made breakfast for him we had quite the discussion on the validity of turkey bacon being *real* bacon. He said that they were *strips of turkey* and it's disrespectful to pigs everywhere to call what I was cooking up bacon. When it came time to eat, though, his feelings on the subject didn't keep him from downing six pieces of my faux breakfast meat.

Spring swings through the kitchen are her way out, grabbing a travel mug and adding some coffee to her cream before she leaves for the day and Landon and I sit down to eat.

"Can I ask you something?" Landon says as I pour him some coffee.

"Anything," I tell him with a confident smile.

"If the circumstances were different…if I weren't Landon Scott, the guy who was hired to find you…if I was really Landon Scott, random guy who works in securities…would you have told me about your past?" He looks at me with genuine inquiry.

"You want to know if I would have ever really let you in." It's a legitimate question, but I'm not sure how to answer it. I don't know what he knows about my past and I'm not prepared to lay it out there, even now, not until I have answers from Dad. "I don't know. I was running from someone who I believed had my father killed...someone I believed was going to kill me, too, if I didn't cooperate with him. I would never have wanted to put you in danger."

Landon presses his lips together and nods, not sure how exactly to respond. "Will you tell me the whole story one day?"

"Yes," I answer truthfully. Once I have all the answers from my father I'll be able to tell Landon everything. I just have to fill in the blanks of my own questions first. "Can I ask *you* something?"

"Of course," he smiles, seeming to feel better now that I've agreed to let him in on all the details at some point.

"If you hadn't been brought into the ER, and I hadn't met the blonde, when would you have told me the truth?"

"Well, I was honest when I told you I was worried I'd be left behind as soon as you knew. I was sure there would be a combination of being focused on your father and being totally pissed at me for lying to you. I never expected to fall in love with you. I mean, I've been doing this a long time, Jenna, and I've never, *ever* gotten close to anyone like I have you. I never wanted to," he tells me. "But, I've been in Chicago for over six months now and your father was getting impatient, so I imagine I would have had to tell you soon. I told him a few days ago that I was running my last lead, but that I thought you might be his daughter."

"So...how long have you been doing this? Finding people who don't want to be found?" I ask. "This doesn't seem like something you just decide one day you're going to do."

"I became a kind of *reverse* skip tracer shortly after I got out of the military. I stumbled upon it out of necessity. The S Squad had a pact. We had each written letters to our families that would be delivered only if we were killed in combat. The pact was that whoever survived would deliver the letters by hand. The Navy would send the official messenger to their homes, but we wanted someone who knew us to personally connect with our loved ones with our last words to them. We *hoped* we'd *all* make it home, but never thought it'd be only one of us. So, I had to deliver all three letters.

"The problem was that Kyle had a falling out with his family before he enlisted and hadn't been in touch with them since. By the time I got to deliver his letter, the address he had for them wasn't any good and there was no forwarding address. The rift was so bad that they moved without tell him." Landon gives an annoyed sigh before continuing. "Their son was fighting for their freedom and they didn't bother to tell him they moved. It took everything in me not to punch his asshole father in the face when I finally did track them down. He showed little, if any, emotion. His mother, on the other hand, was a mess. Clearly the problem had been between Kyle and his dad."

"That sucks. So how did that lead to you becoming this *reverse skip tracer?*" I ask him.

"Well, a skip tracer helps people get lost who don't want to be found. Whoever helped you get *lost* would have been a skip tracer." I guess Dad didn't tell him about Oz, which would make sense since it seems something has happened that Dad couldn't get my whereabouts from him. Dad wouldn't have gone into all of that and would have just stuck with the mission at hand of finding me. "As a reverse skip tracer, I *find* people. Word got out with some other guys I knew in the Navy and they got me connected with some people who were willing to pay me whatever it took to find people who may or may not have wanted to be found."

"Why would you do that? If someone doesn't want to be found, why would you unearth them like that?" I ask with a bit of annoyance in my tone.

"Sometimes people skip town because they owe someone a lot of money," he begins.

"Yeah, and some people skip town because they're running from something terrible," I counter, using myself as an example.

"Hey...I've also found a lot of people who were *happy* to be found. Long lost families, birth parents, children given up for adoption, people who had crazy inheritances coming to them. It's a job, Jenna. A *very good* paying job that's allowed me to see parts of the world I would have never travelled to otherwise," Landon explains in defense of himself. His voice is strong after my challenge.

I hadn't thought about the fact that Landon's job has him travelling all the time. I lower my head as I wonder what this will mean for us. Now that his job of finding me is complete, does he have another job waiting in the wings? Will his next job have him convincing unsuspecting women that he's interested in them just so he can get as close as possible? Or will this new job take him to the other side of world for an undeterminable amount of time?

I'm about to express my fears when Landon's cell rings. He pulls it out of his pocket and stands as he answers it. "Yes sir…excellent. Of course, but she's right here if you'd like to tell her yourself." *It's my father! My father is on the other side of that phone conversation!* "Of course. Yes, I'll be sure to tell her. Yes. Yes. Excellent. We'll see you then."

"He didn't want to talk to me?" My face squishes together in sadness and confusion as Landon ends the call and drops his phone back into his pocket.

"He didn't want your first conversation in six years to be over the phone. He knows you have a lot of questions for him and was sure that once you got his ear you wouldn't be able to hold back," Landon says.

"Well…he's right. So when will he be here? When can I see him?" I ask excitedly, momentarily forgetting about my own fears of abandonment by Landon.

"He wasn't able to get a flight out until later, so it'll be 8:00 tonight before we can meet with him. He's already made reservations at Fronterra, so I guess we're going out for insanely good Mexican food tonight," Landon smiles.

"Ok, then. I have ten hours to figure out what I'm going to wear." I stand

and a little laugh escapes me as I realize I'm actually nervous about seeing my father tonight. Landon gives me a confused look. "I was 19 the last time my father saw me. I'm not a kid anymore. I've grown up. I have a career and a life…and you. My dad was always really protective of me, and while I'm ecstatic he's alive and I'm going to see him tonight, I just want to make sure he knows I'm all grown up and doing really well."

"I'm sure he's fully aware of that, Jenna." Landon wraps his arms around me, calming my nerves. "Are you ok? You were looking a little off when I answered the phone."

"Yeah…I'm fine," I tell him. There's no sense in bringing up my concern about our future now. There's a lot to think about for tonight and Landon and I will just have to cross the bridge of his job when we get to it. We'll consider all the options when it comes time.

We eat breakfast and Landon leaves me to my silent thoughts. I have so many questions for my father. I'm not sure which to ask first, after I wrap my arms around him, that is. I want to know what happened after I left him in the park. How long did he lie there, alone, and who rescued him and took him to a hospital? What has he been doing all this time? Why didn't he just ask Oz where I was and come for me himself? Has something happened to Oz? Most of all, I want to know how he's able to safely come for me now.

"Tell me about your dad," Landon says as we climb back into bed. He's back down to just his boxer briefs and I question the sanity of stopping him from taking my clothes off last night.

"No."

"No?"

"No. I've spent the last month completely avoiding as many real conversations about family as possible. And I've been really inconsiderate in not asking about your family at all, only because I was afraid you'd ask about mine. So, since you've already met my dad, I think it's my turn to ask you about your family," I tell him.

"I only know your father as my employer, not as my girlfriend's father. You're supposed to tell me about him so I know what I'm headed into." Landon pulls me closer and I rest my head on his shoulder, engulfed by his strong arms.

"I see your point, but…"

"But?"

"But I really want to know about your family. I've missed really knowing someone. I've had to keep from asking about people's lives so I could remain guarded about mine. If I didn't open the door to knowing about my friends' families, then no one would knock on mine and my secret would stay safe. I want to know you, Landon. Please, let me have this right now." I feel Landon's arms tighten around me followed by him kissing the top of my head.

"What would you like to know?" he asks softly, giving in to my plea.

"Tell me about your mom and dad," I say.

"Well…my dad was a cop and my mom was…a mom. She had the dance studio, but mostly stayed home while Dad brought home the bacon. *Real* bacon, by the way," he teases. I poke his side giving him a retaliatory tickle. "She was only at the dance studio a couple of days a week."

"Do you really have a sister or was that just part of your story?" I ask. Being an only child, I'm hoping he says it was true. I'm seeing a long life with Landon and to have a sister, even if an in-law, will be amazing.

"Ouch! Yes, I have a sister. Her name is Amy and she still lives in Miami, just like I said. Her husband's name is Steven and her daughters are Isabella and Jordan, who are ten and eight."

"What's your mom's name?"

"Lucia."

"And your dad's name?"

"Michael."

"Well, I can't wait to meet all of them. I hope your mom likes me. Maybe

I'll have to dance for her approval," I laugh.

"If that's the test, you'll win her over immediately! You have nothing to worry about. I'm the one who's biting my nails over here about seeing your dad tonight." Landon takes his arm from around me and moves so he's facing
me. I follow and mirror his position on my side.

"Are you kidding me? You have absolutely nothing to be worried about. You found his daughter! I'm pretty sure that makes you boyfriend of the century!" I lean in and kiss Landon with the intent of making it quick. Landon has other plans and pulls me in and on top of him. His hands are quickly on my back and under my shirt, pressing me closer to him. He's careful not to cross the line I set last night. I don't think either one of us wants our first time together to be under these circumstances. There's too much to think about…too much on my mind for me to be able to really get my head in the game. Once things settle down I'm sure we'll fall into a normal groove, but now is not the time.

We eventually agree a nap is in order since we got very little sleep last night, and I want to look rested when I see Dad. I don't want him to think I'm not taking care of myself.

As I drift off, lying there in Landon's arms, I think as I did this morning about just how perfect my life is in this moment. I have the job of my dreams, the guy of my dreams, and as if it were a dream, my father is alive. Life truly couldn't be any more picture-perfect.

Chapter 11

Landon goes back to his hotel to shower and change and is back at my apartment at seven. When I let him in I'm wearing my robe, still undecided about what I should wear.

"Holy crap! It looks like your closet threw up!" Landon laughs as he enters my room.

"I can't decide what to wear. I'm kind of freaking out here," I say. I'm too anxious about seeing Dad that I can't think clearly. I flop myself on the bed and look up at Landon. "Help me."

"Ok, ok…You're freaking out for no reason. This is your dad, not some blind date. You'll look beautiful, and grown up, and established in whatever you wear, Jenna." Landon pulls me up off the bed and holds me for a moment.

"Thank you. Never in my wildest dreams did I ever think this would be happening. I'm still trying to process the whole thing. I'm glad it was you he sent to find me."

"Me too. I've been impacted by a lot of the cases I've worked, but this has been life-changing." Landon takes my face in his hands and kisses me sweetly. "Now, let's get you dressed. Hmm…not something I thought I'd ever say."

We both give a small laugh and turn our attention to the mess on my bed. I uncover a few of the stronger possibilities and show them to Landon. I've got a dress and a couple of skirt and pant outfits. In the end we decide that my blue wrap dress with the elbow-length sleeves will give the impression I want. It's comfortable and classy, but not too dressy that I don't look or feel like me. It's actually the dress I wore to my nursing school graduation a few years ago. Spring picked it out when we went shopping for graduation outfits.

"You look beautiful,' Landon tells me as I slip on my heels. I've pulled my hair into a low ponytail behind my ear. My hair is dark now and I don't want Dad to be distracted by that. I want him to see my face and know it's me. "Are you ready?"

"Yes. No. Maybe we should have left already so we can be the first ones there. Or maybe we should be late so we can make an entrance. That'd be so weird to walk in together, don't you think? I mean him and us, not you and me. I don't want to see him for the first time at the reservation podium of a restaurant. What do you think?" I'm so excited and nervous that I'm starting to get really flustered.

"Hey. It's ok. He's probably more nervous than you are. He has to look you in the eye and explain why he let you think he was dead all this time. He's got a lot more to worry about than you do. You just have to show up and love him." Landon smiles at me and takes my hand. It feels like the safest place in the world and immediately makes me feel more at ease.

He's right. Dad came looking for me, and knowing him, I know he cares more about who I am than what I look like or even what career I have. It's crazy, but even after all this time, and thinking he was dead, I just want my father to be proud of the person I've become.

We arrive at the restaurant and are seated right away at 7:45. This is good. I can sit, maybe even have a drink before Dad gets here. Landon sees worry on my face again and covers my hand with his on my knee under the table.

"You ok?" he asks quietly.

"Yes. Just nerves bubbling to the top again. I'll be fine. I'm thinking I may need a glass of wine sooner than later, though," I laugh softly.

"I'll get right on that." Landon squeezes my hand and then releases it to take the wine and mixed drinks padded book from the center of the table. "Um, Jenna…when your father gets here…let's not jump into telling him about our relationship right away. I haven't told him and I don't know how he's going to feel about it."

"I'm sure it's going to be fine, Landon. He can't be upset. He's the one who brought us together, after all," I smile. Landon smiles back and looks up and behind me, his smile changing from one of sweet adoration to something more generically pleasant. He nods before looking at me.

"He's here. Are you ready?" he asks.

"I think so." Butterflies swarm my stomach and I wish we had gotten here even earlier so I could have had that drink already. I stand and straighten the skirt of my dress before turning around.

Oh, shit.

Panic and raging fear rush through me and I stumble back a moment, catching myself on the table. I can feel the blood drain from my face and am sure it's turning pale, maybe even translucent. I can't breathe as I begin to search out the closest escape route.

"Jenna, what's wrong?" Landon says, steadying my incredibly unsteady legs.

"That...that's not my father, Landon," I tell him.

"What are you talking about?" Confusion paints Landon's face as the man who he thinks is my father approaches.

"Hello, Veronica," the man says politely.

"Senator Dellinger," I reply. I push down the lump in my throat with a hard swallow and try to regain a normal breathing pattern before I pass out.

"Sir," Landon says by way of greeting the man before us.

"Why don't we sit down," the Senator instructs. We do as he says and take our seats.

"Excuse me, Senator, but...I'm confused. Jenna, what do you mean he's not your father?" He directs his attention back to me, but I can't form the words.

"Jenna, the man asked you a question. Don't be rude. Answer him,"

Dellinger says. His salt and pepper hair and dark eyes make him look as menacing as he really is. And with his black suit, he sits there calmly like some don, giving orders to the family with full expectation of them being carried out. Not what you'd expect the Senator for Connecticut to look like.

Fear and panic are being replaced with anger and rage. I intentionally move the knife at my setting away from me so I don't do anything stupid. "Senator Dellinger is not my father. He is, however, the man responsible for my father's murder."

I keep my eyes on Dellinger as I call him out and make sure he knows that I hold him responsible for killing the only family I had left.

"What? Why? Why would you have me find her if she's not your daughter?" Landon asks. He doesn't know what I know, which is that the only reason Dellinger would go to such great lengths to find me is because he needs me. He needs the skills that I possess. The skills my father taught me.

"The situation with your father was an unfortunate means to an end. Now," he says picking up the menu. "What's good? I hear this is the best Mexican restaurant in Chicago." Dellinger looks over the menu, completely ignoring Landon's inquiry.

"What the hell is going on?" Landon raises his voice and pulls down Dellinger's menu causing the Senator to stiffen.

"I'll tell you what's going on. Henry Dellinger needs something and I'm the only one who can get it," I say with a straight face.

"Meaning…" Landon's irritation is more than evident. Here he was, thinking he was bringing two long lost family members together and the reality is that it was all a lie.

"The Senator is a collector. The only problem is most of the things he collects are already owned by *other* collectors. When they won't sell to him, or when he's outbid at auction, he sends someone to retrieve what he believes should be his. He coerced my father into doing it for him for years, and, since my father bragged about teaching me everything he knows about breaking into the unbreakable, he thinks he can coerce me into doing his dirty work for him, too. Unfortunately he's gone to all this trouble for nothing."

"Why lie to me about who she is?" Landon asks Dellinger.

"I wasn't going to tell you that I needed you to find the only person who has the skill set to break into a sealed, glass case and retrieve the last piece of a collection I've spent 15 years searching for. A father needing to find his long, lost daughter was much more compelling, don't you think? Now, I had hoped to eat before we got down to business, but since you're cutting to the chase and laying all the cards on the table…" Dellinger pulls an envelope from his inside jacket pocket and sets it on the table.

"Don't. Don't say a word. I'm not doing whatever it is you've come here to tell me to do. I don't work for you and I'm not afraid of you," I declare.

"Are you sure you don't want to think about that first. I mean, you are fully aware of what happens when my instructions aren't followed." Dellinger narrows his eyes, bringing new meaning to creepy.

"If you think for a second you're going to hurt Jenna and not end up paralyzed from the neck down, you're quite mistaken," Landon warns. He's leaning across the table defensively.

"I knew you had gotten close to her, Mr. Scott, but perhaps I underestimated just *how* close. And I have no plans of harming Miss Matthews. She is, after all, the key person I need in getting what I want," Dellinger says.

"Well, you're out of your damn mind if you think I'm going to cooperate with you. There is nothing you can say or do, no amount of money you could offer me, that would make me comply." I straighten my posture, asserting my position in refusing whatever it is he's about to offer.

"Your life isn't that important to you, but I know a few others' who might be." Dellinger lifts his hand and motions for someone to come to him.

I hadn't noticed them before, but two men dressed in dark suits approach and stand next to Dellinger where he's seated. One of them looks like an MMA fighter with a bald head and tattoos running up his neck to the side of his face and back of his skull. The other looks like he just graduated from MIT, glasses and all. I would bet there's a pocket protector under that jacket.

The MIT guy pulls a tablet from the attaché case he's carrying while MMA guy stands and looks menacing. A few taps and swipes to the tablet and he hands it to Dellinger who looks at it for a moment before turning it around. On the screen is a high and angled view of my living room apartment. Spring and Matt are sitting on the couch watching TV, completely unaware that they're being monitored. Dellinger swipes the screen to the left a few times, revealing different rooms in my apartment with each screen. He swipes it again and the next view is of Mercy's living room.

"I swear to God if you hurt them…"

"Good. You've got the picture then. Now, inside this envelope is your ticket and hotel information. When you arrive, my contact there will connect with you and give you the rest of the instructions." Dellinger's smug look makes me want to punch him, but I won't for the very reason he chose to meet in a place like this. He knew I wouldn't make a scene.

I open the envelope and find it contains an itinerary and a plane ticket to Paris.

"This ticket is dated for two days from today. How am I supposed to leave for France in two days? I have a job! I can't just pick up and leave for four days!" I've raised my voice and a few of the guests in the restaurant turn their heads to see what my fuss is about.

"I'm sure you'll be able to work something out. You're a very resourceful girl," he says. "My contact will let me know when he has connected with you and that everything is in place. And don't think of

137

skipping town, Veronica. I found you once, I can find you again. Only next time, you'll *know* it's me."

I push my chair out and stand up slowly. "Fine." Dellinger smiles approvingly at me and the picks up his menu and begins to review it. I push past MMA guy and head straight out the front door of the restaurant and out onto the sidewalk. I inhale deeply then let it out along with all the fear, anxiety, and anger I composed inside.

"Jenna!" Landon calls to me as he exits the restaurant. "Oh, my God, Jenna! I'm so sorry. Obviously I had no idea!" He tries to put his arms around me but I pull away. "Jenna…"

"Listen, Landon…I have to take care of this, ok. When I get back…I guess we can talk about what's going to happen with us," I say.

"You *guess* we can talk? What's there to talk about?"

"I should never have let my guard down. You brought him here, Landon. Now, I know you didn't know, but you could have. You should have. Did you *not* do any kind of background check to confirm if what he was telling you was true? One little background check and you would have known that Senator Henry Dellinger is not my father!" I begin to walk down the sidewalk in the direction of my apartment.

"Hold on a second! He had things a father would have of his daughter's. He had your laptop, pictures of you…he said that he and your mother were never married which was why your last name was different than his. He played me, Jenna. How is that my fault?" I'm walking faster and Landon is actually working to keep up with me.

"Ok. I get it," I say. "Regardless of any of that I have to focus on what he wants right now. I can't underestimate him. He *will* hurt Spring or Mercy, or both. Wait." I stop in my tracks. "How would he know who I was or where I lived? And Mercy?"

"I told him about you last week. I also gave him Sarah's name so he probably had her place wired, too. I don't know where Mercy lives, so he must have had a second guy come in and follow you to find out what your weak spot would be," Landon explains.

I begin walking again as I remember him telling me earlier today that Dellinger was pressuring him for an answer. I really can't blame Landon. The Senator gave him enough evidence that he wouldn't question me being Dellinger's daughter, but none of that matters now. I have to go to Paris, meet up with Dellinger's guy, and get this over with. Spring and Mercy's lives depend on it.

"Will you stop?" Landon shouts, grabbing me by the elbow. "Why does this change things between us?"

"Because once this is over, I have to run. I have to get as far away from here as possible so he can't hurt me or anyone I love ever again," I reply matching his volume.

"I'll go with you," he says taking me by the shoulders. "I'll go with you and we can be together. Don't leave me, Jenna. I can't lose you."

I step toward Landon and place one hand on his chest over his heart and the other on his cheek. I try to think of something to say as the cars and taxis whiz by and the people on the sidewalk walk on with no clue as to the steps I'm about to take to preserve the lives of those I love most. I look into Landon's eyes, wanting so desperately to believe that he's right. Believe that we could be together, but even if it were possible, I can't ask him to do that. He has a family who loves and depends on him. He can't just drop off the grid like that.

A cab stops a few feet in front of us and two women step onto the sidewalk. I move quickly to the open door and turn back to Landon.

"I have to go. We'll talk when I get back." I close the cab door and leave Landon standing speechless on the sidewalk.

Spring and Matt are still on the couch when I walk in the apartment 20 minutes later, having settled myself into a happy place before even putting the key in the door. I can't barge in again in a frazzled state. And I cannot tell her that Landon and I are over. After the cheating incident she'll think the worst and then Mercy will raise hell and a baseball bat.

"Hey! Where's Landon?" Spring asks. She's laying her body across the couch with her feet on Matt's lap. They really are so sweet together.

"Yeah, where's lover boy?" Matt and Landon have only met a few times. Between their schedules, it's been a challenge. But, I suppose that doesn't matter now.

"He has an early morning, so we called it a night," I tell them. The words have barely left my mouth when there's a quick knock at the door, followed by Landon letting himself in. "What are you doing here?" I ask him, my tone not reflecting that everything is just fine and dandy between us. "I mean, I was just telling Matt and Spring that you had an early morning and that's why you weren't here."

"I was able to change some things around. We have to talk about this trip," he says with a smile. He's putting on a show for my friends, which I appreciate, but I still wish he hadn't come here.

"What trip?" Spring sits up and turns around on the couch with her inquiring eyes.

"Oh, um…" I stutter. I hadn't decided what I was going to tell her, or anyone for that matter, about this trip. How do I explain a four day trip to Paris?

"Jenna didn't tell you yet? I'm surprised she didn't say anything as soon as she walked in," Landon begins. "I'm taking Jenna to Paris in two days. I asked her to marry me and she said yes!"

Spring bolts up from the couch and practically slams into me as her arms wrap around my neck. "Holy crap! I mean, congratulations! Oh, my God! I'm so happy for you! Where's the ring?" She grabs my hand but, of course, there is no ring.

I'm still stuttering, not knowing how to catch up in this impromptu lie Landon has begun.

"Well, it was really a spontaneous thing." Landon takes my hand and puts it on over his heart the way I did less than an hour ago. "There I was with her tonight, and she was just so beautiful. I looked into her eyes and knew what I've known all along. This is the woman I want to spend the rest of my life with. As soon as the shock wore off of me asking her to marry me, she said yes."

I hate you. How the hell am I supposed to leave you to keep you safe when you say and do something like that?

"Isn't that right, babe?" Landon prompts when I'm still standing there with my mouth agape.

"Uh...right. I didn't say anything when I came in because we wanted to tell you together." I wrap my arms around Landon's waist and put my head on his chest. I don't know how I'm going to get over him.

"I can't believe this! I knew once you stopped cataloging every guy's faults that you'd fall in love! Wait...are you going to Paris to get *married* in Paris?" Spring asks with mixed emotions.

"You can't say anything to Mercy, or Demi and Jack, ok?" I tell her. It's one thing to lie to Spring, which I absolutely hate doing. It's another thing to lie to *all* of my friends. I don't want their last memory of me to be that I deceived them.

"Yeah, Mercy would freak out if she knew you were going to get married and she wasn't a part of it." Spring has never spoken truer words.

Mercy would have my head on a platter if I left her out of something like this. Fortunately for my head, it won't be necessary. I'll come up with some reason as to why we didn't go through with it. I tell them all we decided it was too fast and that we're parting ways, still friends. Then I'll tell them I need some time to get away, pack as much as I possibly can into Oz's oversized duffle bag, and walk away.

"Are you crying?" Spring asks. Tears are filling my eyes at the thought of the outright lies I'll be telling them, but more because I'm going to have to walk away from the only family I've had since Dad died.

"You swept her off her feet, huh, Landon," Matt chimes in. He's a good-looking guy, tall with olive skin and black hair. He has this way of walking that makes him look like he's sauntering everywhere.

"Yeah, I guess I did," Landon says as he takes my hand. "Lucky me."

"I'm going to walk Landon out…" I begin as I open the front door and nudge Landon into the hallway. Spring hugs me again and tells me how excited she is for Landon and me before I close the door behind me. She's a totally low-key, non-fru-fru dress kind of girl so it's no wonder she's not freaking out like Mercy would about being a part of my wedding…my fictional wedding. I won't be surprised if when she and Matt get married if she isn't wearing shoes and has a crown of daisies in her hair.

"Thank you for the cover story. Obviously you'll have to stay out of site while I'm in Paris, but you'll probably head back to Miami anyway." I tell him as I push the button for the elevator.

"I'm not going to Miami, Jenna. And…it doesn't have to be a cover." Landon won't release the lock he has on my eyes, not that I want him to. He takes my hand and turns as the silver elevator doors close, standing there in silence, staring at our reflection. I don't refuse his hand because I want to appreciate the moment I have with him.

A gust of warm, night air slams into us when we leave the coolness of my building and step onto the sidewalk. We both stand there, silent for a few minutes, neither of us sure what to say. He doesn't want me to do this on my own, but I can't put him at risk. This is the price of being owned by Henry Dellinger. I either do his bidding, or I spend the rest of my life running, saying goodbye to everyone I love and never getting close to anyone ever again. Oddly enough, I'd rather spend the rest of my days alone than to do any more than I have to for that slimy snake.

"I don't know what to say. I wish things were different. I wish I had come to Chicago just to go to school. I wish we had met under different circumstances, but...there is far too much for me to focus on right now that I just can't..."

"I'm not leaving you. I don't care what the situation is, I'm not giving up on us. I meant what I said outside the restaurant and what I said upstairs...all of it." His eyes are piercing and begging me to let him in.

"I need you to let me get through this thing in Paris. I'll be home in a week, and then...I won't leave right away. Please, Landon. I know Dellinger and I need you to trust that I'm doing the best thing." My pleading eyes find his in hopes of conveying how much he needs to trust me right now.

"You've been alone for too long, Jenna. You've spent the last six years being so closed off that you don't even know how to let someone help you in a time of crisis...someone who would lay down his life for you. And you're crazy if you think I'm letting you go and that I'm going to walk away while you throw yourself headfirst into this."

"I need to go now. I still have a lot to figure out in the next two days," I say, completely avoiding the truth of his statement. Dellinger forced me into a place of hiding, not just geographically, but emotionally. And this situation is the exact reason why I spent so long avoiding relationships. I knew if Dellinger found me one day that I'd be forced to pick up and leave everyone I loved.

Landon shakes his head and looks away, frustrated by my unwillingness to let him join me on this kamikaze mission. Seeming to give up, Landon hails a cab and I stand there, having as many moments with him as I can before I head off into what could prove to be either a life of perpetual hiding, or death. The cab pulls up quickly and Landon takes me in his arms. I press my ear to his chest and listen to his heartbeat, each thud reminding me why I'm pushing him and everyone else I love away.

He kisses me and I reach my hands behind his head, making the kiss last as long as possible. It ends all too soon when Landon takes me by my shoulders and concentrates on my face. There's a glimmer in his eye. A shine that tells me my efforts to push him away are futile. Part of me is rejoicing in that because I truly don't want to lose him. The other part of me is really scared. My Navy Seal boyfriend is just brave and in love with me enough to do something drastic. My hope is that drastic doesn't equal stupid.

Chapter 12

My flight from Chicago to JFK in New York was uneventful, which is exactly what you want in a flight. Well, it wasn't completely uneventful. I got to the gate and discovered that my seat was in Business Class. At least the rich bastard splurged on a comfortable seat for me.

The 24 hours leading up to that flight were more eventful than I would ever care to relive. First, I had to explain to my boss that I'm apparently so in love that I've agreed to get married in Paris on a moment's notice, with no regard whatsoever for the effect this will have on my job or the other staff. Fortunately I have four weeks of vacation and a hopeless romantic for a boss. She moved some things around and even offered to cover for me so I could *follow my heart and marry the man of my dreams*.

Then I had to make her promise she wouldn't breathe a word of why I was gone to Mercy. I had a huge fight with her before I left because all I would tell her was that I was going out of town for a few days to clear my head. She's not used to me being so cryptic, but what else was I going to tell her?

The worst part was when Demi came over yesterday. She still hasn't told Jack about the baby and was going to do it today. I promised her that I would be there for her, that she wouldn't be alone, and when it came down to her needing me the most I had to tell her I couldn't be there. All I could give her was the same, pathetic excuse that I was going out of town to clear my head. She left my apartment in tears which made me feel like total shit and has only served to fuel my hatred for Senator Henry Dellinger.

I had a very brave and partially transparent conversation with Spring before I left this morning. I don't know how this whole thing is going to go down. I'm confident I know what Dellinger wants, but I don't know who his contact is there and I certainly don't trust him. I don't know if this guy is going to have my back or get me caught and take whatever he can get his hands on and run.

I needed Spring to know a few things before I left and maybe never came back. I told her that things aren't necessarily what they seem and that if I didn't come back it would be because I didn't make it and that she was to contact Oz. I gave her the last information I had for him and said a prayer that he's still there. I don't want to die and him not know. I told her that I had been on the run when she met me and that my past was catching up with me. She asked if Landon was part of my past and I told her that he wasn't. I wish I could say that he's at least part of my future, but that's not true either.

Spring promised to keep my secret and I promised to tell her everything when I got home. She told me to be safe and not to give up. She also told me that when it seemed like I was in a dark and lonely place to remember how much Landon loves me. "Just thinking about how loved you are can make all the difference in the outcome of what seems like a hopeless situation," she said. I wish I had her optimism.

I mill around the airport near my gate since I don't have a long layover. I've got my ear buds in my ears and am listening to random songs on a Favorites playlist. I barely listen to a whole song, skipping on to the next one to see if it suits my mood. I see the boarding attendant pick up the phone and realize she's making an announcement. She calls for passengers in Zone 1 to board. I double check my boarding pass and realize that I can board.

I walk the long, extended bridge between the building and the airplane and the flight attendant checks my boarding pass to direct me to my seat.

"Bon jour Miss Rockwell. Your seat is right this way," the sweet-looking flight attended says to me in a soft French accent. I begin to move to the right where it appears the business class seating is, but the attendant leads me to the left. I follow behind her and step into an area with maybe 20 seats. No, they aren't seats. They're space-age, Star Trek-style lounging pods.

"Are you sure this is where I'm supposed to be?" I ask her in disbelief. I can buy that Dellinger would set me up in business class, but this is just too much. Although, now that I think about it, it makes sense that he would flaunt his money and power this way.

"Yes, ma'am. This is your seat right here, closest to the window. Can I get you anything before we take off?" she asks.

"Um…you can show me how to work this seat," I tell her as my cheeks turn red from embarrassment. Could I look and act more out of place?

The kind girl doesn't hesitate and with a smile proceeds to show me all the bells and whistles I'll be able to enjoy during the 11-hour flight to Paris. She offers me lounging clothes and a wool blanket if I want to be more comfortable while I sleep in my chair that converts into a real six foot bed. She also tells me that I have a wide range of movies on demand that I can watch on my personal video screen. That's all before she shows me the massage feature on my seat that also has a personal telephone. Finally, she explains that I'll be able to enjoy a cocktail before a meal that will clearly make this the fanciest French restaurant I've ever been in.

"If you have any other questions or needs, please do not hesitate to ask. We're here to ensure you have a wonderful flight." We smile at each other and I sit awkwardly in my pod.

"Well, I suppose I should just get comfortable," I say out loud to myself.

"I suppose you should."

I turn toward the voice and find Landon standing next to the aisle seat.

"What are you doing here?" I ask him with mixed emotions. I'm mad that he didn't leave me to do this on my own like I told him I wanted, but I'm also happy for the same reason. Any girl who tells you she doesn't want the guy she's madly in love with to come chasing after her is lying.

"I told you I didn't care what you said. You're not doing this on your own." Landon sets his bag down and begins to get himself settled very matter-of-factly. I smile, deciding to let us have this time together now.

But…once everything is over, and I have to disappear…well, I'll figure out how to break his heart later.

"I was thinking about what you told Spring, you know…the cover story you gave her," I begin as Landon sits.

"Let's talk about that when all this is over and we're warm, lying in your bed," he says. He takes my hand and threads his fingers through mine.

I want to tell him that I would absolutely marry him. That the idea of spending the rest of my life with him is the happiest thought I've ever had. I want him to know in his heart just how madly in love with him I am. That way, when I have to leave, when I have to walk away, he'll know it's because I love him so much that I would sacrifice a life with him if it meant ensuring his safety.

It's not long into the flight when the attendants start their rounds through what I found out is called the La Premiere class cabin and began offering cocktails and other cold beverages before dinner. We both opt for something simple, so Landon orders a Jack and Coke while I ask for gin and tonic. We sit quietly for a moment before Landon breaks the silence.

"I'd still really like to know about your dad," he says quietly. His inquiry pricks a tender place in me that I had been ignoring since Dellinger, not my father, walked into that restaurant. I haven't dealt with the tremendous disappointment that was. To say I was thrilled and overjoyed to see my father would be an understatement. When it wasn't him, I was devastated. I couldn't consider those feelings, though. I've had to plan out my deception to my friends and think about how I'm going to disappear. It's only now that Landon is bringing him up that I'm really thinking about him.

"He was really great," I begin. "He and my mom were married for 15 years before she died. He used to say she saved his life. He had been in a lot of trouble when he was younger. Grew up on the wrong side of the city, got involved with some bad people, ended up in a gang. He would tell me stories of those days and I always found it interesting how each guy in the gang fell into his own role. Leaders, lackies, muscle…my dad discovered that he had these mad lock picking skills. He could crack any lock or safe that wasn't coded. He eventually developed this skill, this *way*, of getting into sealed display cases. He said that's where the really valuable stuff always is, and that the people who can afford those kinds of pieces can also afford to have special cases for them.

"Once he honed his skill, he and Oz decided they were tired of the junk the guys were grabbing from pawn shops and they'd try to hit some more upscale places. It started out with consignment stores and moved to specialty collector shops, and eventually homes in Georgetown and Foggy Bottom. He had a rap sheet from when he would pull jobs with the gang, but he never got caught, not once, when he started hitting the better places with Oz."

It feels strangely wonderful to talk about Dad. I've never really talked to anyone about him. I certainly never told my friends in high school about my dad's past. Some of them had parents in politics and government. I only wanted them to know my dad as the owner of a really successful business, not some former thug. You put something like that out there and that's all people remember.

"So, if your dad was living the gang life, how'd he meet your mom? Was she part of the gang, too?" Landon asks. His body is turned almost completely toward me. It's one of the things I love about him. When we talk, he gives me his full attention.

"Oh, God, no! My mom was as straight and narrow as they come! They met at a party of a girl they somehow both new from high school. They both said they saw each other and just *knew*. They got talking and the rest, as they say, was history. Mom convinced Dad he could have a better life if he left the gang, so he did. He eventually convinced Oz to leave, too, so they started their own business. They got married a year after they graduated from high school and had me five years later," I tell him.

"A good woman will make any man change his ways," Landon smiles.

"Well, you can take the boy from the wrong side of the tracks, but you can't take the wrong side of the tracks out of the boy. Dad was proud of his skills and often joked that he wished he could patent them," I say with a small laugh. "When I was a kid I would watch him in his work room. He fixed household stuff in there all the time because our house was falling apart. But sometimes, I'd find him in there putting glass cases together and then breaking into them. And he would buy these locks that were supposed to be so intricate that no one could pick them, but Dad laughed in their faces and picked every one. You already know that he taught me how to pick a lock, which, as you witnessed, is actually a very handy thing to know. But as I spent more time in there with him, he would show me how to do more and more.

"It wasn't really a big deal, but after Mom died, it was kind of how we coped together. It was just an activity to me, something that made me feel like I wasn't alone. He took such good care of me then. He always did."

"I'm so sorry, Jenna. It sounds like he was a really great dad. That's rarer than you know." Landon tucks a lock of hair behind my ear and brushes my cheek with his thumb. All I can do is nod. "So…how did he end up getting connect with Dellinger?"

"Dellinger's home was robbed and Dad's company was hired to replace the locks that night. Dellinger had some display cases that got smashed. Dad was thinking out loud and commented that it was such a lazy way to pull a job. Dellinger overheard him and asked what he meant. Dad, not being one to shy away from bragging on himself, told Dellinger that when he was a lesser man, he used to pull jobs like this, only with style.

"The Senator is a collector. He displays some of his findings, but he likes to keep most of it locked up. He's the rich, arrogant type who finds complete satisfaction in just knowing that he has things that you can't have, and he doesn't like knowing that someone else has something that he wants. When he sets his sights on a piece, he makes it his. Sometimes that means bidding at auctions until he puts the other bidders to shame, and sometimes that means sending someone to get what he believes should be his. He comes from old money and has plenty of new money, too, so that's never an obstacle."

"So Dellinger threw more money at your dad than he had ever seen and offered him a job *recovering* what he wanted," Landon says.

"I was so mad at my dad when I found out. I mean, that was the life that my mom had rescued him from and there he was falling right back into it. But, things were really, really tight after Mom got sick and stopped working. And then we had all her medical bills that insurance didn't cover. We were in such a desperate state that I guess Dad didn't feel like he had a choice. He didn't want to live that life again. We were poor but we were so happy. Dad decided that he if was going to do this that most of the money would go toward paying for my college. But, since I couldn't take any of that money with me, Oz paid for my college and set up a nice nest egg when he helped Veronica Matthews drop off the face of the earth." I take a deep breath remembering the night I escaped and left my father to die under a tree.

"And because your dad bragged that he taught you everything he knew, Dellinger hasn't forgotten that and now has a job that requires the skills only you and your father possess."

"Yes."

The flight attendant comes by and collects our empty glasses, shaking us from this serious conversation. We give her our orders for dinner and wine and a few minutes later she's back with the most elaborately plated meal I've ever seen. I know I should enjoy every morsel of it because I'm never going to have the chance to travel like this again. I don't know if I'll have the same treatment on the way home. Hell, I don't know if I'm even going to make it home alive.

We eat and talk and treat our dining together like a normal date, despite the fact that we're flying 35,000 feet in the air in the lap of luxury and I'm headed into an unknown situation. After dinner Landon suggests we watch the same movie on our personal screens so we can continue to enjoy this time together. I agree since there's no need to rehash the maniacal madness of Henry Dellinger. There will be enough to deal with once we get to the hotel and Dellinger's person makes contact with me.

We watch our movie and then sleep longer than I knew a person could sleep peacefully on a flight thanks to the full size bed my seat turned into. Otherwise, we have a pretty uneventful flight. It's 11:00 am in Paris when we arrive, but 5:00 am body time. We go through customs and make our way to find our bags. As we enter the baggage claim area there's a man in a suit holding a sign with my name on it.

"Geez! The Senator sure does know how to make an impression," Landon chortles.

"I know, right?" I add. "I'm Jenna Rockwell," I tell the driver. He nods and welcomes me to Paris, noting that he thought he was only picking up one passenger. I advise him that plans changed and he would be transporting both Landon and me. When he tells me he'll have to charge an additional fee for the extra passenger, I tell him that's fine and he can simply add it to the bill. Why not? It's not my money.

We get our bags from the carrousel and are sitting comfortably in the back of a limousine within minutes. I try to keep my eyes open and enjoy the scenery but it's futile. I slept on the plane but didn't exactly get eight hours.

Landon nudges me to a more conscious state as I feel the limo come to a stop. The door opens and he gets out first so he can help steady me when I stand. The hotel looks like a huge mansion and is definitely not a Holiday Inn.

"Bienvenue! Welcome to the Shangri La Hotel. Are you checking in?" the man behind the counter greets me.

"Hello, yes, I am checking in. The last name is Rockwell," I tell him. Landon is standing next to me with his arm around my waist. I'm grateful because on top of not feeling so great, I'm beginning to get nervous.

"Of course, Miss Rockwell. I have a reservation for you, but it only shows one guest. Will you be joined by your companion?" he asks in his lovely French accent. I totally get the appeal of this ridiculously sexy language.

"Yes, thank you," I say.

"Alright, Miss Rockwell, here are your room keys, and, oh, I see there's a note on your reservation. There is a package for you. Un moment s'il vous plait." The clerk walks into a back room leaving Landon and me standing there with puzzled looks on our faces. He returns with an envelope and slides it across the counter to me. I shove the envelope in my pocket feeling like its contents are better suited to be read in the privacy of our room.

Pulling our suitcases behind us we find the elevator and then our room, which is absolutely exquisite. The furniture and linens are white with blue accents throughout. It's light and airy and far too romantic. I told myself I wouldn't cut things off with Landon until all of this was over and we got back to Chicago, so I can't get swept up in the fact that we're in the most romantic city on the planet. If I take things too far with him I'll cloud my judgment and won't be able to follow through with what I have to do to keep him and my friends safe.

I flop myself onto the bed and shut my eyes out of sheer exhaustion. I don't know how people travel like this all the time. Although, I should give some credit for my fatigue to the circumstances for which I'm traveling.

"Jenna, come see this," Landon calls to me. I peek out of one eye and see that he's pulled the white and blue floral curtains open. From what I can see, the skies are blue and it looks like a beautiful day.

I force myself to get up and drag my body to the open balcony doors where Landon is standing. *We have a balcony. Nice.*

"Wow." This one breathy word is all I can muster. We are literally less than half a mile from the Eifel Tower. The view is so amazingly perfect I'm convinced it must be on a postcard in the lobby.

"My thoughts exactly," he says, wrapping his arms around me and pulling me to him. We stand there in the shadow of the most iconic symbol of romance and I let him hold me. It feels good to be so close to him, to take in the time that I have to be his and for him to be mine. This time is fleeting and I know that in the too soon future it will all end.

Landon strokes my hair, soothing and calming my already tired body. Within seconds my body is betraying my mind and is responding to his touch. I don't want to get ahead of myself, but…

Before I can stop myself I reach up and pull Landon's face to mine, our lips crushing together with immediate passion. I lift his shirt off of him and grab his jean belt loops to pull his body as close to me as possible. In one, smooth move Landon lifts me up and I wrap my legs around his waist as he carries me to the bed. I rip my cardigan off and Landon does the rest by pulling my t-shirt over my head and throwing it to the floor.

"I love you so much, Jenna," Landon whispers in between kisses to my throat.

"I love you," I echo as I grab and pull his body on top of mine. I want him. I want him more than I've ever wanted anything. The desire to have him is intoxicating and I'm overwhelmed with need.

Landon's hands touch and pull and kneed my body, intensifying my longing. We roll over and I my lips work hard to kiss every inch of his muscular chest. He runs his fingers through my hair, pulling ever so slightly. I find his belt and unbuckle it, ripping it through the loops and tossing it to the floor. I begin to unbutton his jeans but he pulls me up and I straddle him, finding his lips waiting for mine. I press my mouth to his for only a moment before biting and kissing his neck.

Landon undoes my jeans and flips me over onto the bed so he can strip me of the rest of my clothes. In a flash, he's removed his jeans and our almost naked bodies are entwined together, kissing, grabbing, gasping for air. My body is so ready for him, and I can feel how ready he is for me.

"Thank God you changed your mind. I don't know what I would do without you, Jenna," he pants between kisses.

But...I haven't changed my mind. When all is said and done I still have to leave.

I slow my kissing, easing my body away from Landon. I've done what I just told myself I wasn't going to do. But, God, how could I blame myself. The Eifel Tower is outside our window for crying out loud. I need to calm down and remain focused. *Sex will cloud my judgment.* This needs to be my mantra. As badly as I want him, if I sleep with Landon, it will make it that much more difficult for me to let go of him, and for him to let me go.

"What's wrong?" Landon asks as we both catch our breath.

"Nothing. I...we already said that we didn't want our first time to be under these circumstances," I tell him, referencing our conversation the night he revealed my father, well, who he thought was my father, was still alive.

"What's wrong with these circumstances? We're in Paris, the Eifel Tower is literally outside our window. Who cares how we got here. We're here, Jenna." Landon rolls to his side and places his strong hand on my bare stomach and running his finger just under the lacey trim of my panties. He has the most amazing touch. "I love you."

It's hard to breath. I love him, too, and it's difficult to say no when I want him so much. But I can't. I can't intentionally pull him even closer to me when I know I'm going to have to push him away.

"You're right. The setting is perfect, but... I need you to understand where my head is right now. It's not that I don't want you, Landon, because there aren't enough words in the human language to express just how much I do. It's that I've got a task ahead of me that is going to compromise everything I am, everything I swore I'd never be, and is the very reason I ran away from DC and left Veronica Matthews behind." I stand up and find my clothes when I realize I can't have a serious conversation in just my underwear.

Landon takes a deep breath and runs his fingers through his hair, then covers his face as he exhales. He stands and comes to me on the other side of the bed. "This is really difficult for me, Jenna. But, I know I need to keep my emotions in check and stay on task with you. That's why I'm here…so I can help you through this whole thing. I've, well…I've never been so in love with someone before. You've done something to me…touched my life and changed me in such a way that I will never be the same. I let my feelings for you take over and now is not the time for that. I promise I'll be more in control."

I don't know what to say. I want to tell him that I feel the exact same way about him. I want to tell him that I wish the cover story about us coming to Paris to get married wasn't a lie. I want to tell him that in another life I would commit to marrying him in an instant because that's just how in love I am with him. I want so badly to lose control with him, let him fully undress me and make love to me in the shadow of the Eifel Tower…but I can't.

"Thank you for understand," I say instead.

"So…do you think we should see what's in that envelope?" he asks. Landon releases me and finds his shirt on the balcony. I'm glad he's putting it on because Landon's bare chest is far too distracting.

"I guess we should. I don't know what it could be. Dellinger said his guy would contact me, and I can't believe he would just leave a letter with the hotel desk clerk." I pull the envelope from my purse and tear it open. Inside the folded letter that at a glance I see is from Dellinger are dozens of slips of what look like paper money. They're grey and yellow and are marked with a 200. "Is this French money?"

"Yeah. Each of those is 200 euros, which is a little over $150. How many are in there?" Landon says.

My eyes get wider as I count each bill and add up the total in my head. "There's 3000 euros here. What the hell am I supposed to do with 3000 euros?" I hand the money to Landon and read the letter.

"That's almost $4,000," he says. I'm impressed with his ability to do the conversion in his head like that. It's just another testament to his brilliance.

"What? He says I'm going to need to buy a dress and look like I fit in at some charity event at the American Ambassador to France's home tomorrow night. Why is he sending me to a charity event?"

"Maybe that's where this thing is that he wants," Landon suggests. "Does he say anything about when his person is supposed to contact you?"

"No, just that the event is tomorrow night and he'll send a car to pick me up at seven." I sit down on the side of the bed, hit again with the fatigue that this traveling is having on me.

"At some point Dellinger's guy is going to contact you. Why don't we lie down for a while so we can both be well rested and in a better frame of mind when we hear from him? It's been a long few days and we could both use the rest." Landon rubs big circles on my back and I lean in, putting my head on his shoulder. Despite my telling him that I needed to do this on my own, I am so happy he's here with me right now.

It's 4:00 pm when we close the curtains and darken the room as much as possible for our nap, and 8:00 pm when a loud knock on the door wakes me. I rub my eyes as I get up and go to the door. I turn the table lamp on so I can see but not wake Landon.

When I open the door, the light from the hallway is a bit blinding and I rub and squint my eyes until they adjust. When I move my hand from my face and my eyes can see clearly again, I see a man standing in front of me. I rub my eyes again, not believing what I'm seeing as he stares into my eyes.

"Ronnie?"

"Dad?"

Chapter 13

"It *is* you. Your hair is darker, but…your eyes…your mother's blue eyes," he says softly.

"Dad!" I throw my arms around him and squeeze. "You're alive!"

"Oh, Ronnie! I can't believe it's you! You've…you've grown up." Dad's arms hold me tight and it feels so good, just like when I was a little girl. "What are you doing here?" he finally asks.

"What am *I* doing here? What are *you* doing here?" His question jogs me out of my state of elation and the conflict of my father's presence here is suddenly very real. I argue with myself that there's a good chance I'm dreaming, but when I hear Landon's voice and feel his hand on my shoulder, I'm certain that it's all real.

"Babe? Are you ok? Who is this?" Landon asks. He's giving my father the once over in a protective analysis.

"Who is *this*? You have a boy in your room?" my father questions. It's amazing how quickly he has taken himself back to the days of being my protector.

"Are you kidding me right now? First of all, I am 25 years old. Second, he's not a boy he's a *man*, and his name is Landon. Third, you have no place to question why I'm here and who I'm with until you give me the best damn reason in the world for why *you're* standing here right now," I declare.

"I'm Jenna's father," he says by way of answering Landon's question. "And that's no way to speak to me, Ronnie."

"It's a little hard for me to be happy right now. You have no idea what I've gone through in the last three days, not to mention the hell I went through in leaving you to die under a tree in the middle of a DC park, so you'll have to excuse me if I don't jump up and down," I tell him. I do want to be happy. My father is alive, and it's for real this time. But the fact that he's standing here tells me he's the contact Dellinger said would get in touch with me, and that's not a good thing.

"This is really your dad, Jenna? He really is alive?" Landon is a shocked as I am.

"Yes, I'm her father. A real Sherlock you've got there, Ronnie." Dad always had a sharp wit, but he's being kind of an asshole. What's gotten into him? "Can I please come in before hotel security is called?" Dad asks. I move to the side and let him in, turning on the rest of the lights with the switch by the door.

He looks almost the same. He's lost some hair, and what's left is a blend of dirty blonde and white. There are lines around his grey eyes, but what sticks out to me the most is just how hard he looks.

"You have some explaining to do," Landon tells him.

"Who the hell are you?" Dad rebuts.

"I'm the guy who's in love with your daughter. The guy who has been there for her during the one of the worst times in her life." Landon puts his arm around me in a visual demonstration of his place in my life.

"You *do* have a lot to explain, Dad," I reiterate Landon's statement. "How are you still alive? And if you've been alive all this time, why didn't you try to find me? Oz has known where I am this whole time. But, more than all of that...you're *still* working for Dellinger?"

"It's hard to explain, Ronnie," he starts.

"Stop calling me that. I haven't been her since you sent me away six years ago. You chose my new name, use it," I tell him harshly. Until I hear him out, I can't let him in. He's still working for Dellinger, by choice, and therefore falls into the unfortunate place of being untrustworthy.

"Well, you certainly have grown into the strong woman I always hoped you would. Maybe with a little smarter mouth than I expected, but I suppose you get that from me." Dad moves further into the room.

"Why are you not dead? What happened the night I left you in the park?"

I ask.

"Ok, ok. You're right. I owe you an explanation. Dellinger's search was intensifying. It wasn't going to take much longer before he realized that all of his leads were going to be dead ends. He started suggesting that he'd be closer to finding it if there were *two* people with my expertise who were looking for it. I knew he was going to go after you. I didn't want you to have the life that I had been trapped in. So…I gave myself a deep enough wound to make it look as bad as it did. You were 19 and I knew the day would come when he'd suggest bringing you in, so I had everything arranged with Oz for you to leave town and start over. I'm sorry I put you through that, but I did it to save you, Ronn…Jenna." Dad looks at me with hope painting his face. He doesn't want me to hate him for deceiving me the way he did.

"Why didn't you try to contact me and explain everything? You let me believe you were dead. You let me believe I was all alone," I tell him.

"I said I was sorry. I did what I thought was best." Dad raises his voice a bit, not happy that I would challenge him.

"We've all experienced the lengths Dellinger will go to get what he wants, but you have no idea how what you did impacted her. You could show a little more understanding," Landon says with a strong, protective tone and stance.

Dad stands and I step in before this gets completely out of hand.

"I think what Landon is trying to say, Dad, is that once things were calmed down you could have found me. You could have let me know what happened and why things had to be the way they were. And, really, you could have told me from the beginning. You didn't have to scare me into leaving with a bloody wound," I say as I work to minimize the rising testosterone. "Instead I've spent all this time thinking I left my father to die alone in the middle of a park under a tree. I still have nightmares."

"I was sure Dellinger was monitoring every move I made. He was getting crazier and crazier about finding it. I was afraid if I tried to contact you he'd know," Dad explains.

"Know what? What is it that he's trying to find? Is that why we're here?" Landon asks, clearly confused by the familiar conversation my father and I are having.

"He's trying to find the last 1913 V Nickel. There were only five made, hence the V, the Roman numeral five. He has the first four and has been on an insane hunt for the last one," I tell Landon. "They sell at auction for upwards of three million dollars."

"So that's why we're here? He thinks the American Ambassador to France has this V Nickel?" Landon's tone and stance have morphed and tell me he's in action mode. He's starting to assess the situation and formulate a plan.

"He may or may not think the Ambassador has it. My orders always include looking for the V Nickel among the other coins he's after, but…I think he sent Jenna here because he knows," my father begins.

"Knows what? Could you two please stop with the cryptic talk," Landon face tells me he's tiring quickly of the conversation between my father and me.

"That I have the V Nickel," I answer.

"How do *you* have it?" Landon asks.

"I found it years ago. I gave it to…Jenna…for safe keeping. I always intended to use it as a last resort. Sort of a get-out-of-jail-free card," Dad tells him.

"Well, then this is simple. If what he wants is the V Nickel, we give it to him." Landon's posture has changed and he now seems more relaxed, as if the solution to this unimaginable situation just revealed itself.

"No," my father says quickly.

"Why not, Dad? You just said you gave me the V Nickel for safe keeping. You told me to hold onto it like a winning card. You said I'd know when to play it and *now* is the time. If I give him the Nickel, maybe he'll let

ANNALISA GRANT

you go? You can come to Chicago with me. You'd love it there, Dad." My father crosses the room and opens the curtains and then the balcony doors.

"I can't do that," he says flatly. He's staring out at the city, all lit up like in a movie. The Eifel Tower is glowing and sparkling. It's majestic. "Dellinger has too many good contacts. If I don't have his name to use, I have nothing."

"What are you talking about?" I ask, confused.

"I can't go back to DC. Oz thinks I'm dead, so I have no stake in the company I helped build. And what would I do in Chicago? Where am I going to make this kind of money? Not just from Dellinger, but...you won't believe what some people will pay for the things I find. I have more money in a Swiss bank account than I could have ever imagined. So much that I can send you half of it and you'd never have to work another day in your life." I can't believe what I'm hearing my father say. He doesn't want out from under Dellinger's thumb. He wants this life.

"You aren't *finding* things, you're *stealing* them. And I don't care about your money." I look at my father, searching for the man I once believed he was. A man so disgusted by the life he was coerced into with Dellinger that he just told me he faked his own death so I wouldn't get caught in it, too. But...that was never real. I sit on the bench at the end of the bed, broken.

"That's why you told me to take the Nickel. As long as it was still out there, Dellinger would keep you around and you'd have a steady job," I say. Everything is quickly becoming clear. "He never coerced you, did he? Never threatened to pull me in with you. Or maybe he did and you were afraid I'd join you, and then you'd have to share the profits. You just stood there and lied to me. You faked that whole scene in Constitution Gardens for yourself. You jumped at the chance to flaunt your skills and make some great money along the way. You never could resist the opportunity to brag on yourself. How long?" He told me it all started after Mom died because he was

162

desperate for the extra money we needed, but now I don't believe that for a second.

He hesitates before answering me, knowing he's uncovering all the lies. "You were nine."

"Mom was in the middle of cancer treatment hell!" Rage is filling me and I feel my blood begin to boil. "Were any of those late night work calls for actual work or were they all for your ego-prodding criminal side job? Do you know how many times *I*, as a nine-year-old little girl, got up in the night with my mother to hold a bucket next to the bed so she could throw up? That should have been *you*!" I shout.

"Jenna," Landon comes to me and takes my hand in his trying to calm me down. If I get much louder our neighbors are sure to call hotel security.

"No, Landon! He was out there, stealing people's prized heirlooms and investments and selling them for mad money, *on top of* being paid to get the things Dellinger was after. All the while we were living in a piece of shit house that was falling apart and my mother was pacing out her pain meds because we supposedly couldn't afford to get the prescription filled every month. You let her suffer! You let her die!" I allow Landon to physically hold me so I don't give into my instinct and use all the fighting training my father gave me to beat the shit out of him for what he did to my mother.

"I tried, ok?" my father rebuts. "I tried for years to be the man your mother wanted me to be, but I couldn't. I even took precautions, safeguards in the beginning, because I *really* did take the first jobs because of the money. Your mother's medical bills were already starting to pile up and I knew she was going to worry about that. But…I wasn't made for fixing locks and helping people break into their homes when they locked themselves out. I was made for more than that. Dellinger saw that in me. He recognized that I could be doing so much more with my skills." His pathetic excuse flows off his lips with no effort whatsoever.

"You make me sick. I will gladly, and quite easily, go back to the days when I thought you were dead because that's what you are to me. Dead. The man I thought was my father died a long time ago. I don't know you. I don't *want* to know you," I say now feeling the calm after the raging storm. It's hard not to feel ridiculous after being fooled so terribly for so long.

"Did you bring it with you? The Nickel. Do you have it?" he asks, completely oblivious to the damage he's furthered in me. "I'll…take it off your hands…so you don't have to carry this burden anymore."

"No, I didn't bring it with me! But…I'll tell Dellinger we didn't find it so you can go on living your tragic excuse for a life." The worst part about all of this was that he let Mom die thinking she had helped him turn over a new leaf…that he had been living a life on the straight and narrow. I suppose that's better than living her final days knowing she was married to a big, fat liar.

"I still need your help. I told Dellinger the Ambassador's home was a two person job. The coins he's after are in one location, but the coins I'm after are in another. I can get into both of them. I was just going to use whoever Dellinger sent to distract the extra security there will be tomorrow night. But, since he sent you…"

"You didn't know Dellinger was sending Jenna?" Landon asks skeptically.

Dad doesn't answer right away, which is answer enough for me. "No." *Liar.*

"You can get the coins from one case while I get them from the other. It'll make the job a lot faster," he continues. "Dellinger will get the coins he wants, and I have a buyer ready for mine." It's like I'm looking at a complete and total stranger. It doesn't occur to him for one second that what he's asking me to do is against everything he and my mother ever taught me about being morally conscious. It appears his instructions to me on the subject were more *do as I say, not as I do.*

"You have lost your damn mind if you think I'm going to help you!" I say loudly.

"This is the biggest payout I've ever had and you're not going to screw this up for me. You have to help me. I'm your *father*," he says sternly. He steps forward aggressively and Landon puts his hand against my father's chest to stop him.

"Not anymore you're not." I grab my purse and sling it across my body as I swing the hotel room door open and fly out into the hall.

I luck out and the elevator doors are opening as I approach. A woman exits and I practically throw myself in. I press the lobby button a dozen times, willing the doors to close before Landon or my father finds me. I storm out of the elevator before the doors are completely open and push my way through the front doors and out onto the sidewalk.

The sky is dark but there's a glow from the Eifel Tower and other night life in this amazing city. I walk for a few blocks, not knowing where I'm going. I stop when I realize my heart has stopped racing from anger and lean against an iron gate surrounding a nearby home, or maybe it's a hotel. Everything is so beautiful here. I wish I could really enjoy being in Paris, France, but I can't. Even if I don't change my flight to leave tomorrow, there's no way I could truly enjoy myself here. My experience in France has been tainted, like everything I thought my life was before.

I turn around and walk back to the hotel and make a bee-line for the bar. They must have been trying to make it easier for American guests with only a rude sense of the French language when they named it Le Bar. Perhaps it's an inside joke about how Americans think they're speaking French by add *Le* to the front of everything.

"Que puis-je obtenir pour vous?" the bartender asks as I take one of the empty seats at the counter. I give him a tight lipped smile and shake my head while shrugging my shoulders. He smiles and translates his question for me. "What can I get for you?"

"Oh, right, of course. I'll have a gin and tonic, double gin," I say.

He places my order in front of me on a small white napkin and gives me a nod and a smile.

"I can charge this to my room, right?"

"Of course, m'dame."

"Perfect. Keep them coming," I tell him as I take my room key from my back pocket and slap it on the bar. If I'm going to drink my sorrows away, Henry Dellinger is going to pay for it.

Drink after drink, the only thing I think I can do is ask myself two questions: How did this happen? How did this become my life?

If only Mom hadn't died. Stupid cancer. She would have found out about Dad. She was just too sick when he picked up with Dellinger to know...and he knew that. He played her. He took advantage of her illness and fed his own selfish desires while she lay dying in their bed.

"Asshole," I say to myself out loud. The bartender looks around and I shake my head at him. "Not you. Sorry."

"Well, I hope you're not talking about me." Landon sits next to me at the bar and immediately orders a Jack and Coke.

"No. Not you either," I say.

"You've had me worried sick. I asked the guy at the front desk if he had seen you. He said you walked out of the hotel so I went to find you. I thought you might have walked to the Tower. I've been looking for you for hours. Now I feel stupid for not having come down here first," he says. He takes his wallet out to pay for his drink but I stop him.

"No, no, no. Drinks are on me. Well, they're really on Dellinger, so...drink up!" I pick up my glass and clank it with his, sloshing my gin and tonic around a bit too hard. Some of it spills on the bar. "Oh, no. What a waste of good alcohol," I slur.

"You're drunk," Landon says.

"I'm not drunk. I am fully aware of what is going on right now," I say in a half-inebriated attempt at convincing both of us.

"Oh, really?"

"Yep! I am fully aware that my father is a selfish bastard and that my entire life was a jacked up lie. How's that for being aware?" I take the last swallow of my drink and Phillip, my new bartender friend, brings me another.

"How many of these have you had?" Landon asks before he lets me take a sip of the new drink Phillip has presented me.

"Well, let's see...what time is it now?"

"It's 12:30 am," Landon tells me."

"Aha, but that's the funny part. It's not! See, it's 12:30 am here, but my body thinks it's 6:30 pm yesterday. So, really, I guess I did start drinking a little early for me." Landon lets go of my drink and I take a long sip.

"Everyone's family is jacked up, Jenna," he says.

"Jacked up is putting it lightly. But what would you know, Mr. All-American, mom stays home and bakes apple pies?" Landon's police officer of the year father and picture perfect mother could hardly have anything that resembled a jacked up family. I rest my chin in the palm of my hand and wait for Landon to give me some watered down story about what he thinks is jacked up about his family.

"Because I lied to you."

"Yay! More lies!" I raise my hands like I'm cheering with pom-poms and flop them onto the bar. "I can't wait to hear this."

"You know what...you *are* drunk and I don't want to tell you when you're like this. I honestly am not sure if you're going to remember it or not." I can see Landon almost physically close himself up. I've never seen him do that.

I put my drink down and do my best to give him my attention. He's right...I'm pretty buzzed right now, but not so much so that I can't have a conversation with him. I'm just super honest when I've had a few drinks in me. So, this might be an interesting conversation, but a conversation nonetheless.

"No, I want to know. What was the lie?" I ask with all the seriousness I can gather.

Landon hesitates, not totally sure he wants to do this, but I take his hand in mine and look into his eyes so he knows that I'm really here.

"Well…my dad *is* a cop and my mom *did* stay home. What I didn't tell you was that my mom stayed home because she had to. She wasn't allowed to work. My dad controlled everything she did. Where she went. What she wore. What she ate and drank. When she woke up and went to sleep. How much money she spent, if he even let her spend any. And…" Landon pauses, deciding how straight forward to be about what he's about to say. "If she messed up…he beat the shit out of her."

"Oh, my God, Landon, that's awful. I'm so sorry." I grab his hand and squeeze it with both of mine.

"Don't be sorry. It was my life. All I knew. When I got to be 11 or 12, the day after a beating, I would pretend to go to school. I'd walk toward the bus stop but then I'd hide behind Mrs. McGrew's trees until I saw my dad leave for work. Then I'd go home and take care of my mom. Some days she couldn't walk. I'm sure he at least cracked her ribs on more than one occasion." He takes a long drink of his Jack and Coke. I wish I knew what to say. My dad was a selfish liar, but he would never have physically hurt my mom.

"I had so many tardies and absences that eventually the school called my dad. That's when he beat the shit out of me, and how I got this scar." He points to the scar above his right eye that I noticed the night of our first date. "He came at me and I was going to fight back. I wasn't going to cower on the floor like some frail lamb. He gave me one good right hook and I went spinning down, hitting my face on the corner of the coffee table. Mom took me to the doctor to get stitches. She was good at lying about her injuries, so she knew just what to tell them. After that, Mom wouldn't let me stay home to help her."

"Did she ever call the police?" I ask. It seems obvious to me, but I've never been in that situation before.

"Once, when I was 13. Mom got her worst beating that night for embarrassing Dad in front of his cop buddies. But, as he said, it was her fault in the first place for making chicken for dinner when what he really wanted was steak."

"What about the dance studio, and your sister?" I ask.

"Mom used to own a dance studio. My dad convinced her to give it up, but she really did teach me how to dance. My sister..." he sighs. "My sister is married to a dickhead just like my father, and her daughters will probably do the same. So, yeah..."

Landon's eyes are dark and sad and all I want to do is make that go away. I cup his face with my hand and try to comfort him somehow.

"I don't need your pity, Jenna. I didn't tell you that so you would feel sorry for me or so you would think that your family life was great by comparison. I told you so you would know that I understand in some way about feeling like your life was a lie." He takes the last gulp of his drink and puts the glass back on the bar with a little more force than he has before.

"I don't pity you, Landon. I love you, and hearing that you had to go through something like that is just about the worst thing I've ever heard," I say to him. "But...I bet your mom is really proud of the man you've become."

"That's the other thing. What I told you about delivering the letters for my buddies who died was true. Except...I found all of their families without any trouble. It was my family that was the problem. Well, my mom. I got back into town after I had been discharged and went to see my mom. Dad retired not long before I came back and was home, which I wasn't expecting. He didn't give a rat's ass about me or what I had survived. I asked where mom was and he told me he didn't know. A year prior, he came home from work and she was gone. I hadn't heard from her in a while, but that wasn't unusual. It takes months to get written letters to deployed troops, and internet service is spotty, if anything.

"I went to her best friend's house and asked her where Mom was, but she wouldn't tell me. All she would say is that my mom loved me and wanted the best for me and that Mom made her promise she wouldn't tell me where she went. Mom always hated that Amy and I grew up seeing what we did, and she wanted better for us. I went to Amy to try and help her, but she wouldn't leave. I told her how Mom got up the courage to go and she could too, but it didn't matter. She's stuck and he's beat her down so much that she doesn't have the will to even try. I've spent the last six years looking for my mother. The more jobs I got, the more resources I had to expand my search for her. My dad died last year and all I've wanted is to find her so she can know she doesn't have to hide anymore."

"I'm so sorry, Landon. I didn't know…"

"You knew what I wanted you to know. We're not all that different." Landon moves my unfinished drink away from me to the back of the bar and motions to the bartender that we're done. He brings the bill and I sign it without looking. I don't care how much we just spent. Dellinger has been free with his money thus far, there's no reason to think he wouldn't buy me a few glasses of liquid courage.

Landon steadies me as I stand and we walk slowly to the elevator and back up to our room. I can't walk too fast as the room begins to spin when I do. I'm coming down from my inebriated state and am transitioning into drinker's remorse, regretting having drunk so much.

"Crap! I left my room key on the nightstand when we laid down. I didn't think to grab it when I came after you. Where's yours?" Landon asks when he doesn't find his room key on him.

"It's in my back pocket," I tell him. My body is pressed face-first to the wall. "You'll have to get it."

"Well, the night's not a complete loss. At least I get to grab your ass," he laughs.

"Such a gentleman," I tease.

The door opens and Landon helps me inside. I flip the switch on the wall that controls several lights in the room. As soon as the room is illuminated, the picture of what happened in here while we were gone becomes clear.

Our room has been ransacked.

"What the hell?" Landon exclaims.

"So I'm guessing this isn't the result of you beating the shit out of my dad," I say with a little bit of disappointment.

"Uh, no."

I shake my head, sure of why our room has been completely turned over. "When did my father leave?"

"We shared a few colorful words after you left, and then I kicked him out when I came to find you," he tells me. "You think your dad did this? Why?"

"Yes," I tell him with absolute certainty. The fog seems to be clearing from my head. Nothing like a dose of reality to really kill the buzz you're coming out of. "Because he didn't believe me when I told him I didn't bring the V Nickel with me. And he'd be right."

I pull my purse off my body and sit on the uncovered bed with it. I pull out a small, black velvet sack from my bag, open it, and turn it over. Onto the bed falls the last of five 1913 V Nickels Senator Dellinger has been searching for over the last, at least, ten years. I've had it in my possession since I left DC.

"This is worth three million dollars. Wow." Landon picks up the coin and examines it.

"Yep. They weren't supposed to put Liberty's head on it. It was supposed to be the Indian's head. They made five of them when the mistake was discovered and printing halted." I stand up and go into the bathroom to get some headache medicine from my toiletry bag.

"Are you ok, Jenna?" Landon calls to me.

"I'm good. Just needed something for my headache," I tell him when I'm back at the bed. I think about telling him that I'm going to change my flight in the morning, but decide that I won't tell him at all. I'll need to put some serious distance between us while I settle exactly what I'm going to do. I need to figure out when I'm going to leave Chicago and where I'm going to go and I won't be able to do that with Landon near me.

"We've got a lot to sort out tomorrow. Let's get some sleep and approach it when both our heads are clearer." Landon takes me in his arms and kisses the top of my head. "We'll figure this out, Jenna. I promise."

We settle into bed and I find my happy place in Landon's arms, thinking about how lucky I would be to have him by my side forever. He managed to grow up in an abusive home and break the cycle of violence to become the opposite of everything his father was. He's kind and caring and generous. He's done nothing but protect me and promise to never leave me. I take comfort in knowing I'll be protecting him, Mercy, Spring, and the others, when I leave Chicago. If I'm not near them, Dellinger won't be able to use them as leverage to make me do his dirty work. I may have the same skills as my father, but I spent the evening discovering that I'm nothing like him. And that makes me strangely sad.

Chapter 14

Landon pulls the curtains open and even with my eyes closed the light shining in is so bright it hurts.

"Oh, my God... did we wake up on the sun?" I whine as I roll over and pull the sheets over my head. I slept hard, which was a combination of jet lag and gin and tonic. I wish I had drunk enough to forget about what happened last night, but I didn't. I remember everything from opening the door and seeing my father, alive, to coming back to our trashed room after attempting to drown my sorrows.

"Well, the sun is pretty bright at 11:00 am," Landon says by way of explaining the blazing light coming in through the balcony windows. He sits by me on my side of the bed and brushes the hair out of my face. His fingers trail my jawline until his hand comes around and cups my face as he kisses my forehead. "It's time to get up, beautiful."

"I smell coffee," I whisper, still not able to use my full voice. I stretch and sit myself up in the bed, rubbing my eyes while they get fully adjusted to the light.

"Breakfast! I ordered eggs benedict and French toast, although I'm pretty sure they just call it toast here." Landon's light laugh brings a smile to my face and for just the tiniest of moments this feels like something other than it is. It feels like Landon and me being together in the most permanent sense of the word. It feels like a honeymoon in Paris. It feels like forever.

"Thank you. That was very sweet of you." I pull myself out of bed and run through my morning routine of brushing my teeth and washing my face before I eat. After that, Landon and I enjoy a truly marvelous breakfast in almost complete silence.

This morning, with my headache dissipating and the growl in my stomach being satisfied, my mind is reviewing the events of last night.

There's so much to think about. Aside from deciding when or if I'll tell Landon that I'm going to change my flight home to today, I'm battling this gnawing feeling that there's more to what my father told me. His wording, his phrasing, was off. Clearly I don't know my father like I thought I did, but I still know him well enough and am confident he's hiding something.

"What it is?" Landon asks after about 30 minutes of silence and what I'm sure was me making odd *I'm in thought* faces. I've been replaying everything Dad said last night. Analyzing the tone, the verbage, even the delivery. I don't think sending me here is all about Dellinger playing a sadistic trick on me.

"What he said last night...the way he said it. Something just isn't sitting well with me," I tell him.

"Of course it's not sitting well with you, Jenna. Your father burst every bubble you had of him last night. Nothing about what he said should be ok with you," Landon says. He takes another sip of his coffee and a bite of his French toast. It's hard to avoid the look of elation with each bite. It's the most heavenly French toast either of us has ever had. It reminds me of the morning Landon was waiting for me outside my apartment and I shared my croissants with him.

"It's more than that. When he asked me about the coin, even after his speech about how he tried to be on the straight and narrow, and how Dellinger can't get his hands on the Nickel because then he wouldn't need my father anymore, he asked me if I had the Nickel with me. He said 'Did you bring it with you?' He wasn't concerned about the safety of the coin. He wanted to know where it was, if I had it on me. He offered to *take it off my hands*. He *needs* the coin," I explain.

"Do you think he's already made a deal with Dellinger? Maybe he's told him if *he* finds the coin he wants more money, and that's the payout he was talking about. If Dellinger gets the coin from you, your dad won't get the payment he's counting on. Seeing you here, maybe he realized this was his chance to get it. I mean, it's not like he could show up in Chicago and ask you for it," Landon suggests.

"That's a possibility." I sigh, feeling the weight of everything and having no idea how to relieve any of it. "I don't know what to do. Despite the lies and deception, he's still my father. I can only imagine what Dellinger would do if he knew Dad had been stringing him along all this time. I mean, Dellinger has used my father to collect hundreds of other pieces for him, but he has been psychotic about finding *this* coin.

"Part of me wants to just give the coin to my father and let him decide what to do with it. It's not like I'm going to have anything else to do with him. But the other side of me wants to give the coin to Dellinger and know that my father will pay for what he did to me and my mother." It's not like giving the coin to Dellinger would free me from him now that he's found me, especially since Dad may face a real execution once Dellinger knows how my father deceived him. But, maybe it would buy me some time in between getting back to Chicago and determining when I would need to leave town. "Maybe I should get them together and threaten to split the coin down the middle. Then we'd find out who values it more. Better yet, I wish I had two coins. I would give one to each of them and let them figure out what to do."

"If you mean that, not the splitting the coin part, but the two coins…I have an idea." Landon puts his coffee cup down and pushes himself away from the small café table where we've been enjoying our breakfast on the balcony. Circumstances being what they are, it's sad that I can't relish the fact that I'm eating breakfast on a balcony of the Shangri La Hotel in Paris in the shadow of the Eifel Tower.

"What's your idea?" I ask him with a wary eye.

"I actually thought of this last night when you showed me the coin. I, well, I know a guy. Actually, he's the reason Dellinger found me. Christie's hired me to find an art forger and Dellinger has a Christie's Frequent Buyer's Card. Anyway, Christie's sold a Van Gough and a Monet belonging to this guy, " Landon tells me, using air quotes with the each artist's name. "He got almost a half a million for each. He would have gotten away with it if the woman who bought the Monet hadn't had a friend challenge its authenticity. Turned out the friend had recently acquired the same painting in London earlier that year. Both pieces had to be evaluated again, so it took a while to get to the point where they needed me. From what I understand, the appraiser had a hell of a time deciding which one was real. Christie's doesn't like to involve the authorities if they don't have to. It makes them look bad if they can't spot a fake.

"When I found the guy in Germany, we kind of hit it off, so we struck up a deal. I would tell Christie's that someone else he crossed must have gotten to him first because I found him in the morgue, and the guy would owe me as many favors as I needed from him. He's very good at what he does and I thought I might need him to forge some documents of identification for me when I found my mom." I can see it still pains Landon to even mention his mother. It must be so difficult to have been searching for her for so long and have every overturned rock come up empty.

"So what are you suggesting?" I ask.

"You want two coins? Let's make two coins."

"I don't know, Landon. I was just talking. It sounds risky. What if they can tell it's a fake?" I'm already nervous about what Dellinger is capable of. If we give him the fake and he finds out, I don't know what he'll do.

"He is *very* good at what he does," Landon says with confidence.

"And he can do coins?"

"He can do anything."

"Well...I guess it's worth a shot," I say. "Where is he? Is he in Paris?"

"He's in Versailles, about 40 minutes from here by train. If we leave now, we can be there within the hour." Landon stands, a man on a mission.

"Ok. Let me grab a shower first, though," I begin.

"We really don't have time. I don't know how long it will take him to make the coin, so we need to get there as soon as possible. We still have to get you a dress for tonight and be ready when the car picks us up at seven," Landon interjects.

"I'm not going tonight, Landon," I say flatly. I can't believe he would even remotely suggest I go through with this.

"You have to go. Dellinger got you on this guest list. You're going to have to make contact with the Ambassador to prove that you were there," he tells me.

"But Dellinger probably suspects that I have the coin already," I reply. "What difference does it make?"

"He probably does. But we don't know that for sure. So, if there's even the slightest chance that Dellinger thinks the Ambassador has the coin, you have to go tonight and make contact with him so Dellinger knows you were there. You can't act like you're on to anything they may be doing. Not Dellinger. Not your father." Landon has joined me on my side of the table, crouching down next to me so we're eye-level with each other. He puts his hand on my knee and the warm feeling that his touch brings courses through me.

"I hadn't thought of that." I cover Landon's hand on my knee with mine and lean my forehead against his for a moment before he pulls me to stand with him.

"Out of curiosity…why didn't you just use the coin as leverage when Dellinger cornered us in Chicago? You could have played that card and made a deal with him."

"After what I thought he had done to my family, I never wanted him to have it. I still don't, but, now that I know it wasn't all him, that my father willingly participated in Dellinger's schemes, I'm not quite as adamant about it. I'd happily throw it in Lake Michigan if I could."

Landon nods, understanding what I'm saying, and doesn't add anything to it. I throw my hair into a messy bun on my head and put on a pair of jeans and a t-shirt. Slinging my purse over my body, Landon and I walk out the door in less than 15 minutes and are on the train to Versailles in 25.

"How do you know he's going to be around when we get there?" I ask Landon about the mystery art forger whose hands I am placing the success of this plan in.

"He owns a small antique store. Well, he doesn't own it. The woman who took him in when he was a teenager owned it. He runs it now that she's dead. He'll be there," he answers.

Landon holds my hand the entire train ride to Versailles and I take the time to pretend that this is just a lovely vacation for the two of us. The ride is beautiful and it's the first time I've been able to really enjoy the beauty of France.

We walk the few blocks from the train station to the antique store and I stop Landon before we walk in.

"I'm nervous about this," I tell him. "Not nervous. I'm scared. I'm scared about this whole thing, Landon."

"Good. It's the first time you've been really honest with me about your feelings. Now that you're being real, I can protect you without arguing with you." Landon kisses me quickly and then holds my gaze with his beautiful brown eyes. "Trust me."

I nod, making a conscious decision to trust him. I don't know that I have any other options at this moment. At one point I considered emptying my bank account from here in France and finding someone who could do for me what Oz did in setting up a new identity, but I couldn't bear the thought of not seeing Spring or Mercy again. I want to leave them some kind of note before I disappear, however deceptive it may be. That was also the thought process that brought me to the conclusion that I would wait until Demi had her baby before I disappeared. I promised I would be there for her. I already let her down by taking off to Paris when she wanted me there when she told Jack. I can't leave before I hold her hand in the delivery room and watch her bring her little baby into the world.

A bell at the top of the door rings as Landon pushes it open. It's a small store filled with things that would fetch far more in the States than what they're being sold for here. I scan the shelves and tables wondering what kind of rich history some of these items have. Then it dawns on me that there are probably several reproductions of expensive pieces in here that this mystery man has made himself to fool buyers. I sure hope Landon knows what he's doing.

"Je suis à vous dans un instant," a man's voice calls.

"We don't have a moment," Landon calls back having understood the French phrase.

A man who looks to be around our age and of average height, definitely shorter than Landon, appears from behind a curtain that separates the front of the store from the back room. He's wearing jeans and a white dress shirt with the sleeves haphazardly rolled up and an open brown vest. His bronze hair is shaggy and he's wearing wire glasses like John Lennon.

"Holy shit! It's Landon Scott! How the hell are ya, man?" The familiarity between the two is a little surprising. Landon said they had hit it off, but I didn't have the idea that they were this friendly.

"Hey Jace! You stayin' out of trouble?" Landon asks as they give each other a firm handshake.

"Never! Who's your lady friend?" he asks enthusiastically.

"Jace, this is Jenna. Jenna, this is Jace." Landon motions between the two of us and I extend my hand to shake his.

"It's nice to meet you," I say.

"Likewise. What brings you guys to Versailles? Honeymooning in Paris maybe?" Jace raises his eyebrows as a teasingly hopeful gesture.

"No...not yet," Landon smirks. There it is. That smirk. With all the intensity we've faced over the last several days, I didn't realize how much I missed that sexy smirk of his. "I'm actually here to call in a favor."

"Absolutely. What can I do for you?" Jace doesn't hesitate in agreeing to do whatever it is Landon is going to ask. Landon must have gotten him out of some hotter than hot water for him to be so agreeable.

"I need a replica of a coin." Landon looks at me and nods so I pull the coin from my purse and show it to Jace.

"No fucking way! This is a 1913 V Nickel!" he says with amazement. "Where did you get this?" he asks me.

"Where I got it isn't important. Can you make a replica of it?" I say.

"This isn't your average collectable. This is some serious shit here." Jace inspects the coin, turning it over in his hand several times before pulling over a large magnifying glass with a light around it and examining it there. "Oh, man! This is the real deal."

"We need a copy of it. Can you do it?" Landon asks, reiterating my question as Jace keeps his eyes on the coin.

"Can I do it? That is the most insulting thing you've ever said to me. Of course I can do it." Jace sets the Nickel on the top of the counter and I immediately pick it up. I don't want any sleight of hand going on. Give me a few hours. I have to make the mold, pour the metal, let it cool, and make sure it looks like it's 100 years old."

"Why don't we go find a dress for you while Jace works on this?" Landon suggests.

"No."

"No?"

"No. I'm not letting that coin out of my sight. It's the only card I have left to play and I don't trust Jace not to take advantage of the situation and leave us holding a fake...no offense," I say.

"None taken. I wouldn't trust me either," Jace says. "Stick around while I make the molds and then take the coin with you while I work on the copy."

"I can live with that." I say.

"Great. Wait until you see how this works," Jace begins. "Years ago I had some Spanish medallions I was copying and…"

"We're short on time here, Jace," Landon says cutting him off.

"Right. Come into my work room." We follow Jace behind the curtain and into an office space. I look at Landon with curiosity, my brow furrowing with confusion. There are no doors to another space, and I don't see anything in this office that looks like it could be used in any way to create a mold or melt metal. Landon just smirks and nods his head, gesturing at Jace. With a smile of his own, Jace pulls the back of a large bookshelf toward him like a door, revealing a hidden passage.

"Really?" I say in astonishment.

"Oh, yeah." Jace winks at me and Landon pushes him through the entry way. "You'd be hard pressed to find a building or home around here that doesn't have a least one secret passage. They had some serious wars roll through this part of the world you know."

"No need for the history lesson, Jace," Landon says firmly.

This is more like it. We enter a room that looks like a cross between a mad scientist's lab and a great artist's studio. One side of the room has Bunsen burners, glass jars like the kind from my 11th grade chemistry class, protective glasses, and gloves, among other sciencey-looking tools. The other side has two easels, paints, smocks, and jars full of brushes.

Jace pulls a box big enough for a pair of shoes out of a supply closet along with a couple of round trays that look like small, shallow cake pans. When he's removed the contents from the box, and everything seems to be set up, he hold his hand out to me, palm up.

My heart begins to pound inside my chest. What if this doesn't work? What if something happens to the coin in the process? I'm worried and I can't hide it from covering my face.

"It's going to be fine, Jenna," Landon says, trying to comfort me.

"I promise. The last thing I want to do is ruin such an incredible artifact." Jace gives me a reassuring, tight lipped smile.

"I'm trusting you with my life here. You know that, right?" I say to Jace.

"I know." Jace's hand is still held out for me to give him the coin.

I take a deep breath and place the coin in his hand. He begins to work quickly, using some kind of rubber based compound. He presses the coin into one of the trays with the rubber substance in it along with a straw so as to make a well of sorts, and lets it set for a moment. It doesn't take long for the rubber to set. He flips the whole mold out of the pan and pulls the coin out. He does the same thing with the other side of the coin in the other pan. When he's done he removes the coin from the mold and gives it to me. My heart has officially stopped racing now that I have the Nickel back in my possession.

"So now what? What's next?" I ask him.

"Next, I use both sides to pour the nickel and make an exact replica," Jace says with some vanity. He takes great pride in his abilities. I hope that pride never costs him an important relationship the way my father's pride has cost him ours.

"Won't the nickel be too hot for the mold?" I ask, concerned the heat will melt the rubbery material.

"This is a special, a little more high-tech, material. You can't exactly buy it online, if you know what I mean," Jace answers cryptically.

"And you have actual nickel?" I question. Jace nods. "How?"

"Do you really want to know?" he asks, looking at me over his glasses.

"No, I guess not." The less I'm privy to here, the better. "Just be careful to make sure the front and back line up just as they do on the original. And there's a little discoloration near Liberty's chin. And…" Landon puts his arm around my waist, stopping me mid-sentence.

"He's got it, Jenna. I wouldn't have brought you here if I wasn't sure he could do this." Landon's reassuring words don't completely take my worry away, but they do help. "You've got the coin in your hot little hand, so let's take care of getting your dress for tonight, ok?"

"I guess shopping beats hanging around here for the next however many hours."

"Ok, that one *did* sting a little." Jace winces at my comment so I lean in and kiss him on the cheek. "I'm good now."

"Good, because that's the last time my girlfriend's lips are getting anywhere near you," Landon tells him as he takes my hand and begins to walk us to the secret passage.

We get halfway into the shop when Landon asks me to wait for a minute. He goes to the back of the store where Jace is still working and I wander around the small store stuffed with antiques. I scan the shelves and tables displaying some of the most beautiful things I've ever seen and even find a few things that I love. There are some gorgeous pieces of white china with gold embellishments around the rim of the plates and cups, and a porcelain doll that reminds me of one my mother had when I was a little girl. I think she said her mother had given it to her. I wish I knew where it was now.

I look at pieces of art and what look like Tiffany lamps to me, but I could be wrong. I have no idea what a real Tiffany lamp looks like. I have no idea if those dishes are fine china or not. That's what would make me the perfect customer for Jace. He could show me any item in this store and give me some convoluted story about its ancestry, telling me about how there are only a few of whatever it is left and that I'd be lucky to have it in my possession. I would be completely unsuspecting.

But not Dellinger. And not my father.

I'm not sure how to execute this idea of passing a fake coin to one of them at all. Do I give it to my father for betraying me? Do I give it to Dellinger for swooping in and inviting my father back into the world he tried so hard to leave? Or do I throw them both in a bag and pick one randomly to give to each of them. They're big boys. Let them duke it out for themselves.

Chapter 15

I didn't want to, but I actually enjoyed shopping with Landon this afternoon. Getting to spend someone else's money didn't exactly hinder my fun. And since it was Dellinger's money, I bought the most expensive dress and shoes I could find. We walked through a shopping area of Versailles that Jace told Landon was a hidden treasure of stores. That must have been what Landon went back to ask him before we left.

Again, there were moments when we forgot about why we were there in the first place. We laughed and shopped and even stopped for a bite to eat at a little sidewalk café. Perhaps we didn't forget, but chose not to remember. We also used the time to sort through a plan of some kind for tonight with my father. It's a loose plan if anything. There are so many unknown variables that the number of *if this happens then we'll do this* ideas is too many to count.

The only thing that was decided for sure was that I would have to use one of the coins as leverage with Dellinger. I'll give him what he's been looking for and strike a deal. It's the only shot I have at not having to run. I let Landon lay out his plan and agreed with him on as many plot points as possible. It's as good a plan as any, but I can't walk confidently in anything until I have complete reassurance that Henry Dellinger is never going to interfere with my life again.

I'm just out of the shower when I hear the hotel room door close and Landon calling out to me that he's back. "I didn't realize you had gone anywhere," I tell him as I emerge from the bathroom wearing only a robe and my hair twisted on top of my head with a towel.

"That's a hot look." Landon smirks and I roll my eyes.

"A paper bag would look hot to you," I tease.

"On you? Yes, a paper bag *would* be hot. You could also make a potato sack look sexy." Landon tosses a garment bag on the bed before giving me a lip-crushing kiss. I part my lips and lift my hands, lacing my fingers together behind his neck. My short robe rises and Landon's hands trail down my sides, discovering that I'm not wearing anything else. His fingers skim over my hips with light, feathery touches before he takes me by the waist and pulls me from him.

"I'm not sure how much longer I can do this, Jenna. I don't think you realize how difficult it is to say no to you." Landon steps away and takes a deep breath.

"I'm sorry," I say softly.

"No, no...*I'm* sorry. I shouldn't have said anything. I'm in total agreement with you that, while this is the most perfect setting for us, these aren't the right circumstances. I guess I'm just...a guy in love." He smiles sweetly and it's hard for my heart not to melt. He's been so understanding about my reasons for not sleeping with him, even though since we got here those reasons have been lies. I can't tell him that we can't have sex because then I won't be able to make a sound decision to leave if I need to leave. I know that once we take that step I'll be even more bonded to him, more in love with him, that I'll be too torn. I can't solidify my relationship with Landon like that until I'm sure Dellinger has taken the deal with the coin and I'm free to move on with my life.

"Everything will be different when we get back to Chicago. Things will be as they're supposed to be," I tell him. It's just as cryptic and full of mixed signals a message I've been sending since he sat next to me on the plane here. I wrap my arms around his waist and let him envelop me with his. It's a warm and safe place and I've decided that I will have and enjoy it as long as possible. "So...where did you go?"

"I went down to get my tux. Concierge had one sent over for me. I gave them my measurements so hopefully it fits like they promised it would," he tells me.

"I'm sure you'll look very handsome. The shower is free," I tell him.

Landon strips down to those eternally sexy boxer briefs of his and heads into the bathroom to shower. I take that time and do my make up at the mirror by the bed and then move back into the bathroom when Landon is done so I can finish getting ready. I take everything in there because, along with the dress and shoes I bought today, I also bought a new black lace bra and panty set to go with it. Landon has seen me in my underwear before, but it would just be cruel to let him see me in this set. It's not just underwear. In any other setting it's an invitation for crazy hot sex.

I step out of the bathroom as Landon is adjusting his bow tie in the mirror across the room. I can see his reflection and he looks even more handsome that I had imagined. I smile at the site of him and he catches my eyes in the mirror. A look washes over him, one I haven't seen before, not even when I modeled the dress for him in the store. He turns slowly and takes me in from head to heel.

The dress I chose is black, with a halter strap that attaches at the farthest points along the top of the bust, reminding me of those retro bathing suits from the 50s. The whole thing is a bit nostalgic, actually. The skirt comes just above my knees and flares at the waist. The red crinoline peeks out just enough, making my only option for shoes a sexy pair of red, Jimmy Choo stilettos with handcuff hardware around the ankle. I've left my hair down and in its natural wavy curl, letting it all fall down my back.

"Oh, my God, Jenna. You look...you look *so* beautiful." Landon kisses me gently on the cheek rather than my lips so he doesn't smudge my lipstick. It's one thing for a guy to tell you he thinks you're hot, but there's something about being called beautiful that means so much more.

"Thank you," I say softly. "You look pretty incredible yourself."

"Are you ready?" he asks.

"As ready as I'll ever be," I say. I grab the red clutch I bought to complete the outfit and walk through the open door Landon is holding for me.

The car arrives promptly at 7:00 pm just as we are stepping out of the hotel and onto the sidewalk. Landon helps me in and then the door closes behind him as we settle in for the drive to the Ambassador's home. We're silent the whole drive as I run through all the possibilities in my head. I'm leaning toward giving my father the real Nickel. He *is* my father and despite what's happened, I can't shake this feeling of loyalty to him. Is it his fault that he got sucked into this life again? If Dellinger hadn't offered him the money he did, would Dad have sought out this life after working so hard to leave it? I blame Dellinger for inviting my father to betray my mother and the work he had done to live an honest life. But...I blame my father for accepting the invitation. Neither one of them deserves the coin. Maybe I will toss the real one in Lake Michigan after all.

The car pulls up to the Ambassador's home. It's a grand, palatial estate that looks like it was built in the 1700s. *Our US tax dollars at work*, I think as I consider the upkeep of a home like this.

We step onto the gravel drive and Landon holds my hand to help me so I don't fall. *I don't understand why they don't pave driveways out here.* There are two secret service men, or whatever kind of security they are, standing next to the front entry. One of them is holding a clip board, while the other is clearly there in case things get out of hand. I'm nervous because Dellinger only got an invitation to this event for me. I'm not sure what they'll do with Landon and I know I can't make it through this night without him.

"Good evening. May I have your name, please?" the security guy with the clip board asks.

"Good evening. Yes, my name is Jenna Rockwell," I begin. I'm about to try and explain Landon's presence with me when the guy interrupts me.

"And is this Mr. Scott?" he asks, looking at Landon.

"Um, yes, it is," I tell him.

"Enjoy your evening." He and the other security guy both nod at us, sending us away and into the vestibule of the house.

"How did they know about you?" I say to Landon with a mix of curiosity and worry.

"Dellinger," Landon reasons.

It makes sense. Dad probably laid into Dellinger for sending me and told him about Landon. They would assume that I wouldn't come tonight without him. Adding him to the list would mean avoiding the scene I would cause in my efforts to make sure he was with me all night.

The estate is just as beautiful on the inside as the outside. There are antiques and heirlooms everywhere. They must be part of this wing of the house...the area where they entertain and display their wealth and prestige for their visitors. I'm sure it's how they play the part and point to the master of the house's important position.

"Good evening. You must be Miss Rockwell," an older gentleman greets me. He looks to be in his early 60s, with greying hair and fair skin. He has a nice smile and seems warm. "I'm Ambassador McKay, but I hope you'll call me Ronald. Henry sent a picture with his email asking me to include you tonight. I hope you're enjoying your visit to Paris."

"Oh, yes, thank you," I say nervously. "It's very kind of you to let us intrude. Please, call me Jenna."

"Nonsense! Any friend of Henry's is a friend of mine...Jenna. You must be Mr. Scott, or shall I call you Landon?" the Ambassador says. He seems so kind. I hate that Dellinger has convince him that they're anything alike.

"Yes, of course. Thank you for including me on such short notice," Landon thanks him as they shake hands.

"I'm always happy to host fellow Americans. I think it's wonderful that we get out and explore other countries. You'll have to meet my wife, Marie," he says to me. "She's around here somewhere. She'll be the beautiful woman in the gold dress," he says looking around a bit to see if he can spot her. "I have to attend to some other guests, but I do hope you'll enjoy yourselves this evening. Please feel free to look around the estate. There's security guarding prohibited areas. Other than that, explore at will. It was lovely meeting you."

"I feel bad for him," I whisper to Landon as the Ambassador disappears into the crowd. "He has no idea what's happening. He thinks Henry Dellinger is a good man and probably gave my father the same warm welcome as he did us. I have to find my father and stop him. I'll give him the V Nickel and then he can make whatever deal or get whatever payout he can from Dellinger."

"That could be dangerous, Jenna. Your father is a man on a mission here. Who knows how desperate he is or what he'll do if you try and stop him," Landon says trying to convince me. I hear what he's saying, but I just can't let my father do this. Enough is enough.

"I have to at least try, Landon. Please." I take Landon's hand and look wishfully into his eyes, begging him to help me.

"Ok. There's a second floor that overlooks the main area here," Landon points out. He's already scoped out the room and determined our best approach. "Let's make our way around the perimeter of the balcony and see if we can get an aerial view of where he is or might be. If we don't see him down here, we'll do a little *exploring*. The Ambassador *did* invite us to, after all." He squeezes my hand and smiles reassuringly at me.

With a deep breath we take our first steps toward the staircase and find our way to the upper level balcony. The view of the room, which seems like such a small word to describe such a grand and elaborately decorated room, is breathtaking. There are no tables set up with food. Only white-gloved servers passing hor d'oeuvres. Everyone looks exquisite and, even though I paid more than three month's rent for this dress and shoes, I feel terribly out of place. In any other circumstance I'm sure I would eventually calm my nerves and enjoy myself in this once-in-a-lifetime opportunity. When will I ever be invited to a place like this again? Never. But my nerves won't calm until we find my father, give him the Nickel, and convince him not to go through with this.

"Do you see him?" I ask as casually as I can. Landon and I have walked as nonchalantly as we can halfway around the balcony.

"No. I'm guessing you haven't either," he says.

"Nope. Let's start exploring. If we get caught anywhere we're not supposed to be, just play dumb and act like we got lost." I nod and Landon takes my hand as we begin down a corridor on the upper level. There are a few guests mingling near the front of the hall, so we keep a low profile as we pretend to admire the artwork along the walls.

"Jace could have a field day with these," I chuckle.

"Who says he hasn't already," Landon replies with a small laugh.

We come to the end of the hall and make a left and are almost immediately in front of a set of ornate double doors. This is the first room we've come to like this. Every other room either had a locked single door, or it didn't have doors at all and offered nothing of interest inside. I try one of the doors and the ornate handle makes a loud grinding sound before it clicks, releasing the door.

The smell of old books fills the air. It's a sight to behold. The room is two stories tall and there are floor to ceiling bookshelves on every wall. The hard wood floors are covered with the largest rugs I've ever seen. There are two spiral staircases on either side of the room, leading to two balconies that are set up as sitting areas. I run my hand along the wooden handrail of the rolling steps that are attached to a bar midway up the bookshelf walls. It's the most overwhelmingly grand room I've ever seen, beating out the grand hall where the guests are all gathered downstairs.

"I bet some of the books are hundreds of years old," I say as I scan the shelves.

"I'm sure there are several first editions," Landon agrees. "I don't see anything that would be of interest to your father or Dellinger in here. Maybe we should try some rooms downstairs."

"First editions would on their list, but there's no way to know where they are in here. Even if the books are alphabetized, it'd take too long to find what you're looking for." I'm mesmerized by the uniformity of the spines and consider the rich history that's contained just in this one room among these books. "But, my father said he was after coins. Finding my him and what he's looking for is going to be like trying to find a needle in a haystack." I shake my head in disappointment, feeling defeated already.

"Hey...don't worry. We haven't been looking that long." Landon is always so good about doing his best to encourage me, even in the most discouraging of situations. I'm going to miss that.

Landon threads his fingers through mine and we walk back toward the door to the hall. We hear the grinding of the handle to the door and both look at each other nervously. I'm prepared to play dumb when Landon pushes me against the bare wall next to the door and crushes his lips to mine. I'm hesitant at first, taken off guard by his sudden need for me. But as the voices of the two men who open the room become clearer, I understand that Landon has opted to play us as lovers who were just looking for a place to feed our insatiable lust for one another.

"Hey! What are you doing in here?" one voice says loudly as the door opens. I don't see them because my eyes are closed, enjoying the way Landon's lips are moving with mine.

"Oh, my God...I'm so sorry," Landon says, feigning embarrassment as he pulls away from me.

"You can't be in here," one of the men scolds. It's the same voice that first questioned our being in this room. The other man isn't speaking, which is kind of making me nervous.

"Sorry. Paris! And, seriously guys...look at her. Can you blame me?" Landon motions to me, causing the silent guard to crack a creepy smile and raise an eyebrow. "We're leaving."

Landon and I scurry out into the hall and back downstairs into the grand area where the 200 or so other guests are socializing. There's no sign of my father and there was nothing upstairs remotely resembling anything that would house the coins my father wants to find.

"What are we going to do? We can't find my father, and by the number of men in black suits all of the corridors down here look like they're off limits," I say with hushed panic.

"Stop panicking, Jenna. We haven't been here that long. There's still time to find your father and stop him. We've been everywhere we're allowed to go. Let's just work our way around the room. Ok?" Landon's calming and even tone are helpful in this moment and I am once again so glad that he's here. If I were alone, I don't know what I'd do.

We spend the next hour walking around the room and chatting with various people. Some of them are dignitaries from other countries who happen to be in France, while some of them are commoners like Landon and me. I met both a judge from England and one of the Ambassador's neighbors. She's ridiculously wealthy like everyone else here, but she's not connected like some of the others. By the time we find ourselves in the same spot we were an hour ago, I feel completely crushed.

"We might as well go, Landon. I'll contact Dellinger when I get back to Chicago and tell him that my father disappeared on me, but that I have the coin and I'm going to give it to him. It's my only option at this point."

"We'll find him," Landon begins. Before he can continue, we're approached by the two men who caught us making out in the library upstairs. They don't look happy.

"Come with us," the one who speaks says. It's not a question, but a directive.

Landon and I look at each other with puzzled faces. We were in the library over an hour ago. We didn't touch or move anything, and we certainly didn't take anything. Why are they coming for us now?

They lead us through a door where another one of their team has been standing guard. The room is filled with displays of antiques and heirlooms, but none of them are coins of any kind.

"Wait here," he speaks again with the same low, monotone voice. They both exit through a door on the opposite side of the room.

"There's nothing to worry about," Landon says.

"I hope you're right," I tell him.

A few silent minutes later the duo returns through the same door with my father in tow. Landon and I followed the men here but my father is obviously being brought in with a more aggressive approach. He's wearing a tuxedo like Landon and I can't help but think he looks handsome. I've never seen him so dressed up before, and it actually looks really good on him.

"Ronnie!" Dad calls to me. I wish he would stop calling me that. "Are you ok?"

"Yes, I'm fine. Why wouldn't I be? And stop calling me that." My tone and delivery are flat so I can communicate my lack of attachment to him.

"Sorry. I forgot," he says defensively.

"Where have you been? We've been looking everywhere for you," Landon says.

"I didn't think you were coming, so I've been working the job alone," he says. They caught me upstairs. I was just about to cut into the seal of a case when they walked in. Why'd they bring you in?" my father asks.

I furrow my brow in confusion. I guess we didn't hit all the rooms that weren't guarded.

"Oh, good. You're all here," the Ambassador says as he comes through the main door to the room. "Let's move them to a more private location."

The Ambassador walks to the back of the room and pushes against a panel on the wall. The panel clicks and a door-shaped piece pops open. He pulls it open and the security twins escort us through the hole behind him.

Jace wasn't joking about the old houses having secret passages.

The room is bare but looks like it may have been used as some kind of storage at one point. The dirt on the subflooring sounds like sandpaper beneath our feet, and the poor lighting makes for more shadowy places than I'm comfortable seeing.

"Is everything alright, Ronald?" I say. I don't offer any information about us snooping upstairs, just in case that's not why we're here. Although, with my father having been brought in as well, I'm afraid that all of our snooping has been a red flag to the security team.

"Did you enjoy your self-guided tour of the east wing upstairs?" he asks. The Ambassador's demeanor has changed completely. Gone is the warm and congenial man we met earlier. The man standing before us is cold and serious.

"Did we go somewhere we were not supposed to?" Landon asks. "We followed your instructions and there didn't seem to be any security anywhere we went." He shifts his body so he's inches closer to me, enabling him to slide his arm around my waist.

"I'm not really concerned about where you may or may not have gone on your tour as I am about the item Jenna has with her. The coin, please," the Ambassador says.

"I don't know what you're talking about." I look at the Ambassador and try not to let my terror show. What happened to Mr. Congeniality? Where's the man who I thought had been duped to think Dellinger was some kind of stand-up guy. It was all an act. But...how? Why?

"Is she going to play games?" he asks my father. "If she's going to play games we can certainly even the playing field."

Just as soon as the words have left his mouth and he gives a nod, the security guys who brought us in here are on Dad. One of them forces him to his knees while the other one takes out a gun. He doesn't point the gun at my father, but holds it up in a way that tells me this is not the first time he's done this.

"Dad…" My voice is shaky, but I feel Landon's grip on me tighten, reminding me that I'm not alone.

"He wants the coin, too. Just give him the coin," Dad says.

"I told you I didn't bring it with me," I say.

"Jenna…please," he begs.

"I don't have time for this," the Ambassador says with a bored tone. "I have guests to get back to before they realize I'm gone."

"She must have it on her. It wasn't at the hotel," my father says hurriedly with fear in his voice.

McKay motions to one of his men and he moves quickly to me, reaching for my arm.

"Don't fucking touch her," Landon says calmly. He takes me by the waist and give both the security guard and Ambassador McKay a look that tells them he's not afraid of them.

"I knew it!" I begin to charge at my father, but Landon still has me and physically holds me back. "Is this some kind of game to you?" I shout.

"No! Ronn…Jenna…they caught me breaking into one of the display cases. I told them I had something to bargain with if they wouldn't hurt me. I told him you had the V Nickel. If you give it to him he'll let me live." Sweat is dripping down my father's face from nerves.

I don't say anything. I just watch him, waiting to see what he does next, what he says.

"I said I didn't bring it with me," I reiterate slowly.

Something is off here. Why would they kill him? McKay is a United States Ambassador. He could have my father arrested without any trouble. Why eliminate him? What else does he know?

"Please." He squeezes his eyes shut as the security guy presses his gun against the side of my father's head.

The Ambassador breathes a heavy and annoyed sigh. "I should have known better than to trust you. She doesn't have the Nickel. He's obviously lying. Kill him."

"Wait!" Landon shouts.

Chapter 16

Landon steps forward and holds his hand out as the gun pressed to my father's head is cocked.

"What if we do have the coin? What is it worth to you?" Landon says quickly.

"Finally, someone who understands." The Ambassador nods his head and the guy uncocks the gun and removes it from my father's temple where it has left an indentation. "Stand him up."

"What are you doing?" I whisper to Landon.

Landon takes me by the neck and presses his forehead to mine. "I'm not going to let your father die. I don't care what you think you're feeling for him right now. You mourned his death once. I can't let you do that again."

He's right. I can't lose my dad again. I can hate him later, but at least he'll still be alive.

"Ok," I tell him.

"I have the V Nickel." Landon lifts his hands as if in surrender. "I'm going to reach in my left pocket and get it." I watch him move his hand slowly to his pocket as I hear the cocking of the gun again. I don't look to see who it's pointed at this time, but I would assume it's at Landon as a protective measure.

Landon pulls a small, black velvet pouch from his pocket and holds it out. Silent security guy takes it from him and hands it to the Ambassador. His eyes widen as he opens the pouch and turns the coin out into his hand.

Even in the lower light I can see how shiny it is. Is that the real one or the fake? Was the real one this shiny, or is this the fake one and it's too shiny? For as many times as I turned that coin over and over in my hand, somehow I can't remember anything about it now. I compared both coins when we got them from Jace and remember thinking how remarkable it was. There's no way anyone could tell them apart with the naked eye.

"After all these years...I've finally beaten him," Ambassador McKay says eerily.

"You beat *who*?" Apparently I've lost my mind and have no hesitancy in asking this mad man about his cryptic statement.

"Henry Dellinger, of course," he says obviously.

"What did Dellinger do to you?" I ask. *Who hasn't Dellinger screwed over?*

"Henry and I used to be great friends. We went to law school together, got married within months of each other, had the same political dreams. Almost 12 years ago he and I ran against each other and three others men for the two Senate seats in Connecticut. I assumed we would team up...run campaigns that would support each other as the best candidates. Well, you know what they say when you assume. Henry ran a dirty campaign against all of us, but it seemed especially filthy when it came to me. Maybe it's because I thought we had been such good friends that it stung as much as it did.

"Well, every time it seemed that I was getting ahead, he fired something more damaging than the thing before. I ended up spending most of my campaign explaining the horrible accusations and lies he was constantly hurling." Ambassador McKay turns the coin over in his fingers like a parlor trick. "A few years into his first term it came to my attention that Henry was a collector of very rare artifacts. I also came to understand that he had an expert on retrieval working for him. I made him a better offer and so we've spent the last eight years working together. If Henry wanted it, I had to make sure he didn't get it. Of course, we let him have a few so he didn't catch on. Bobby Matthews has been the best employee I've ever had. It wasn't until recently that I discovered the fifth V Nickel was Henry's golden ticket. Now that I have it, Henry never will."

"This was all a set up," I say in disbelief to my father. Even with all the lies and deception I would have never imagined my father would put me in a life or death situation. Dad just looks at me blankly.

"As I've already said, I have guests. Mr. Matthews, you can expect your regular payment plus the bonus I agreed to include." The Ambassador walks toward the secret passage door, followed by his two henchmen. One of the security men has already passed through the door when Landon calls out to them.

"That's it?" Landon challenges.

"Landon…the Ambassador is leaving quietly. I suggest we do the same thing," I say with some chastisement.

"What would you like me to do, Mr. Scott," Ambassador McKay says as he turns around. "You're not going to tell anyone about this. I am, after all, a Unite States Ambassador. No one will believe you. And, I have two security guards who caught you snooping in part of the residential area of the estate. But, if you like, I can have you shot in the knee if you feel that would make our exchange here more gratifying." He nods to the only security guy left. He pulls his gun from the holster under his jacket, cocks it, and shoots at Landon.

"Holy fuck!" Landon yells. I scream and rush to Landon's side. He puts his hand to the side of his head and pulls it away, showing me the blood. I examine the wound immediately and see that the bullet grazed his ear. It'll be sore for a while, but, really, he's fine.

"You should know he missed on purpose. Challenge me again and he'll prove his expert marksmanship to you. Good evening." With that, Ambassador Ronald McKay and his security henchmen leave Landon, my father, and me standing in this barren room.

"I thought I hated you before…" I begin.

"Which one did you give him?" Dad asks.

"What?" I reply.

"Don't play dumb, Ronnie…and don't tell me not to call you that. I knew you wouldn't leave the coin back in Chicago. When I didn't find it in your room I figured you had it on you. I followed you today, hoping to find a good opportunity to get it from you before we got here. But when I saw you walk into Jace's place I knew exactly what you were doing."

"You...know Jace?" I say, stumbling through my words.

"When you deal in antiquities you *have* to know Jace. So...which coin did you give McKay? The real one or the copy you had made today?" My father reaches into his tuxedo jacket and pulls out his own gun. "I really don't want to use this, but I will if I have to."

"You son of bitch. Do you have any idea the damage you've done to this woman? First, not only do you make her think you're dead, but you make her spend her days thinking she left you to die. Then you set her up with Dellinger. You told him the Ambassador had the Nickel and you made him believe that only your set of skills was going to get you in to get it. Of course he'd search for Jenna. You made it clear she was the only one who could do what you did." Landon takes a step forward and my father cocks his gun.

"Don't," my father instructs. He has this look in his eye that, even when I knew he was working for Dellinger all those years ago, I never saw. "I won't hesitate to shoot you, Landon."

"Were you ever the man Mom thought you were?" I ask him. "Or was your entire life together a lie?"

Dad sighs and his eyes now look sad. I fight to feel anything for him because, in essence, the man standing in front of me is not my father. This man...is a stranger.

"I meant it when I said I tried. I don't know if you'll ever know how I tried to create a way out, but...for now...you need to know that I love you, Veronica. And I loved your mother more than words could ever describe. One day you'll understand that being married means you make compromises. There are some things you exchange for other because you want the healthiest relationship possible. Sometimes, though…sometimes, even though you try really hard to make those exchanges, you discover that you weren't made that way. That, as hard as you try, you can't change. Good, bad, or ugly, you're born to be who you are. You don't like it, but sometimes who you are hurts people, so you hide yourself away and pretend to be someone you're not. I hid so much, especially when your mother was sick, but my life with your mother was never a lie. I was who she needed me to be when she needed that guy.

"I know that your life is better without me. You're right to pretend I'm dead, because, inside…I am. So, I'm just going to take the Nickel and disappear. I have a buyer for it that will pay me ten times what McKay did or what Dellinger would. It'll set me up so I can completely drop off the face of the earth."

"You know if you take the Nickel and disappear Dellinger is going to make me work for him. He'll force my hand. He's already forced me to be here by threatening the people I love most in this world. He knows I have all your skills and he's going to send me after every other item for his collection while he searches for you and that damn coin. But…you don't care." Tears are stinging my eyes and I feel a dark sadness fill me in the pits of my soul. It's the same feeling I had when I would cry myself to sleep at night thinking that my father was dead. Mourning. That's what it is. I'm mourning the death of my father all over again.

"Just…just give me the Nickel, Landon. I really don't want to hurt you, but I'll do it if I have to." My father has literally shaken his head to rid himself of the emotions welling up inside him. He knows what he's doing is breaking me, but he still stands there pointing his gun at Landon. "Maybe you need a little incentive," he says as he turns the gun to me.

"Stop…ok…ok," Landon says. He reaches into his pocket and pulls out the small, black velvet pouch carrying the real 1913 V Nickel.

"He's not going to hurt me, Landon. Don't give it to him," I say.

"I can't take that chance," he says. Before I can stop him, he's tossing the pouch to my father who catches it in his free hand. "McKay's coin is fake."

"I'm sorry it had to end this way, Veronica. Despite what you may be feeling right now, I do love you." My father stares at me for a moment. "Even though it was only for a short while, I did love looking into your mother's eyes."

Stunned, I watch my father pass through the secret passage doorway and out of my life forever. I'm silent. I have nothing to say. I have no idea how to tell Dellinger that I don't have the coin, and it won't make a difference for me to tell him the truth about my father scamming me for it. The best I can hope for is convincing Dellinger to hold off on calling me into his indebted service until Demi's baby is born.

I let Landon hold my hand as we walk back through the house and to the front of the estate where there seem to be two dozen drivers waiting to take their passengers on a return ride to wherever they came from. We situate ourselves in the back seat and I even allow myself to rest my head on Landon's shoulder.

"We need to talk, Jenna," he begins.

"No."

"No?"

"No."

That is all I have to say. Now that this is over, and the beginning of my end is drawing closer, I won't be able to emotionally handle being with Landon for much longer. I can't drag things out after we get back to Chicago and am certain of what I must do. It will involve lies and deceit, and most of all, the breaking of Landon's hopelessly devoted heart.

Landon tries several more times to talk with me about what happened tonight, but I shut him down every time. There's nothing to talk about. There's no need to rehash or decompress or strategize.

I lie in bed next to him, unable to fall asleep, wondering if he's asleep or if he's given in to my silence. My future has been decided. Without the last V Nickel to bargain with, Dellinger is sure to send me on the same mission he did my father. He'll hunt and track down whoever my father sells the coin to and I'll spend the next undetermined number of years trying to steal back what I once held in my hand. Along the way, Dellinger will use me to add to his collection things that were at one time just out of his grasp.

The only way for me to avoid this certain future is to disappear. To get as far away from Mercy and Spring, and Demi and Jack and their sweet baby as I can, and to somehow get away from the one person who was able to find me. To say goodbye and not return until Henry Dellinger is dead.

Insomnia has convinced me of my only logical step at this point. I get dressed and pack my things as silently as possible. Landon is definitely asleep because he would never let me pack up and leave like this. The front desk supplies me with a sheet of hotel stationary and an envelope when I reach them 30 minutes later. I begin writing a letter to Landon, sure it's the only way to get out everything I need to say. If I tried to talk with him, he'd only interrupt and convince me that I had other options when the reality is that I don't.

Dear Landon,

By the time you read this it'll be morning and I will have been gone for hours. I'm most likely wandering the Paris airport waiting to get on the next flight home.

The first thing you need to know is that I am hopelessly in love with you, and that is why we can't be together. With the last V Nickel out of my hands, Dellinger will track down the person my father is selling it to, and use me to get it back. I can't live that way, so I have to disappear. If I stay, he'll continue to threaten everyone I love, adding you to those already on that list. I love you too much to put you in that kind of danger.

So...please...do not come back to Chicago. And don't come looking
for me. Spend your time and energy looking for your mom. You need her
more than you need me.

I'm sorry for leaving this way. If I knew of any other way to keep
Dellinger at bay and keep you and everyone else safe, I would do it. It
has to be this way.

I love you.

Jenna

I ask the front desk to deliver the letter by sliding it under the door in an
hour. It's three in the morning, so by the time Landon wakes and finds the
letter, I'll be long gone. I may even be sitting on a plane.

The concierge calls a cab for me and I'm at the airport by 4:00 am. The
next flight to JFK leaves at 7:00 am. I breathe a sad sigh of relief knowing
that there's no way Landon will make it to the airport in time to try and stop
me. Although I anticipate the texts and emails I'll have waiting for me once
I'm back in the States and my cell service resumes.

I stop for coffee and a pastry at one of the airport food stands and sit. I
have a while before my flight so I take my time drinking my coffee and
eating my croissant, thinking back to the day Landon and I decided was our
actual first date. I remember how nervous I was when I saw him sitting at
the café tables outside the coffee shop downstairs from my apartment.

Why would you get a croissant today, Jenna? I scold myself. *Are you a*
glutton for punishment?

I shake my head and force myself to move on to more practical thoughts,
like where I'm going to go and how I'm going to get there. Maybe I can
contact Oz. He'll understand me needing to vanish again and can maybe
connect me with the guy who created my Jenna Rockwell identity. I have
plenty of money, so I can pay him whatever it costs. I used part of the
money Oz gave me for school, but I haven't touched the rest of it at all. It's

been sitting in an investment account for six years and has done pretty well.

My flight is called and I gather my carry on and sling my purse across my body as I make my way through the food court to my nearby gate. I've got about 700 Euros left but have no desire to go to a US bank and have it exchanged. It's Dellinger's money and I don't want any more of it.

I notice a young woman who appears to be traveling with three small children all by herself. I saw her come into the food court earlier and there hasn't been anyone else with them. She bought them some breakfast, but it looks like they're all sharing one muffin and two bottles of orange juice. I don't know if she's just thrifty or if she scrimped and saved for whatever flight they're about to take, but I decide that she would find this money more helpful than I would.

When I approach, I hear here speaking French to the children, who all respond to her in French as well. I pull the folded Euro bills from my purse and extend my hand to the woman. She looks up at me, confused by what I'm doing. I gesture the bills to her again and she slowly reaches up and takes them from my hand. Smiling at her and her beautiful children, I walk toward my gate. A few moments later, when I'm approaching my gate which is next to the food court, I hear the woman calling after me.

"M'dame! M'dame!" she shouts. She must have counted the bills and realized how much money I just gave her. Before I turn behind the wall that separates the boarding area and the food court, I look and see her huddled with her children. She shows them the money and seems to be laughing and crying at the same time.

It's good to know that Dellinger's money was good for something other than buying a pretty dress and some kick ass shoes.

The flight to JFK is four hours longer than the flight to Paris. It's interesting how, even though the plane is flying 500 miles an hour, how the rotation of the earth can still add so much time.

It's 2:00 am when the cab from the airport drops me off at my apartment.

FIVE

I've only been gone three days, but it seems like so much longer. I unlock the door and slide my body into the apartment as quietly as possible. Leaving my suitcase next to the couch, I pull a chair out and find the camera Dellinger had placed to show me how close he could get to me. I do the same in my room and the kitchen. I'll have to get to Spring's room later. He would have just replaced them if I had taken them out before I went to Paris. I figure he needed to know that I believed him when he threatened my friends, and I was far too concerned with how I was going to pull this off anyway. I'll have to find a way to get the one out of Mercy's apartment somehow. Once I leave town and cut everyone off, he won't be able to use my friends as leverage against me and won't have any reason to monitor them.

I go straight to my room and change into a t-shirt and sleep shorts before climbing into bed. I may have just spent three nights at the Shangri La Hotel in Paris, but there is nothing like your own bed. I tried to sleep on the plane, but I just couldn't turn my mind off. Now that I'm in my own bed, I'm hoping sleep comes quickly. Dellinger is going to contact me any day now and I need a clear mind.

"Jenna?" Spring lightly knocks on the door and opens it. "I thought I heard you come in. How was Paris?"

I don't answer. I've been thinking about how I'm going to leave my friends, my family...strategizing for when and where. But, seeing Spring standing here in my room, I realize how excruciatingly painful it's going to be.

The tears come and come quickly without warning. I've broken down, sobbing and unable to form any words. I cried for weeks after I left my father in DC, but this is actually going to be so much harder.

"Oh, Jenna!" Spring rushes to me and lies on the bed, curling up next to me and letting me soak her t-shirt with my tears. "It's ok. It's going to be ok," she says. She doesn't ask me what happened, or even where Landon is.

207

She may be making her own conclusions about what happened in Paris, but she's not offering them now. And, knowing Spring, she won't.

Spring lies there with me until I've cried all I can cry and I finally fall asleep.

And then I sleep.

And sleep.

And sleep.

It's 9:00 pm when I finally wake. There are voices in the living room. Good voices. Voices of people I love.

"Hey guys," I say quietly as I emerge from the hall.

"Oh, my God! You're alive!" Mercy jumps up from the couch and runs to me, throwing her arms and pint size body around me while Demi, Jack, Spring, and Jerry look on.

"I was only gone for three days," I say.

"It was a really long three days," she says, as she hugs me fiercely.

"Do you want to talk about what happened? We know you told her not to tell, but Spring told us about the proposal and Paris." Mercy says.

"No. And I don't want anyone to say anything bad about Landon. I need you all to trust me when I say he didn't do anything wrong, and that us not being together anymore was my decision. Ok?" I tell them.

"What if he shows up here?" Jerry asks like the protective friend he is.

"I doubt he'll do that, but, if he does, I'll deal with it," I tell them. I walk to where Demi is standing and hug her, partly because I just need to hug her, and partly because I need to apologize to her for walking away when she needed me. I don't know if she's told Jack yet, and I don't want my apology to be the catalyst to that conversation.

"I'm so sorry," I whisper to her. "I'm so sorry I left when you needed me the most."

"It's ok, Jenna," she whispers back. "I found out that I was stronger than I gave myself credit. I told him on my own." I pull back and look at her face to gauge how well that conversation went.

"We're getting married," she tells me with a huge smile.

"Oh, Demi! That's so wonderful" I hug her again before I wrap my arms around Jack's neck. "You better be good to them!"

"Don't worry!" he laughs.

"When? What's the plan?" I ask. It feels good to get out of my own head and back into the lives of my friends, even if for just a little while.

"Well...don't freak, but...three weeks." Demi covers her face with her hands and peaks out at me through her fingers.

"Oh, my gosh! That's so fast!"

"I know, but I won't be showing too much, and I didn't want to have to get some maternity wedding dress, and I was definitely not going to have a baby on my hip either," she says smiling.

"Jerry's going to let us have the wedding at Duke's, so we also thought maybe bringing a baby to a bar wouldn't be the best way to start parenthood," Jack laughs.

"Are you sure you're ready for this?" I say to Jack. He's never been one to focus on others before himself in the way you have to when you're married or a parent. It's one of the things that worried Demi the most when she found out she was pregnant.

"Is anyone ever ready for marriage or parenthood?" he answers. "All I know is that when Demi said she could do this on her own if I didn't want to be a part of her or the baby's life, I suddenly couldn't fathom *not* being a part of her life. In an instant I knew that I had something I would be crazy to let go."

"That...that is the rightest answer I have ever heard to any question...ever." I smile, so happy that Jack and Demi are moving forward and tackling this new adventure together. And, while I'm so incredibly happy for them, it makes me sad to know that there's no way Landon and I could face the treacherous road I'm about to travel, together.

Chapter 17

It's midnight when I close the door behind my dearest friends who came to see me in my time of crisis. Staying home from work to nurse my broken heart, Spring called everyone sometime after lunch and they all came running, taking the rest of their day off work to be there for me whenever I woke up. It felt good to see their faces and feel their warmth. It took some convincing to get Jerry to agree not to kill Landon should he ever show up here, but it was nice knowing that he has my back.

Mercy pulled me aside and asked what had happened in Paris. I just told her that when Landon and I got there, and I couldn't go through with getting married, he was hurt and said that it was a mistake to be so spontaneous. That maybe now wasn't the right time for us. I told her I agreed and we decided to go our separate ways.

I couldn't tell her the truth. I know that she would worry and want to try and fix things. She would be impetuous and try to out Dellinger in some way, and that would only mean more backlash from him. No, I had to stick with a story that connected to the cover Spring gave her. It's for the best.

When I wake the next morning, all I can think about is the dance studio. It's been just over a week since that crazy crack head stabbed me. I won't be able to do everything, but I really need to dance right now. And just being around Carina and Marco, watching them dance…it's like therapy. So, I throw my hair into a ponytail, put my dance clothes on, and walk downstairs.

There's a Latin class in progress when I walk in. I hadn't paid attention to the time and only now realize that I'm terribly late.

"Mi amor!" Marco shouts when he turns around and sees me. "We have missed you so much!" He stops the class and rushes to me, hugging me tightly.

"I've missed you, too, Marco," I tell him.

"Where have you been?" Carina asks, making Marco move so she can hug me too.

"Well, there was this crazy woman who came into the hospital early last week. She kind of stabbed me," I tell them.

"No! Oh, my God, are you ok?" Carina asks. Her eyes are wide and I can see that she's very concerned about me.

"It sounds much worse than it is. The wound wasn't too deep, but it did knick some muscle. I laid off it for 24-hours, and it's been healing fine since. It's still a little sore, so just don't make me dance with Marco," I tell Carina, trying to calm her.

"If you say so," she says. Marco kisses my cheek and excuses himself to continue the class. "So…are you still seeing Landon?" Carina raises her eyebrows in anticipation of a wonderfully juicy story about how Landon and I are madly in love and are going to spend the rest of our lives together. Only the first part of that is true, but I can't tell her that and explain why the second half of that statement is never going to happen.

"Well…he has to travel constantly for work, and I have obligations here…it'd be great if it could work out, but it just isn't going to happen." I give her a sad smile and hope she reads it as me just being disappointed and doesn't see that I'm absolutely devastated at the reality of how things have played out.

"In due time," she says. "In due time you will have the love your heart longs for." She doesn't say anything else, which is strange for Carina. In the past she's been more than vocal about my love life. When I haven't connected with someone she's set me up with, she's been quick to move on to the next guy in her attempts to fill my life with love. For her to leave it as she has is new.

I move to the back of the room and spend the rest of the class moving my body to the musical therapy and let the stress and anxiety sweat out as much as possible. I don't move like I normally do when I let the beat and soul of the music consume me and I would dance almost involuntarily. It's a successful session, though, as I feel a bit lighter. With all that is weighing me down, even the smallest amount of relief is more than welcome.

Spring meets me at the door as I hobble into the apartment. "What are you doing home?" I ask her.

"I'm taking a few days off. I wanted to be here for you," she says. She helps me to the couch, putting a pillow under my knee to make my sore leg more comfortable. "Had I been awake when you were leaving I would have told you not to go to dance today. It's still too early, Jenna. But, it looks like you figured that out on your own, huh."

"I had to go, Spring. I'm so full of tension and anxiety...it was the only thing I know that would relieve some of that," I tell her.

"Why didn't you tell Mercy what you told me before you left for Paris?" she asks, sitting on the coffee table and facing me. I shake my head in an effort to keep the thoughts of Paris out of my head, but it doesn't work.

"I knew she would react protectively, emotionally," I say. "Not that I thought you wouldn't want to protect me...it's just...I knew you'd be rational about it, whereas Mercy's first instinct is to go all mother bear. She takes a long time to get to rational thought, and I didn't have that kind of time. Was she as upset as I think she was?"

"Do you think she was pissed beyond measure because she thought you had run off to get married in Paris without your best friends there?" I nod at her sarcastic question. "Then, yes."

"Well, it's all over now, so I guess it doesn't matter."

"So...now that you're back, and still alive, you have to fill in the blanks. You promised you'd tell me everything when you got back." Spring puts her elbows on her knees and rests her chin on her fists, ready to hear my story.

I take a deep breath, calming myself. I suppose, now that things are the way they are, it won't hurt to tell her the truth of my past, so I begin.

"When I was 19 I left my father under a tree in Washington, DC to die. I thought he had been shot by a very powerful man, a Senator, who he had been coerced into working for. And by working for, I mean he was paid to steal antique and heirloom collectables. My father has a very special set of skills that enables him to break into some unbreakable places almost completely undetected." I pause for a moment and raise my eyebrows at Spring to ensure she's following me.

"Go on," she says.

"My father taught me these special skills when I was younger. I had been curious when he would be in his work room…practicing…and he took that as his cue that perhaps I could be as skillful as him. He was right. I took to it. Well, because my father had bragged to the Senator that he taught me everything he knew, and that I was a chip off the old block, my father made arrangements for me to leave DC and start a new life with a new name. He told me that he had ratted out the Senator and that he'd be coming after me to fill my father's shoes."

"What was your name before?" Spring asks. She moves a pillow to the floor and makes herself more comfortable.

"Veronica Matthews," I smile softly.

"I like it. But, I like Jenna Rockwell better." She pats my leg and smiles back at me.

"I like Jenna Rockwell better, too."

"So where does Landon come in?"

"The Senator told Landon that I was his estranged daughter. That we had a falling out and he wanted me found so we could make amends. He showed Landon things I had left in my home the night I essentially escaped. My laptop, pictures of me, dance medals…things a father would have of his daughter's. So, Landon did his job and found me," I tell her. It's hard talking about Landon. I've got to work toward forgetting about him somehow, and this is not helping.

"And Paris?"

"There's a particular thing that the Senator has been after for years, a rare coin. Later, when I knew about my father working for this man, Dad would tell me about leads he had on where this coin was. So, with my father gone, the Senator wanted me to follow the lead in Paris and get it for him. There ended up being two problems with this."

"Only two?" Spring jokes and we both give a light laugh.

"Well, only two to start with. First, I'd already had the coin for eight years. My father discovered it during one of his other jobs and gave it to me for safe keeping. We thought we might need to use it one day as leverage. Second, it turned out that my father wasn't dead. He set me up to bring the coin to Paris so he could get it from me and sell it to someone who would pay him much more than he would have gotten from the Senator…and then he disappeared. My father left me to come home to the Senator empty-handed. So now the Senator is going to track the coin down and send me after it," I explain.

"Why can't you just tell him that you're not going to do it? Or, why don't you threaten to tell the authorities?" She asks.

"Because he threatened the people I love. He threatened you and Mercy directly. I couldn't live with myself if anything ever happened to you, especially if it was because of me." I feel tears filling my eyes and will them to stop. I've cried enough, and no amount of tears is going to change the situation.

"Jenna, he's not going to hurt us. He's just trying to scare you, manipulate you in doing his dirty work," she says, taking my hand in hers.

"You're right. He's not going to hurt you or anyone I love. I was going to wait until Demi has the baby, but since she and Jack are getting married in a few weeks…I'm leaving Chicago."

"What do you mean you're leaving Chicago? You can't leave! Where will you go? What are you going to do?" Spring sits up straight, shocked by my statement.

"It's for the best, Spring. If I'm not here then he can't use you and the others to manipulate me. He knows I'll do whatever I have to do to keep you all safe." I move the pillow out from under my leg and shift my body so I can get up. Spring sits up on her knees and blocks me.

"You aren't going anywhere, Jenna. I think you need to be patient and see what happens. You don't know for a fact that the Senator is going to come after you," she says with bright, hopeful eyes.

Oh, Spring...always so optimistic, even in the most hopeless of situations.

"Promise me you won't say anything to the others about any of this...even after I leave," I say as we stand, choosing not to respond to her hopefulness. She looks at me, unsure of how to respond. Spring wants to be supportive, but she knows that by doing so she'll have to lie to our friends. That's not easy for her to do. "Promise me."

"Ok," she says reluctantly. "But I still think it's going work out." I take Spring in my arms and hold her close. I know that, no matter where I go, what lie of a life I live anywhere else, I'll never have another friend like her.

*****

As suspected, my boss was extremely disappointed that my fairytale, happily-ever-after wedding did not take place. I explained the same story to her as I did the others and she completely understood. I told her that my plan was to throw myself into my work and try to forget about him as best I could. So I suppose I've given myself another apologetic letter to write when I drop off the face of the earth.

Thankfully it's been an uneventful first night back to work. Everyone's meds are in stock and have been delivered as needed, and I don't have any comatose patients on the brink of death. Mercy has avoided talking about

Landon and Paris at all. I can see she's working hard to not verbally murder him, which is helpful. I don't think I'm ready for any conversation about him...or that I ever will be.

"I feel like you're keeping something from me," Mercy says quietly as she sits next to me at the nurse's station.

"I'm sorry. It probably just seems that way since I'm not really interested in talking about what happened in Paris. I don't mean to make you feel like I'm keeping something from you," I tell her. I look down and fidget with the pen in my hand. The absolute worst part about this whole thing isn't the fact that I'll be abandoning the people I love, but that every moment until that day, I will tell lie after lie to them.

"I just want you to be ok. I understand why you didn't tell me about going to Paris yourself. I suppose you knew I would have gone crazy, which is what I did when Spring told me. It was just so unlike you to do something like that. I mean, you went from being a serial dater to falling in love with Landon. It all happened so fast. I guess I was taken off guard by it."

"I was taken off guard, too. I never expected to fall in love with Landon...certainly not so quickly. But, don't worry. Landon and me...we're definitely done," I say. I begin to flip through the charts in front of me, intent on moving on from this conversation.

"That's just it. I don't know what happened in Paris, but I think you're walking away too quickly here. Yes, at first I was really pissed that you were in Paris to get married without me. But the more I ranted to Jerry, the more he reminded me of all the times I told him how much I wish you would find someone who would make you happy. How I wanted you to find the kind of greatness he and I have. And I couldn't deny that when I looked at you and Landon together, I saw that you had found everything I had ever hoped you'd find." Mercy puts her hand down on the files I'm still flipping through, forcing me to look up at her. "So what, you couldn't go through with an impetuous move like getting married in Paris on a moment's notice.

You love him, and he's insanely in love with you. Don't push him away because you're scared. You'll regret it for the rest of your life."

I spend the rest of my shift grateful that all of my patients are sleeping through the night without incident. Mercy and I don't really talk, and since none of the other girls ask me about it, I'm sure Mercy has told them that Paris was a disaster.

The train ride home is as crappy as they come. Usually rush hour passengers don't bother me, but the guy talking loudly on his douchebag ear piece this morning made me want to punch him in the throat. I still haven't heard from Dellinger and it's making me on edge. I can only imagine he's discovered that Dad has taken off and is working to track him, and the coin, down. He'll send me after the coin…and someone dangerous after Dad.

I round the corner and eye the bakery. I consider going inside for my favorite croissants, but I can't. The thought is just a sad domino effect of reminding me of Landon and Paris and all that I'm giving up.

Adjusting my bag on my shoulder I continue walking toward the entrance to my building. All I want to do is get upstairs and crawl into bed. I take four steps past the bakery and that's when I see him, sitting there just like he did the morning I knew my life would never be the same.

"Jenna," Landon says as he stands, shoving his hands in his pockets.

"Why are you here, Landon?" I try not to look into his eyes, but it's nearly impossible to resist them. It's nearly impossible to resist Landon, period.

"It took me a while to pick myself up off the floor after I read your letter. It's a pretty shitty way to break up with someone. Add the fact that we were in Paris, France, and it rises in competition with breaking up via text message," he says.

"Landon…" I try.

"I'm not done." He takes in a deep breath and pulls his hands out of his pocket. "I don't care. I know you're only saying goodbye because you think you have to. The truth is, you don't. If you really believe you have to run, then I'm coming with you." Landon takes the back of my neck in his hand and presses our foreheads together. "I love you, Jenna, and I'm not letting you go."

"I can't ask you to do that," I say. "I won't let you do that. You still haven't found your mother. You can't abandon your search for her just to follow me to God knows where. And I can't guarantee that Dellinger isn't going to find a new you to find me." The idea of Landon giving up looking for his mother is heartbreaking.

"You're not asking me. I'm telling you. And, the truth is, if my mom wanted me to find her, she would have made sure I could. I have to let her go…because I think that's what she wanted. She wanted me to stop taking care of her. She wanted me to have a better life than what we had with my father. I have that better life with you," he tells me. My chest tightens as Landon talks about his mom. I can see that this conclusion is still painful for him.

"It won't be some romantic adventure, Landon. It'll be a life of constant lies and deception…so much that we'll forget what we've even told ourselves. That was my life for the first two years of being here in Chicago. I may have to live that life again, but I won't let you. I love you, too, and that's why I'm doing this alone." I force my body to pull away from Landon's and walk toward the door to my building.

Landon grabs my arm as I start to move past him. "I found you when it was just my job. How much harder do you think I'm going to work to find you again now that I'm in love with you? Let me help you. Let me take care of you."

"You can't just swoop in here like you're going to rescue me. Until you fell for Dellinger's lies and found me, I was doing just fine taking care of myself." I jerk my arm away from him, trying a new approach to getting rid of him: bitch. Being honest about wanting to keep him safe obviously isn't working. He's clearly going to have to hate me in order to walk away. "Your own mom doesn't even want you coming after her because she's tired of you thinking it's your job to take care of her. Get the clue, Landon. She doesn't need you to save her and neither do I!"

I leave Landon standing on the sidewalk, stunned and clutching his gut from my hurtful and insensitive words, and walk into my building. Saying those words to him were harder than writing him the letter in France. I hate that being so awful to him was the only option I had, the only card I had left. I push the button for the elevator because I just don't have the strength to walk up four floors today. I step inside and drop my bag on the floor as I lean my physically and emotionally weary body against the back wall of the elevator. The doors close in front of me and I realize that the only thing left to do now is let the tears fall.

Chapter 18

It's been a week, and still no word from Dellinger. I have a feeling he's waiting until he's tracked my father down, along with whoever he sold the V Nickel to, before he contacts me. He'll probably just send one of his thugs to come get me. That makes me think I should I go ahead and write the letters I want to write to Spring, Mercy, and Demi and have them ready. I don't think that Dellinger is going to allow time for me to leave any kind of proper goodbye.

Spring still calls or texts me a few times a day to make sure I'm still here and to make sure I'm doing ok. It's also been a week without any word from Landon, which is what I wanted. My approach of hurting him has apparently worked and he's walked away, just like he needed to do. He'll get completely over me, and someday I'll get over him, and we'll both be the better for it. I shake my head to rid myself of thoughts of Landon. It's hard to do, but in time it will become easier.

Now seems as good a time as any to start sorting through my things. It won't be much longer before Dellinger puts me to work and I figure I should have a bag packed and ready to go. It's going to start getting cold here in Chicago in the next month or so, and unless he's sending me to Australia, I guess I should pack jeans and pants. I grab a few pairs from the closet and throw them into the oversized duffel bag Oz gave me when we left DC. I never got rid of it because I was sure I'd be using it again one day to pack as many of my belongings as possible before I skipped town again.

I pull some long-sleeved shirts from the top of my closet where I keep seasonal clothes and toss them in the bag. When I open my dresser drawer to pull out essentials like pajamas I'm jolted by the two t-shirts of my father's that I've had all these years to keep him close to me. I look at them for a long time before I take them out and throw them away. Those were the shirts of a man I loved dearly and wanted to keep with me forever. The problem is I found out that man never existed.

I slide the bottom drawer of the dresser open and pull out its contents so I can remove the false bottom and take out the box that's been hidden in there for six years.

"Oh, Mom," I say quietly as I trace my finger over the picture of her and Dad. "Did you know? Did you know he was lying? Did you know what he was doing when he left you so sick all those times? Did you know he hadn't changed, and loved him anyway?"

Opening her locket I fight the urge to rip out the picture of my father. I hate the idea of closing it and leaving my little girl picture to stare at his lying face for all eternity. But…I leave it, believing whether she knew my father deceived her all those years or not, in this locket were the pictures of the people she loved more than her own life. And even if it was for just a short time, there were years when my father did try to be the man my mother knew he could be. I suppose, if I'm going to give him anything, I can give him that.

A knock at the door diverts my attention. I pull the long chain over my neck and let the locket hang. Wearing it brings a small smile to my face and makes me feel a little lighter.

"Thanks, Mom," I whisper.

Opening the door I'm greeted with a huge bouquet of flowers. For a moment I think that it's Landon and I'm immediately unsure about how I feel. But, within a moment, Jerry's face is revealed when he lowers vase.

"Oh, my gosh, Jerry…they're beautiful, but really unnecessary," I say, opening the door wider to let him in.

"They're not from me. They were sitting here when I walked up." He sets the vase full of flowers on the table. "There's a card."

My stomach flutters with both excitement and nervousness thinking that the flowers must be from Landon. He hasn't given up on me after all. The flowers are a beautiful gesture and I love them, but it also continues to make this difficult. He's supposed to think I'm a total bitch for saying what I said to him, not forgiving me and sending me flowers. How am I supposed to get over him when he's being so...so...so *Landon*!

"Oh, well...thanks for bringing them in. I'll check the card later," I tell him. "What's up? Mercy isn't here."

"I'm not looking for Mercy. I came to ask a favor." Jerry looks down shyly and actually shuffles his feet like an embarrassed schoolboy.

"What is it?" I can't help smiling at this buff guy standing in front of me, red-faced like I just caught him with his hand in the cookie jar.

"Well...when I told Mercy that you wanted me to get Sharper Image to play at the reception, Mercy told me to make sure I had them play slow songs too so everyone can dance, and, you know...so Demi and Jack can have an official first dance and all. She said it'd be romantic. She said, and I quote, *girls love that shit*."

"Yeah, that sounds like Mercy," I chuckle. "So what's the favor?"

"Can you teach me how to dance more than just swaying from side to side? This is the first semi-fancy thing Mercy and I have ever done together and I really want her to have all that romantic stuff. Will you help me?" Jerry looks at me with hopeful, puppy dog eyes and there's no way I can say no.

"Of course I'll help you! She's right: we do love that romantic shit." We both laugh and the tension in Jerry's body relaxes. "I've got the perfect thing to start you off," I begin. I walk toward the sound system by the TV but Jerry stops me.

"I can't start today," he says.

"Oh, um...ok."

"It's just...It's after 5:00 and I'm on my way to the bar. Mercy is coming by soon. We'll need to do it on a day when she's working and you're not. I really want to surprise her." I can see the look of anticipation in Jerry's face and it makes me really happy for them both.

"Sure. We've got two days next week like that. Do you think that's enough?" I ask.

"With you teaching me, I'm sure it's more than plenty. Thanks, Jenna." Jerry envelops me in his huge arms. I sigh for a moment, enjoying the embrace of my dear, sweet Jerry. I'm going to miss him.

"So it sounds like you're in pretty deep here," I suggest.

"Yeah. I'm pretty crazy about her, which is putting it mildly," he smiles.

"Any wedding bells in *your* future?"

"We've talked about it, but, Mercy's not in any rush." Jerry clears his throat and looks down for a moment before catching my eyes. "I'm guessing the flowers are from Landon."

"Me, too." I sigh and look at the gorgeous bouquet sitting on my dining table.

"I don't know what happened in Paris, but I do know that guy loves you more than I've ever seen anyone love another person." There's a softness in Jerry's eyes and his voice that I've never seen before. For a tough guy like him to say something so sweet… If only I could change the way things are. If only I could explain to Jerry why things have to be the way they are.

"Jerry…things just have to be this way," I tell him.

"Well…give it time. Maybe you'll see that they don't."

With that, Jerry gives me another hug and kisses me on the cheek before leaving. I try to restrain myself, but as soon as I've closed the door behind him I rush to the dining table and find the card hidden among the flowers. I tear open the 3 x 3 card and my heart stops.

Disappointed you failed your first assignment.
7 pm, Thursday at Fronterra for your next.
HD

And there it is. I have two days before I find out when I'll be saying goodbye to everyone I love. I'll have to stand my ground and tell Dellinger that I'm not leaving until after the wedding on Sunday. After that, I'll disappear, never to be seen or heard from again.

It's strange. Now that Dellinger has contacted me, the anxiety I've been feeling is gone. The not knowing was killing me, but now I can really formulate a plan. I'll go back to Paris and find Jace. Once I get there I'll have to use cash for everything so Dellinger can't track me. I'll have to be quick though. My father said that everyone who deals in antiquities knows Jace. I'm sure Dellinger will waste no time in concluding that I might contact him.

I'm going to need a new identity with new documentation for every aspect of my life. Birth certificate, social security card, driver's license. And I'll need identification with connections to various countries. I'm going to need a lot, so I'll have to make it worth Jace's while, especially because he's going to have to promise not to tell Landon anything. It must have been fate for Landon to follow me to Paris. If he hadn't, I would never have met Jace.

There's another knock at the door. Maybe Jerry changed his mind and wants to squeeze in a little dance lesson before he meets up with Mercy today.

I open the door and a wave of shock rushes through me.

"Oz! Oh, my God! Oz!" I scream and throw my body into his huge arms. I won't let go so he has to walk into the apartment with me hanging off him like a monkey.

"It's good to see you, too, Angel," he says as he puts me down.

"What are you doing here?" I ask, wiping the tears of joy that filled my eyes.

"I heard you were in need of some help," he answers.

"What? From who? Did my father contact you?" I'm stunned and confused and filled with elation all at the same time. Oz is here and something about that makes me feel like I'm going to be ok.

"I did," Spring says, walking through the still open door.

"So you contacted Oz when I was in Paris?" I feel my face squish together, trying to get my mind to make sense of what's going on.

"Yes, but not because you gave me his information. Once it was official that you and I were going to live together, this big teddy bear told me to call him if I ever thought you were in trouble. Didn't you, Uncle Oz?" Spring explains.

"Uncle?"

"Yep. Spring here is my sister Ester's daughter. When you said you wanted to move to Chicago, I knew I could keep an eye on you. I don't know what I would have done if you had chosen to go anywhere else," Oz says. He puts his arm around Spring and draws her to his side. "I hadn't heard a peep from her about you in six years, so when she called, I knew it had to be bad."

"I wanted to tell you he was my uncle, but he wouldn't let me. I was sworn to secrecy. But, when you came to me before you went to Paris, I knew I had to call him," she tells me.

"Wait. Did you ask if your father had contacted me?" Oz asks, confused.

"I didn't tell him anything after that first conversation we had. I figured you'd want to tell him," Spring says. "I'm going to make dinner. You two talk." Spring kisses Oz on the cheek and gives me a hug before she leaves Oz and me in the living room.

"Is your father alive?" Oz asks as we sit on the couch.

"Yes."

"That son of a bitch. Did Dellinger make him do it?" Oz is shaking his head with disappointment.

"Yes and no," I say. I spend the next 15 minutes telling Oz everything that's transpired over the last couple of months. I tell him about Landon and how Dellinger used him to find me. I also scold him over not letting me bring my laptop with me since that turned out to be the main source of the information Landon used to track me.

I explain what happened in France and how, knowing I would bring the V Nickel with me, my father set me up so Dellinger would find me and send me to Paris.

I also tell him about falling in love with Landon and how I have to say goodbye to him because Dellinger is going to use me the same way he used my father, but that I'll be dropping off the face of the earth rather than giving in to that slimy politician's control.

"I can't say I'm completely surprised by Bobby's choices. Your dad tried really hard for a long time to leave the past in the past. He just couldn't, I guess. That's what all the bragging was about. He couldn't stand the idea of hiding his *talent* from the world." Oz sighs and smiles softly at me. "I'm sorry you went through all of that, Angel. And I'm sorry that you've been alone all these years."

"Thanks, but, I haven't been completely alone. Set up, or not, Spring has become one of my best friends in the whole world, along with Mercy and Demi, and Jack and Jerry," I say happily. "They became my family...which is why I have to leave. Dellinger has already threatened them. If I even try to refuse him, he'll come after them.

"Maybe not. That's why I'm here." Oz pulls a folded over, large manila envelope from inside his jacket and hands it to me.

"Is this the other envelope you took from the house the night we left DC?" I ask.

"Yes. The important things you need to know *now* are in *here*," he says, echoing his words to me the night we sat at Paulina's table and ate meat loaf as we discussed the new life I was going to build in Chicago.

I unclasp the envelope and pull a small stack of papers from the pocket. It's all hand-written on loose leaf paper. The first pages contain names and dates, along with notes about someone named Ken Cooper with Bouche and

Renner.

"What's Bouche and Renner?" I ask.

"They're a private insurance company. They insure rare items...like antiques. They are the *only* insurance agency to have offices in every civilized country in the world," Oz answers.

"And who is Ken Cooper?"

"Ken Cooper is the Bouche and Renner agent that Dellinger has had under his thumb for almost 20 years."

I flip through the papers some more and find another few pages with columns titled "Old ID" and "New ID" followed by a column titled "Item."

"I'm sorry, Oz. What are you trying to tell me? I don't understand what any of this means," I say. I'm trying to find the meaning in it all but keep coming up clueless.

"I'm trying to tell you that at least for the first little while, your father really *didn't* want to work for Dellinger. And neither did Ken Cooper. So, your father struck up an agreement with Ken. They would keep track of all the old insurance ID numbers for the things your father stole for Dellinger, and connect them to the new ID numbers Ken was creating so Dellinger could have his newly acquired artifacts insured.

"Ken knew that if anything ever happened, he would go down for fraud and spend a long time in prison. He kept the documents as his own insurance, hoping his cooperation would lead to a lesser sentence. Your father always kept his own copy in case he needed something to encourage Dellinger to cut him loose. He must have stopped tracking with Ken when the pay got really good because there's only about 75 pieces here," Oz explains.

He stopped tracking with Ken because that's when he started working for Ambassador McKay. Once he was on McKay's payroll, it didn't matter if he kept anything on Dellinger.

"So Dellinger only had my father steal collectables from people who also had their things insured with Bouche and Renner? I suppose these are the kind of items that one *only* insures with Bouche and Renner," I muse.

"Yeah. Not just the wealthy either. Christie's and all the other auction houses use them, and every museum from the Smithsonian to the Louvre." Oz watches me, waiting for me to reveal what the wheels in my head have been turning and creating.

"That calculated bastard. He would get the inside scoop from this Cooper guy and that's how he knew how to find what he was looking for. And as long as what he wanted was insured by Bouche and Renner, he could find anything in the world. Cooper would find its original registration and change the ID and ownership. Well this is about to get interesting." The corners of my mouth involuntarily rise a little.

"Why is that?"

"Ambassador McKay is going to insure his fake V Nickel, and so is whoever my father sold, is selling, the real V Nickel. Ken Cooper is going to be sweating when he has to tell Dellinger there are *two* entries with Bouche and Renner for what is supposed to be the last of the five V Nickel's Dellinger is searching for." A giddy feeling wells up inside me, finally feeling like I have the upper hand.

"Well...you certainly have grown up," Oz smiles. "Spring tells me you're a nurse and that you've kept up with your dancing."

"I've just tried to live the life my supposedly dying father wanted me to have. As terrible as what he did was, I'm kind of glad. I ended up living in the city of my dreams, with my dream job, and dream friends. And now that I have this, I'm not going to have to leave it all behind," I tell him excitedly.

"Listen now...don't get ahead of yourself, Angel. You still have no idea what Dellinger is willing to do to get what he wants," Oz warns. He's got that stern look on his face that I've actually missed. He used to give me that look when I would try to sneak ingredients off the counter when he was baking. "You could show him this and it mean absolutely nothing to him."

"Well, if the possibility of being the center of an insurance fraud investigation and being dragged through the political mud in the process doesn't do anything, I suppose I could always go back to the Ambassador and tell him what we did. I have a feeling he'd be happy to have me take the forged coin back to Dellinger. McKay would raise a toast every night knowing that Dellinger was holding a totally fake V Nickel." I raise my eyebrows at Oz and smile.

"You got the best parts of your dad, you know that right?" he smiles back at me and pulls me in for a bear hug. Oh, how I've missed him.

"Hey…dinner will be ready in about half an hour. Anyone up for a drink?" Spring holds up a bottle of wine and spreads a smile on her face.

"I am *so* up for a drink!" I tell her as I stand.

"That's going to take some getting used to," Oz says. "You were a 19-year-old kid when I last saw you. You're a grown woman now and I'm not sure I'm ready for this."

"You just need to hang out with me more, Oz. I hope you'll be sticking around for a while." I take a sip of the red wine Spring just poured and decide to let it sit and open up a bit.

"Just long enough to meet Landon and give him the once over to see if he's good enough for you," Oz says with his mock-dad voice.

"You're not going to get to meet him," I say.

"What happened?" Oz asks. Spring looks at me with sadness in her eyes, already knowing the whole store.

"I cut things off with him, totally pushed him away when it seemed I was going to have a life on the run from Dellinger. He wanted to come with me, but I couldn't let him do that. He deserved better than to be stuck living a lie." I check on dinner as a way to avoid the conversation further, but Spring won't have it. She turns my body around and sends me back to the other side of the counter bar.

"Now that you've got the upper hand, why don't you call Landon? Tell him what's happening and that things might not be as desperate as you once thought. He loves you, Jenna. He wants to be with you and would coming running if you called," Springs says.

"I can't do that. I pushed him away, and pushed hard. I said some terrible things to him to make it easier for him to cut himself off from me. He's never going to forgive me," I tell her. I feel the lump that precedes crying form in my throat.

"I don't know a lot about love, Angel, but what I do know is this: when you love someone, you're willing to forgive a lot. I know your mom forgave more than she should have with your dad. When I asked her about it, she said it was because she loved him, and despite his deception, she knew he truly loved her." Oz's eyes are soft as he tells me about my mother. As I got older it was always a difficult subject for me, but it's nice to hear how strong she was, how much she loved my dad.

"She knew he was lying to her? Even when she was really sick from chemo?" There's a pain in my chest and I'm convinced it's because my heart is breaking again for what my father did to her.

"What your mom knew and when she knew it isn't important. What's important is that she loved him and, right or wrong, she overlooked a lot of his indiscretions. He was always faithful to her and provided for the three of you. Those were the things that mattered most to your mom.

"The point I'm trying to make, Angel, is that if your mom was willing to overlook the things your dad did because she loved him, how much more do you think Landon is going to forgive you for what you said? He's not dumb. He knows why you did what you did."

Oz has a way of convincing a person to do anything he wants. He could use his powers for evil, but he doesn't. He only uses them for good, like the night he got me out of DC. Oz said I had five minutes so I made sure I was done in four.

I want to call Landon. I want to tell him what a terrible mistake I made, and how I jumped the gun in pushing him away. I had no idea when Dellinger was going to rear his ugly head and I should have enjoyed as much time with Landon as I could until then. If I had waited, Oz would be here now with the insurance information, I would be preparing to expose Dellinger, and Landon would still be mine.

I let Dellinger get under my skin and scare me into letting go of the only perfect thing that I've ever had. For that, I'm filled with even more rage. Dellinger is going to pay for he did to my family, and to me.

"I guess. But...I can't even think about trying to mend things with Landon until everything with Dellinger is really fixed. I'm meeting him on Thursday night at Fronterra. He thinks he's going to give me my next assignment. I think I'll just nail his ass to the wall."

Chapter 19

"Are you sure you don't want me to come, too?" Spring says nervously as I'm getting ready for my meeting with Dellinger.

"Yes, I'm sure. I'm feeling confident that it's going to go well, but if it doesn't, you have the copies and you know what to do, right?" I tell her.

"Yes, I know what to do. You and Uncle Oz went over it with me about a hundred times," she says, rolling her eyes at me.

We did go over it with her about a hundred times. It's really important that she delivers it to the right person in Washington and that she gets the other copy to the big national news affiliate here in Chicago, too. They'd chomp at the bit to be the first to release a story about a dirty Senator.

"Where's Uncle Oz?" Spring stand and pulls my long hair out from the top I just put on.

"He's meeting me at the restaurant, but staying hidden. Dellinger will have at least one of his lackies with him. Last time he brought muscle and brains. He'll most likely have them both with him this time, too. One to intimidate me and another to disseminate information to me.

Spring looks worried. I can see the lines of stress on her forehead, and she's wringing her hands, something she only does when she's nervous.

"Hey…" I say, taking her by the shoulder. "It's going to be ok. Oz is going to be there, and Dellinger's not going to do anything to me in a public place like that. I made a reservation under his name, so even if he used a fake one when he had the reservation made, his name would be on the books. But none of that matters because he's going to see what I've got on him and he's going to walk away and find someone else, someone in no way connected me, to do his dirty work for him. Ok?"

"I'm just…I just want you to be ok…ok?" she says quietly, trying to keep from crying. Spring likes to cry even less than I do. We're strong woman and if we're even on the verge of tears, you know it's bad. "I don't know what I'd do without you. And I really don't know if I'd be able to keep all this locked up inside me forever."

"You're not going to have to keep anything locked inside forever. Once this is all over, and I mean *all* over, I'll be able to share more of my life with you guys. I won't have so much to hide anymore. Then everyone will understand why I've been so *not me* lately."

I take a deep breath and check myself in the mirror. I don't tell Spring this, but my outfit was completely chosen on how well I'd be able to move and run in it. I've got on black leggings and a green and white tunic top with a pair of black ballet flats with rubber soles. I'm hoping not to have to employ some of the krav maga or other defense techniques I used on the crack head from the hospital, but I should be prepared for anything. Being optimistic doesn't mean you stop being realistic.

"How do I look?" I ask Spring with a smile?

"You look beautiful…and like you could kick ass," she laughs.

"That's the best compliment you've ever given me." I give Spring a long hug and reassure her that it's all going to work out just fine. I also remind her that Oz will be nearby and he won't let anything happen to me, which is to make us both feel better.

My cab pulls up to the restaurant and I take just a moment before I step out onto the sidewalk. With my bag slung across my body, and my copy of the smoking gun in the case against Dellinger safely tucked away, I enter the restaurant and leave every ounce of fear in the Chicago air.

I tell the girl at the podium that I'm there for Senator Dellinger's reservation at 7:00 pm. She tells me he's not yet arrived and asks me if I'd like to wait for him or be seated. I tell her I'd like to be seated so I follow her to a table conveniently located in the middle of the room.

Our server introduces himself as Trey and I immediately give him my order for a glass of Merlot. I'm halfway through my glass when Dellinger arrives and begins following the same girl into the dining room.

"Oh, good, you found him," I say to her with a cheery smile.

"You're Senator Dellinger? Well then, this is your table," she says with a sweet smile.

"Yes…thank you," he says reluctantly.

I catch Trey's eye and motion for him to come to us. "Trey, the Senator here would like a drink. Wouldn't you, Senator?" I say. I can't hide my smile and wish I had a better poker face. Although, I have to say I'm thoroughly enjoying throwing Dellinger off with my devil-may-care attitude.

"I'll have a gin, straight up, and only the best," he says. He doesn't even look at Trey, but stares me down…trying to figure out what the hell is going on.

"Thank you for the flowers. They were lovely," I tell him.

"I have to say, this isn't the response I expected from you…not at first, at least. It took your father about a year before he was really on board with the fact that I was offering him more money than he'd ever make with his little locksmith company. I saw the fire in his eyes, and I can see it in yours now, too." Dellinger's drink comes and I have to decide if I'm keeping myself from laughing or stabbing him with my butter knife.

"Would you like to order, or do you need a few minutes," Trey asks.

"We're going to need a minute, Trey. Thanks," I say. "There's definitely a fire in my eyes, but it's not what you think. You see, I'm going to make sure you never threaten me or anyone I love ever again." A huge grin spreads across my face. "Take a sip of your drink…Senator."

"Oh, I see. You think you're going to do something like report me to the authorities, or have a reporter poke his nose in my business. You're brave, I'll give you that. But, seriously, who is going to believe you? Your father was a known criminal and after I counter any report with what happened with Ambassador McKay, it'll look like the apple doesn't fall far from the tree," he says.

"What do you think happened in France?" I ask. I'm genuinely interested in what McKay told him. I can only imagine that it's the partial truth. McKay wants to hold onto his *I have the one thing you've been looking for* card.

"Poor Ambassador McKay's security detail discovered you and your father red handed with some of his most prized possessions. He called me when it happened and I persuaded him to let you and your father go," he explains. His arrogance would light a fire of rage inside me if I didn't know I was about to take his ass down.

He didn't mention Landon at all. The Ambassador said Dellinger had contacted him to add Landon to the guest list, but it must have been my father.

"Had I known your father was going to disappear with the coin I would have just made acquiring the coin part of Mr. Scott's assignment," Dellinger continues.

"How did you find the Nickel? You've been searching for so long," I ask.

"I have my usual ways, but sometimes your father provided some very credible leads. It was his lead that took us to McKay," Dellinger tells me. I'm beginning to understand the quiet bragging Dellinger enjoys by having something other people could never have. I'm sitting here listening to how McKay and my father totally scammed Dellinger and, I have to say, it feels pretty good.

You know he's going to sell it, don't you? How long do you think it's going to take to track it down this time?" I say.

"All you'll need to worry about is retrieving the things I send you after. Make no mistake, I'll find that coin again." He talks to me like I'm a little girl and I don't need to concern myself with grown up things. He has no idea the arsenal in my possession right now, but I'm about to attack.

"Ways like, say, when someone files to have their newly acquired 1913 V Nickel insured?"

Dellinger's face goes white from the initial shock of my informed statement.

"So you've done some digging have you? Impressive. You might be more useful to me than I had originally thought," he says, regaining his composure.

"Thank you for the compliment, but I didn't do any digging. It seems my father did one thing right before he turned into your soulless minion." I pull the envelope from my bag and place it in front of him. He eyes it and then me, not seeming to be sure if he wants to know what's inside. "If you don't want to open it, I can do it for you." I begin to take the envelope back, but he slams his hand down on it so hard that he breaks the side plate it was resting on.

I shake my head ever so slightly, letting Oz know that I'm fine. He's only there in case things get so crazy that I can't handle it. Right now, I've got this level of crazy under control.

Trey comes rushing to us, asking the Senator if he's ok. "I was trying to swat a fly," Dellinger says flatly. "Everything is fine." Trey removes the broken plate and returns in a flash with a new one.

Henry Dellinger's eyes are cold and hard as his anger rises. He hasn't even seen what's in the envelope, yet he's enraged. It's not that the envelope may or may not contain damaging information. It's that I *dared* to challenge him. He's *the* Senator Henry Dellinger, the distinguished representative from Connecticut, and *nobody* challenges him.

Dellinger opens the large envelop and pulls out the photocopied documents. He quickly thumbs through them once and then reviews each page carefully. It takes him a full four minutes to review each page. I start to get a little nervous, thinking that maybe Dad wasn't as detailed as he should have been to make this a slam dunk. But when the three minute mark hits, and a bead of sweat rolls down the side of Dellinger's face, I know that I've got everything I need.

"You think this proves anything?" he has the audacity to say.

"I don't think the names, dates, and numbers prove anything on their own. But if it took me all of 30 minutes to do a simple online search for where most of these items were last sold, for how much, and by whom, how much deeper do you think the police are going to take it? They'll press hard in to Ken Cooper and he'll cry like a baby when they tell him how long he'll spend in prison for insurance fraud," I say. I let the words roll off my tongue like honey.

"Whatever fraudulent activity Mr. Cooper has committed at his job has nothing to do with me." Dellinger downs the rest of his gin and motions to Trey for another.

"Really? You're serious," I begin. "You don't think they're going to track the original insurance number to original owner and then track the new insurance number to you…and see that you have no proof of purchasing the item? Please tell me you're not that stupid. You're a Senator. You represent a state of people who are counting on you."

The rage that filled Dellinger's eyes only a moment ago has turned to fear and that one bead of sweat has turned into a tie-loosening heat that is making Dellinger shift uncomfortably in his chair. He's losing it.

"Ok, Miss Rockwell…you've made your case. How much to keep you quiet?" His voice shakes a little as he speaks, throwing me completely off.

"Oh, my God. I thought it was just a caricature, but you're one of those people who really thinks money is the answer to everything. That was your whole point in the lavishness of sending me to Paris. First class, most prestigious hotel in the city, thousands of dollars to buy a *dress*. Money is a toy to you. You pay off, buy off, and threaten whoever you can so that you can keep all your dirty little secrets." I take a sip of my wine, satisfied that the night has been a success.

"You're sad. You're a sad man who's done nothing but live off his family's wealth and privilege. I feel sorry for you. You haven't even built

237

any great power with the opportunities you've been given. You won your first election by mud-slinging someone who was supposed to be a good friend. After that I imagine not too many people were willing to go up against you and your smoke and mirrors, diversion campaign tactics, which is how you've kept your seat in the Senate.

"You talk a big game with your muscly thug by your side and your hidden cameras, but you're not going to do anything. I'm sitting here with evidence that is going to crucify you in Washington and your first instinct is to throw money at me."

"Would you rather I threaten your life and the life of your friends again?" he asks, annoyed that I haven't gotten to the nitty gritty of my demands.

"Well that's just a silly question," I reply sardonically.

"*What* do you want?" Dellinger raises his voice and draws the attention of several guests seated around the dining room. "You've made your point, Miss Rockwell. Just tell me what you want and you can have it."

I see the fear in his eyes again and it dawns on me that I am the only person in his life who has ever called out his shit. We spent all this time being afraid of him like some mysterious Boogie Man when all we had to do was stand up and tell him to go away. I don't think it would have mattered if I had these papers or not. If I had walked in here and laid out a clear plan to smear his name through the media, I think he would have sweated just as much.

"It's simple. Leave me, my friends, Landon Scott, and my father alone...forever."

"After how your father betrayed you, you care whether he continues working for me or not?" Dellinger's arrogance is creeping back and all I want is for this to be over.

"How my father and I work through our personal family issues is none of your business," I tell him. "Do you understand?" He nods. "Good. Because if I find out that anything has happened to my father, I'm going to blame you. I don't care where he is in the world, I will blame you. He wouldn't have picked up this life again had you not invited him into it and, therefore, he wouldn't be on the run from you."

"Are we done here?" Dellinger asks with defeated annoyance.

"Yes." I stand and put my bag across my body, leaving Dellinger with a copy of the evidence of insurance fraud. Taking a step forward, I lean into his ear I say, "You might want to reevaluate your relationship with Ambassador McKay. I forged a copy of the V Nickel and gave it to him. Not knowing he had a copy, he was giddy at the thought of having something you wanted *so* desperately."

"Miss Rockwell!" The Senator stands and calls after me. I stop and turn back, tilting my head as I look at him. "Who has the real coin?" he asks hopefully. It occurs to me that this might be the one thing that he actually cares about, but I'll never know for sure.

"As far as I know, my father has it, and I trust you're going to keep your word."

I leave the Senator standing in the middle of the restaurant dining room and walk swiftly out onto the sidewalk. I hail a cab and am met by Oz as soon as I slide into the back seat. I let out the breath it feels like I've been holding since Dellinger walked into the restaurant, and let tears of relief fill my eyes to overflowing.

I lean into Oz and let him hold me like he used to when I was a little girl…back in the days when I would refer to him as my other dad. He was always there for me, and now that my dad never will be again, I'm really glad to have him.

"You did good, Angel. You did good."

Chapter 20

There's a knock at the hotel room door and Mercy scurries to get it. We put our card out last night for room service breakfast this morning and we're all just giddy about it. Mercy, Demi and I are staying at a nice hotel just a couple of blocks from Duke's. Jerry sprung for the hotel saying that it was every girl's right to stay in a fancy hotel the night before her wedding. He continued by saying that he didn't know what Jack had planned for their honeymoon and wanted to make sure she had at least one pleasant memory from the day.

He was kidding, of course, but it was still a lovely gesture on his part to do something so sweet for us even beyond what he's already doing by closing the bar and covering all the food and non-alcoholic drinks. He said he had to draw the line somewhere.

Demi thanked him profusely and said her only stipulation on any part of the wedding was that Jack was not to show up to their 3:00 pm wedding still hung over from the night before. Jerry held Jack's bachelor party at the bar last night and I'm sure he didn't let Jack get too crazy. He'd have the pregnant bride and his own girlfriend to deal with if he did.

"I am starving!" Demi declares. "Where are my pancakes?"

"Good grief, woman! It's like you're eating for two!" Mercy jokes. "Oh, and please do not puke today. Your dress is way too gorgeous and I cannot handle puke."

"You're a nurse! How can you not handle puke?" Demi asks as she smothers her pancakes with syrup.

"Hey…we all have our limits," Mercy says seriously, but then cracks a smile. "You've actually been doing pretty good in that department, haven't you?"

"Yeah…it's been great. I've been nauseated, but I haven't thrown up once. Although, by the time this baby comes, if I never see another whole wheat Ritz cracker again, it'll be too soon! Those are the *only* thing that sooth my queasiness."

"Alright, ladies," I interject. "I have a surprise for you. I know we said we were just going to go natural and do our own hair but…I hired the girl who does my hair to come do ours! And she's bringing one of the girls from the salon to do our makeup, too!"

Squeals of *what!* and *oh, my God!* echo through the room as both girls jump up and hug me.

"Oh, Jenna! You truly are the greatest ever! Everyone has been doing so much for us. Jack and I don't want you guys to think we can't afford anything. I mean, we're not swimming in cash but…" Demi starts, but I cut her off.

"No one thinks that. We would all just rather you save your money for that little baby. He or she is worth far more than anything you two could spend your money on today," I say.

"Yeah, let Jenna pick up the tab!" Mercy jokes. "You know she's got loads of money!"

I once told Mercy about the inheritance I got from a distant uncle – aka Oz – and that after school I wasn't touching any of it. That I was saving it for something great and by great I really meant was in case I had to leave town. But, now that I'm not leaving, I guess I should start thinking of something else I could do with the money.

The girls from my salon arrive and we talk and take turns eating and ordering more food. The closer we get to the wedding, I don't think Demi is going to eat. And then once we're there, I think she'll forget to eat altogether. So my objective is to make sure there's food here constantly so I can trick her into munching all morning.

By 2:15 all of our hair and makeup is done and we're all sufficiently stuffed. Fortunately, all of our dresses are very forgiving. Demi told Mercy and me to just find something really pretty in colors that made us look and feel good. That was harder than it sounded, but, we found the same dress in two different colors and bought the same shoes that would go with both. It wasn't until we saw Demi's dress that we realized just how perfectly they all fit together. They're all empire waists with a flowing chiffon skirt that hits just at the knee. Mercy's and my dress are halter tops that tie with the same soft chiffon around the neck. I almost didn't even try the dress on because it reminds me so much of the dress I bought in Versailles with Landon, but it really was beautiful on the rack and Mercy and I both agreed that we looked more than fabulous in them.

Demi's dress is a gorgeous, soft white, strapless dress with gold beads and threading embellishing the bust. With her hair up and makeup done, she's simply radiant.

"Demi…you're stunning," I whisper, trying to keep my tears at bay.

"You two look amazing. That royal blue is gorgeous on you, Jenna. And, Mercy…I had no clue how incredible emerald green would be on you. I'm blown away." Demi starts to tear up too and before we know it, we're all dabbing our eyes to keep from messing up our makeup. "You have no idea what you two mean to me. I couldn't do this without you. You've both helped me see just how lucky I am to have Jack. I think we were all so uncertain of how he would react to the baby…if he could grow up enough and take responsibility. But now…sometimes I look at him across the room and think about how happy I am. This man makes me so happy and I know he's going to be a great husband and an amazing dad. Thank you for everything."

We all dab our eyes preemptively before the tears come and catch them as soon as they appear. With deep breaths and hugs all around, we walk down the hall of the hotel to the elevator with excited anticipation.

Demi found a florist who agreed to do just three bouquets and one boutonniere for the wedding. Jerry got his sister to come and do a little decorating by putting white table clothes on the tables and setting little votive candles in the center. We worked through how the whole bar needed to be set up so there was an actual aisle and chairs on either side. And because Sharper Image is a surprise, we got some pipe and draping to hide the stage. I told Demi it was to cover the messiness of the stage so all their wedding pictures wouldn't look like they were in a bar.

We get downstairs at the hotel and are prepared to hail a cab for the two and a half blocks, but there's a limo and a driver holding a sign with Demi's name on it.

"Um…that's me," Demi says. "Jenna, did you hire a limo, too?"

"No. This one is not on me," I say. "It must be a surprise from Jack, or maybe Jerry."

"If it's Jerry, he didn't tell me," Mercy says. "I'm sure it was Jack. Get in girls! We have a wedding to get to!"

The Sunday traffic is horrendous for some reason. It's taking us twice as long to drive there as it would if we had walked.

"So, Jenna…" Mercy says. "Have you heard from Landon?"

"No, I haven't," I reply shortly. "And today is about Demi and Jack so I am not talking about my tragedy of a relationship with Landon."

"It doesn't have to be a tragedy, Jenna. You're still in love with him." Demi says.

"Of course I'm still in love with him, but…there's so much you guys don't know about Paris, and the things I said to him that pushed him away. It'd be a miracle if he ever forgave me." I don't want to, but I have to dab the corners of my eyes to keep the tears I feel stinging them from rolling over and messing up my makeup.

"You won't know if you don't at least reach out to him and try," Mercy tells me.

"You have to tell him what you want from him," Demi says.

"What…just call him and tell him that I'm still in love with him and that

I want to spend the rest of my life with him? You guys weren't there. You don't know…" I murmur.

"We would know if you'd tell us," Mercy says softly.

"Now is not the time or the place to talk about this. Today is about Demi and Jack. Let's just focus on that, ok? After the wedding you can drown my romantic sorrows with me and some cookie dough ice cream."

The car stops in front of Duke's and Mercy and I get out first, making sure Jack is inside. Demi's dad is outside waiting for her. When she steps out of the car he can barely hold it together and immediately begins to wipe his eyes.

"You look like a million bucks, Dem. A million bucks." Demi's dad is a born and bred Chicagoan and spent some time in some of the rougher parts of the city when he was younger. He's a little rough around the edges himself, not so great at sharing his feelings, so this just might be the best compliment he's ever given her.

"Thanks, Dad." Demi gives her dad a kiss on the cheek and he looks at her like she's his pride and joy. It warms my heart because I remember that there was actually a time when my father looked at me that way…before Paris.

I go inside and make sure everything is all set up and ready before Demi and her dad come in. Spring is going to get the door when Mercy and I are at the front of the room and it's time for Demi to come in.

"You look gorgeous, Jenna," Jerry says as he kisses my cheek. "Thanks for helping with the dance stuff. I think Mercy is going to be really happy when we do more than shuffle and sway from side to side on the dance floor."

"Thanks, Jerry. You were a good student. You picked it up really fast! I know Mercy is going to flip. Oh, and thanks for the limo. That was really cool," I say.

"What limo?" Jerry says, puzzled.

"You didn't send a limo to pick us up at the hotel?" Jerry just shakes his head. "Hmm…must have been Jack. Where is he, by the way?"

"Back room. I've kept him in there for the last half hour to make sure he didn't see Demi. Mercy's orders," he tells me with a small laugh.

I find Jack in Jerry's office, pacing back and forth.

"You ok in here?" I ask, startling him.

"I'm great. Jerry threatened me within an inch of my life if I came out of here. I'm glad to see you. That means Demi is here and I'm that much closer to making her mine." Jack leans against the desk and smiles like a fool in love and it's the greatest smile I've ever seen on anyone.

"She's just as excited as you are," I tell him. "We made sure she ate today. Lots, actually. So don't worry if she doesn't eat too much this afternoon. Just offer her some fruit periodically if you don't see her eating. Gotta keep her and the baby's strength up! You ready?"

"More than ready. Let's get this show on the road." Jack stands straight up and follows me out into the bar.

I poke my head out the door and let Mercy, Demi, and her dad know that it's time. I'm the last one to get my flowers from the florist as she's already delivered them to Demi and Mercy. They're a sweet mix of seasonal end-of-summer flowers that work surprisingly well with both Mercy's and my dress. Of course, anything looks beautiful against the bride's soft white dress.

The music for Mercy and me starts playing and we make our way down the short aisle to the front of the bar. There are normally a dozen small tables barely big enough to seat four people filling this area. Jerry's sister has performed a miracle with how she's rearranged the whole bar for the ceremony. The tables are lining the walls so that no one can sit at them. Their chairs are being used for guests anyway. She's draped pink and white chiffon around the room to cover the exposed brick walls. There are lines and lines of little white lights behind the chiffon to make it glow. It's a really cool look with the contrast of the brick being covered by these soft materials and light. I hope Demi loves it as much as I do when she comes in.

Demi's music starts to play and her mom stands up to cue the rest of the 50 or so guests to stand with her. The light from outside is so bright behind Demi and her father that we can't see them until Spring closes the door behind them. When Demi sees how transformed the bar is, her face lights up. And when Jack and Demi come into each other's view, they both start to cry.

The reverend takes them through the ceremony and I can't help but giggle a little at the thought that this is probably the first wedding he's performed in a bar. I'm sure he'll have a great story to tell.

Demi said she didn't want them to write their own vows. She's always felt like that was a super personal thing and it always makes her uncomfortable as a guest. So they did the standard vows that were just as beautiful. They say *I do* and Jack gives her the sweetest first married kiss I've ever seen, but I may feel that way about every first kiss at a wedding.

The ceremony ends, pictures are taken, and the tables lining the walls are moved in just enough to create space but also make room for dancing.

"Demi, my incredible wife," Jack says holding the microphone that's been threaded under the pipe and draping. "I have a gift for you. Well, this is my first wedding gift to you." Demi looks at Jack, standing where only moments ago they said their vows, with a suspicious look in her eye.

Before she can say anything, Jerry and Matt pull the draping down, revealing Sharper Image on the other side. I swear Demi's scream was heard by dogs on the other side of the city. She was more excited than I ever anticipated she would be.

Without hesitation she grabs Jack and kisses him like there is no tomorrow. "Thank you! Thank you! Thank you! Best husband ever!" she chants in between kissing him.

"He's never going to live up to this mega gift ever again," Mercy says with her trademarked sarcasm.

"Yeah, but every time they have an argument and she wants to talk about how he's screwed something up, he's going to have this to refer to. *Uh, I got you your favorite band for our wedding*, I win!" Jerry laughs.

The band plays a few of Demi's favorite songs while some people eat and drink or just mill around. When they begin a slow song I watch Jerry take Mercy's hand and lead her to the dance floor. She settles in for their standard shuffle and sway, but Jerry wastes no time in showing off the moves I taught him. Before she knows what's happening, Jerry has Mercy moving all over that dance floor in beautiful and sexy fluidity. I sigh, happy that they've found each other.

I scan the dance floor and spot Demi and Jack, and Matt and Spring. Something churns inside me as I watch them smile and hold each other close. The smile I was wearing fades. I didn't want to feel this way today, but I guess this is harder than I anticipated it was going to be. I've never been the girl who was jealous or felt like a third or fifth wheel because her friends were all with someone and I wasn't. I was always happy for them. I *am* happy for them.

I wish Landon could be here with me, but I nailed that coffin shut and there's no way I can pry it open. I move behind the bar and start tidying things up. It's a little after 6:00 and I know Demi and Jack will be heading out soon. They've just got to cut the cake and then all the official wedding moments are done.

"Can we have everyone's attention, please?" I hear Jack say through the microphone. "First of all, thank you all so much coming today. We know it was short notice, but you all know that I'm not that great of a planner, which might be why I just got married in a bar," he says and we all laugh. "Demi and I are so grateful for all of your love and friendship. We couldn't have pulled off such an incredible day without you. So we want to raise a toast to all of you and wish you all the happiness that we have today." Everyone raises their glasses and gives a cheer.

"Before we cut the cake, there's one tradition that we didn't want to leave out: the bouquet toss and the garter!" Demi says too excitedly.

I hate this tradition. A bunch of desperate, single women in the middle of the room, clawing at each other for a shot at a bouquet of flowers that is somehow supposed to determine whether they're the next one to get married or not. Then, there's a group of single guys desperate to get laid so they push and shove each other so they can grab the garter and get a little leg action when they put it on the single tramp who punched another women for the bouquet. Good times.

"We'd like to do things a little differently, though," Demi begins. "Instead of having all the girls and all the guys out here, and make you fight your way for the bouquet and garter, Jack and I have decided to give the bouquet and garter to two people who are more than crazy about each other and are destined to live a long and happy life together. We're going to call them up here and they're going to share a special dance."

I come out from behind the bar and look for Mercy and Jerry. I wonder if his pleas for dance help were because of this. I bet he set it all up with Jack and Demi so he can propose!

"Would you all please clear the dance floor for Jenna Rockwell and Landon Scott?" Demi finishes and looks at my stunned face.

My heart stops and Landon emerges from the other side of the room. Has he been here the whole time? My legs feel like cement until Spring comes behind me and nudges me, forcing my first step. Landon stands in the middle of the floor, holding out his hand. I bite my lip to keep from exploding into the ugly cry.

"You're here," I say quietly.

"I'm here," he says.

Landon takes me in his arms and holds my hand in his at his heart. Music starts to play but I don't pay enough attention to it to recognize what it is. We move together silently for a little while, neither of us sure what to say to the other.

"What are you doing here?" I ask.

"Mercy called me. She told me if I didn't get my ass back here and make things right with you that she was going to let Jerry use my head for batting practice. So…" Landon smiles and I give a breathy laugh..

"They don't know anything," I say. "Well, Spring knows everything, but the others don't," I tell him.

"They do now," he says. "Spring called me first and asked when I was coming back. I told her you made it clear that you didn't want me around and that's when she let me know that you had given her the whole story…and when she told me that Dellinger was off your back. Why didn't you tell me, Jenna?"

"I was scared. I was mean and unkind, and I pushed you away on purpose." Tears fill my eyes and I can't keep them from falling over. "I'm so sorry, Landon."

"There's nothing for you to be sorry for, Jenna." Landon looks into my eyes, locking ours together. By now Demi and Jack have joined us on the dance floor and invited everyone else to dance as well. "You didn't push me away. Dellinger did. Your father did. If you didn't feel like we were all in danger, you wouldn't have pushed me away," he says a bit sternly.

"I'm still sorry. Can you ever forgive me?"

"I sent a limo to pick you up at the hotel, didn't I?" Landon smiles and flashes that sexy smirk and I think all might be right in the world.

"Well played, Mr. Scott. Well played." I smile, relieved that at least for now, everything seems to be moving in the right direction. There's still something that's weighing on me, though. "I'm still scared, Landon. Your job…"

"My job isn't nearly as important as you are. I work for myself and I just gave myself early retirement."

"But…"

"You want to argue with me about my plans to spend forever with you?" he says. I nod and Landon puts his hand behind my neck and pulls me to him. Our lips press together and I don't hesitate for a moment to give in. I've missed him so much and I'm so hopeful that we can love each other the way we did before the craziness of my father and Henry Dellinger.

"I have to ask you something," Landon says, releasing me from our kiss. He steps back and somehow the crowd parts like the Red Sea. "I really would have done this in Paris had you let me."

As if on cue, the band has stopped playing and I see that Demi and Jack, and Mercy and Jerry are responsible for the space we've been given. The four of them are standing there like proud parents filled with excitement for their little girl.

In a moment Landon is down on one knee, holding a black, velvet ring box. My heart is pounding and more than the feelings of love I have for Landon, right now I'm feeling so incredibly grateful. This dream had died and now it's been brought back to life. There isn't a long road of recovery and forgiveness ahead of me. Landon understands why I did what I did and he kept his promise to never leave me alone. I want to shout out my answer right now, but I have to give Landon his moment to say what he needs to say.

"Jenna...there is no one else I want to spend the rest of my days with. Please, please, *please*...marry me." Landon opens the ring box and I'm too shocked to answer. There's no ring. Where the ring should be gently nestled between the satin is a coin. Landon stands and comes closer to me, seeing the shock and confusion on my face.

"I don't understand," I stutter.

"I had Jace make two copies. This is the original, and last, 1913 V Nickel," he says.

"So that means..."

"Both Ambassador McKay and your father have the copies. When I went to get my tux from the concierge, I had them put this one in the hotel safe," he explains.

"Why didn't you just tell me? We could have still given them the fakes and then used the real coin to bargain with Dellinger," I offer.

"I tried to tell you that night, but you wouldn't listen to me. You just shut down...and then you left," he says. It's still painful to think about. "You said that after what he did to you and your family, you never wanted him to have it. I agreed with you and took measures to protect it. And...from what Oz tells me, you didn't need that coin as a bargaining chip with Dellinger. He told me about the insurance information and said you played Dellinger like a fiddle...said he was sweating bullets," Landon smiles. "I'm proud of you, Jenna."

"You talked to Oz, too?"

"After Spring called I was determined to do everything I could to make this moment happen." Landon brushes my cheek with his thumb and that warm feeling that I've missed comes rushing through me again.

"I can't believe you arranged all this for me. I really can't believe what you did with the coin." I can't stop smiling.

"I love you, and I was just trying to protect something that was important to you. If you needed the coin to deal with Dellinger, of course I would have given it to you earlier. But, you kicked ass without it and now...now you can use it for whatever you want. You can keep it for posterity...sell it and put the money away as a guaranteed nest egg...buy your dream house." Landon sighs and smiles. "So...I look kind of dumb standing here holding a ring box with what everyone thinks is just a nickel. If you wait any longer, this is going to end up online as the worst proposal ever." he smirks.

I look at Landon looking at me and I feel warm. It's the first time I think I've really realized that I can do and say whatever I want. I can let people in and share my life with them. Before Landon crashed into my life I had come to terms with the fact that, no matter how close I got to anyone, the closest they would ever get to me would be arm's length. All that has changed now. Something inside me has opened like a book.

I look at Landon through blurry, tear filled eyes and somehow all I can see is that sexy smirk of his. Yeah...I could look at that smirk every day for the rest of my life.

"Jenna...marry me," he whispers.

"Yes."

"Yes?"

"Yes."

THE END

Acknowledgements

Thank you to my friends and family for their continued support, encouragement, and excitement for this unexpected and wonderful journey I am on. I am constantly humbled and honored by you.

Thank you to Michael Canales for the incredible cover art! You have an amazing eye and I'm truly grateful for your work.

A huge thank you to my amazing agent, Italia. I am honored to be one of your cubs and excited for all that the future holds for us! You can meddle any time you want!

Also by AnnaLisa Grant

The Lake Trilogy: The Lake, Troubled Waters, Safe Harbor

As I Am

For more information, visit:

AnnaLisaGrant.com

Facebook.com/AuthorAnnalisaGrant

Cover art by Michael Canales

FIVE

Proof

Made in the USA
Charleston, SC
13 March 2015

EMMA
Every Day

A Trip to Grandma's

by C.L. Reid

illustrated by Elena Aiello

PICTURE WINDOW BOOKS
a capstone imprint

Published by Picture Window Books, an imprint of Capstone
1710 Roe Crest Drive, North Mankato, Minnesota 56003
capstonepub.com

Library of Congress Cataloging-in-Publication Data
Names: Reid, C. L., author. | Aiello, Elena (Illustrator), illustrator. |
Reid, C. L. Emma every day.
Title: A trip to Grandma's / by C. L. Reid ; illustrated by Elena Aiello.
Description: North Mankato, Minnesota : Picture Window Books, an
imprint of Capstone, 2022. | Series: Emma every day |
Audience: Ages 5-7. | Audience: Grades K-1. |
Summary: Emma and her brother are staying at their
grandmother's house for a full week; she has packed her favorite
stuffed toy and the recharger for her cochlear implant, but she is
a little worried about feeling homesick—but with her grandmother
keeping her busy, and the help of a new deaf friend named
Nick, the week flies by. Includes an ASL fingerspelling chart,
glossary, and content-related questions.
Identifiers: LCCN 2021006175 (print) | LCCN 2021006176 (ebook)
| ISBN 9781663909305 (hardcover) | ISBN 9781663921949
(paperback) | ISBN 9781663909275 (pdf) Subjects: LCSH: Deaf
children—Juvenile fiction. | Cochlear implants—Juvenile fiction. |
Grandmothers—Juvenile fiction. | Grandparent and child—Juvenile
fiction. | Friendship—Juvenile fiction. | CYAC: Deaf—Fiction. | People
with disabilities—Fiction. | Grandmothers—Fiction. | Friendship—
Fiction. | Cochlear implants—Fiction. Classification: LCC PZ7.1.R4544
Tr 2021 (print) | LCC PZ7.1.R4544 (ebook) | DDC [E]—dc23
LC record available at https://lccn.loc.gov/2021006175
LC ebook record available at https://lccn.loc.gov/2021006176

Image Credits: Capstone: Daniel Griffo, bottom right 28, bottom
right 29, Margeaux Lucas, top right 28, Randy Chewning, top left 28,
bottom left 28, top left 29, top right 29, bottom left 29

Design Elements: Shutterstock: achii, Mari C, Mika Besfamilnaya

Special thanks to Evelyn Keolian for her consulting work.

Designer: Tracy Davies

TABLE OF CONTENTS

MEET EMMA

EMMA CARTER
Age: 8 Grade: 3

SIBLING
one brother, Jaden
(12 years old)

PARENTS
David and Lucy

BEST FRIEND
Izzie Jackson

PET
a goldfish named Ruby

favorite color: **teal**
favorite food: **tacos**
favorite school subject: **writing**
favorite sport: **swimming**
hobbies: **reading, writing, biking, swimming**

FINGERSPELLING GUIDE

MANUAL ALPHABET

Aa   Bb   Cc   Dd   Ee

Ff   Gg   Hh   Ii   Jj

MANUAL NUMBERS

0   1   2   3

Emma is Deaf. She uses
American Sign Language (ASL)
to communicate with her family.
She also uses a cochlear implant
(CI) to help her hear some sounds.

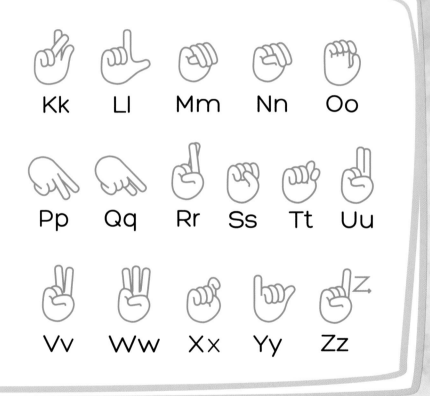

Kk Ll Mm Nn Oo

Pp Qq Rr Ss Tt Uu

Vv Ww Xx Yy Zz

Chapter 1
The Big Welcome

"Do I have everything?" Emma

asked Ruby, her pet fish.

She looked around and picked

up her favorite stuffed animal.

"Oops!  I can't forget Fluffy or this stuff," she said.

She put the batteries and charger for her cochlear implant (CI) into her bag.

"I think that's it," Emma said. "Bye, Ruby."

Emma was going to stay with her grandma for a week. She was very excited, but she was nervous too.

After a few hours, the car stopped in front of Grandma's house. Emma and Jaden hopped out.

"Have a good week," Dad signed. He hugged Emma and Jaden.

"Have fun  with Grandma," Mom signed. She gave them both a big hug too.

"I love you," Emma signed.

She blinked back tears and tried

to smile as she waved goodbye.

"Let's go in the house and eat.

I made spaghetti, meatballs, and

cookies," Grandma signed.

Emma wasn't sure she could eat.

Her stomach hurt.

Chapter 2

Homesick

That night, Emma had a hard time falling asleep. When she did sleep, she dreamed that something terrible had happened to Ruby.

Emma grabbed Fluffy and ran to
Grandma's room.

"I think something bad
happened to Ruby," Emma signed.

"Ruby is okay. You had a

nightmare," Grandma signed.

"You can sleep with me."

When Emma woke up the next morning, she put on her CI and went into the kitchen. Emma wasn't hungry for breakfast.

Just then, Muffin,  Grandma's sweet cat, rubbed against her leg.

"I miss Ruby," she said.

"It's a nice day. Let's go weed my flower garden," Grandma said.

"Mom would love these flowers," Emma signed.

"You can take some home for her," Grandma signed.

It was raining the next day.

Grandma said, "Let's drive into town today. I need to buy cat food, and you can each pick out a toy."

They each got a yo-yo.

The third day Grandma said,
"Let's work in my vegetable garden
today. You can pick ripe vegetables."

"Dad would like these vegetables,"
Emma signed.

"You can take some home for
him," Grandma signed.

Chapter 3

A New Friend

The next day, Emma and Jaden

stood on Grandma's front porch.

Emma played with her new yo-yo.

She liked being with Grandma,

but she was ready to go home. Just

then a kid carrying a soccer ball

walked up the driveway, waving at

Emma and Jaden.

"Hello, my name is Nick," the boy signed. "What are your names?"

"Emma and my brother, Jaden," Emma signed. "Are you deaf?"

"Yes. Are you deaf?" Nick signed.

"Yes. I use a CI," Emma signed.

"Jaden is hearing. We are visiting
my grandma."

Grandma stepped out onto the

porch, smiling.

"Hello, Nick. How are you?"

she signed.

"Great!" he signed.

Grandma looked at Emma and

Jaden. "Nick moved here a few

months ago," she signed.

"Cool," Emma

fingerspelled.

"You want to play soccer?" Nick

signed, looking excited.

"Yes!" Jaden and Emma signed at the same time.

Emma, Jaden, and Nick played soccer for an hour. Emma forgot all about feeling homesick.

That night after dinner Jaden signed, "Let's watch a movie."

"I will make popcorn and lemonade," Grandma said.

Emma sat on the couch beside Grandma. She munched on popcorn as they watched the movie with the closed captions (CC) on the TV.

"I can't wait until I can come

back and visit you," Emma signed.

"Anytime, sweetie. Anytime,"

Grandma signed.

LEARN TO SIGN

sleep
Close hand in front of face.

night
Move hand down
and away from body.

grandmother
1. Make the sign for "mother."
2. Bounce hand away from chin.

sad
Move hands down in
front of face.

blanket

Bring hands to shoulders.

cook

Move hand back and forth.

cookie

Rotate C shape.

I love you

Combine the shapes I, L, and Y.

GLOSSARY

closed captions (CC)—the text version of what is being said or heard (such as a doorbell, knocking, music, etc.) on the TV show or movie that is shown on the screen

cochlear implant (also called CI)—a device that helps someone who is Deaf to hear; it is worn on the head just above the ear

deaf—being unable to hear

fingerspell—to make letters with your hands to spell out words; often used for names of people and places

homesick—missing your home

nervous—feeling worried

sign language—a language in which hand gestures, along with facial expressions and body movements, are used to communicate

TALK ABOUT IT

1. Would you like to be away from your home for a week? Why or why not?

2. How do you think Emma felt when her parents left?

3. Talk about some things you can do when you feel nervous.

WRITE ABOUT IT

1. Make a list of three places you would like to go for a week. Then make a list of all the items you would bring to each place.

2. Emma feels nervous being away from home. Write about a time you felt nervous.

3. Pretend you are Emma. Write a thank-you note to Grandma for your fun week.

Ruby

ABOUT THE AUTHOR

Deaf-blind since childhood, C.L. Reid received a cochlear implant (CI) as an adult to help her hear, and she uses American Sign Language (ASL) to communicate. She and her husband have three sons. Their middle son is also deaf-blind. C.L. earned a master's degree in writing for children and young adults at Hamline University in St. Paul, Minnesota. She lives in Minnesota with her husband, two of their sons, and their cats.

ABOUT THE ILLUSTRATOR

Elena Aiello is an illustrator and character designer. After graduating as a marketing specialist, she decided to study art direction and CGI. Doing so, she discovered a passion for illustration and conceptual art. She works as a freelancer for various magazines and publishers. Elena loves video games and sushi. She lives with her husband and her little pug, Gordon, in Milan, Italy.